Odyssey of the Butterfly

by

Fran Heckrotte

2013

Odyssey of the Butterfly
Copyright © 2013 by Fran Heckrotte
All rights reserved.
First Edition

Published: April 2013
ISBN: 978-1-939950-03-1

This book is Published by
Novel Ideas Publishing, LLC
Beaufort, S.C., USA

E-mail: novel_ideas_publishing@hotmail.com
Editor: Alexa Hoffman, auth2b@gmail.com
Cover Design by Patty G. Henderson,
http://www.pattyghenderson.com

Visit Us at http://www.novelideaspublishing.net

ACKNOWLEDGMENTS

I want to give special thanks to the people that helped me bring this book to fruition.

For brainstorming the ideas behind several of the stories, Annabelle is the one who took me to places my imagination would never have ventured.

Alexa, you're a gem. Copyediting has got to be the most tedious task in the production of a book. Thank you for your dedication and professionalism. I would recommend you to anyone wanting a quality job. In fact I just did. Alexa can be reached at the following email address: auth2b@hotmail.com.

For a great cover artist, look no further than Patty Henderson. I can't thank her enough for her patience and willingness to work with me on what was a difficult task. Catching the essence of one story is hard. When five stories are involved it is especially challenging. Patty can be reached at her website: http://www.pattyghenderson.com.

And to all my beta readers and proofers, there are no words that can express my gratitude and appreciation for your time and insight. Thank you Sherry and Pixiey, and those who didn't want your names mentioned.

Odyssey of the Butterfly

Table of Contents:

Daughters

of the Queen

BUTTERFLIES AND MOTHS

IS THERE ANY INSECT more pleasing to the eye than the butterfly or moth? They are the elusive, mysterious creatures flitting from flower to flower, weed to weed, giving life to many plants and destruction to others. They bring us joy and occasionally death. The Monarch butterfly is well known for being poisonous to some predators, but even it is a lightweight compared to the South American Silk moth. Bristles around its body carry one of the most potent defensive chemicals of any animal. The venom is an anticoagulant that can cause a human to hemorrhage to death. Caterpillars can devastate crops, creating enormous economic losses to farmers... and still, when this dangerous, destructive child of nature emerges from its cocoon... spreads its wings... and takes flight, all we see is beauty... and perhaps that is what makes them truly magical.

DAUGHTERS OF THE QUEEN

THEY ARE THE LEPIDOPTERA. Most people know them as butterflies and moths, at least in the English language. Easily recognized, they are found on all of the continents except Antarctica and can be traced as far back as the Cretaceous Period. Perhaps it was due to the appearance of the first flowering plants, perhaps merely coincidental circumstance. Then again, maybe they existed long before that time but their remains have yet to

2

be discovered. Nature makes her own rules in the game of life, whether on this world — or another.

CHAPTER 1

SHE WAS SHENARA, Queen Mother, and challenged by none... for why would one challenge the weakest of the colony? Their survival depended on her ability to lead, not her strength. She kept the colony alive and ultimately the species. Physically, she was the largest of her kind. Her wings were almost twice the size of the others', making her inferior to the ones that reached maturity. Slower moving, her journey always began days in advance of the collective. Distance provided her the time and opportunity to mark safe routes with the irresistible scent of pheromones. They drifted with the winds, eventually settling on the plants and earth. The flights were arduous but necessary if the colony was to succeed in its yearly migrations.

Queens were the Mothers of their species, although they never mated nor bore young. They were chosen from amongst their sister siblings when the time was right. Always white with thin black swirls bordering semi-translucent wings, they were the most visible of their species... and the most vulnerable. Their eyes could be black, green or a deep purple, sometimes glowing in the early morning or late evening light.

Shenara was unusually large, making her a bigger target for predators. She had, however, three offsetting factors that gave her a greater advantage: superior intelligence, greater wisdom and, most important, the vast experience of all her predecessors. A Queen's memories

4

were passed to her Chosen. Millions of miles and thousands of years of accumulated knowledge gave the monarch what no other in her colony possessed — the ability to recognize subtle changes in the world around them and understand the consequences of such changes. She could predict colder winters and warmer summers, extended droughts and torrential storms.

* * *

Shenara lived in a world of extremes — hot and humid in the summer, cold and brutal in the winter. To avoid each, she timed her colony's migration to take advantage of the lush plant growth in spring and fall. Winters were spent in the south, summers in the north.

Only a Queen survived the entire trip. Her colony would faithfully follow her to the first breeding ground, mate, reproduce and die. The offspring, after maturing, then followed the Queen's scent to the next nursery. The cycle was repeated once again before they arrived at their final destination, the cooler summer forests of the north. There the last generation was born, fed and grew strong for **they** alone could make the entire return trip to their winter home, always trailing behind their Queen. As with all life, there would come a time when she could no longer lead and a successor would have to be chosen. Fortunately, Queens lived a long time.

CHAPTER 2

THE AIR FELT STRANGE, warmer, hotter, thicker than normal. Each downward stroke of her wings pushed her higher and further away. Flying was becoming more difficult. She was old and tired and ready for her final destiny.

My time is near, Shenara thought, contemplating all the obstacles that lay ahead of her. *I must choose my replacement soon.* The Queen scanned the roiling mass of orange and black bodies feeding on the milk of the tall, thin-leafed weeds that flourished around them. *But who?* Nowhere could she see white wings until the sun glinted on a small speck laboriously climbing a spindly plant tucked amongst the massive growth surrounding it. Then another pair appeared, and another, followed by six more.

Nine! Nine white daughters struggled upward. Shenara watched intently as the first reached its goal and then dismissed it as unacceptable. She moved too quickly. The next six also were rejected as potential successors for the same reason. Speed was not an asset to be Queen. But the last two, **they** had potential. Every step took a toll on their strength. Neither gave up, a necessary quality to lead, but a certain amount of physical weakness was essential. Survival of the fittest was so ingrained in the genes of each butterfly that challenging the weakest made little sense, a waste of valuable energy, and thus Queens could move amongst their colonies with impunity.

Gliding down for a closer examination of the candidates, Shenara hovered next to one, much smaller than the other, and then moved to inspect her sister. Both had some growing to do but they had potential. That was the only requirement for now.

Come, daughters! she commanded and flew away without looking back. Sensitive to fluctuations in the air, she knew immediately when they left the security of the milkweed. This was their first flight away from the colony and the beginning of a training regimen that would prepare them for the final test.

Shenara hoped one proved worthy. Her strength was waning. If neither fledgling passed, the collective would be without a Queen, without her memories. The colony would be doomed to extinction, an unthinkable consequence. Shenara would bear the responsibility for such a tragedy, for **she** was Queen.

* * *

You move too fast, Rojani, Shenara gently reprimanded. *Conserve your energy. Speed is your enemy, not distance.* Rojani was smaller than her sister, Fenari. The strain of trying to keep up with Fenari and her Queen was exhausting.

How can I keep up with you if I don't fly faster? Rojani asked.

Why do you want to keep up with us? Shenara countered. *Did I command you to? Are we in a race?*

Rojani took a deep breath and exhaled.

No, Mother, but I can't keep up with you by flying slower. I don't understand what you want of me.

I want nothing more than you can give.

Confused, Rojani slowed her beating wings.

7

I am giving you all that I can, Mother. Is that not enough?

Fenari, who had been keeping pace with the Queen, veered off and circled back to Rojani's side.

I think Mother wants us to fly at our own pace, sister. If we allow others to push us forward, we will fall behind.

Very good, Fenari, Shenara said, pleased at her daughter's early display of wisdom. *Survival is about knowing your limitations. Use them to your advantage. You are the weakest of the weak. You must never compete against the others. Your strength will come from patience, endurance and wisdom.*

I only state the obvious, Fenari said, humbly. *Were I small like Rojani, I would have made the same mistake.*

Perhaps, and perhaps if she were larger she would have made the one you have now made.

Before Fenari could respond, Rojani fluttered excitedly up and down, then dashed in front of her sister to make eye contact.

You cannot doubt yourself, Fenari. You must always believe you do what is best. Am I right, Mother? she asked, spinning around to look into Shenara's eyes.

Yes, daughter. I am pleased with both of you. Come! It is time we returned home. There is much work to be done and little time for preparation. A good night's rest will replenish your energy.

Slowing her speed so Rojani could keep up, Shenara led her two daughters back to the safety of the colony.

Go now. Hide deep amongst your brothers and sisters. Your color makes you vulnerable. I cannot afford to lose either of you.

Shenara watched Rojani and Fenari burrow deep amongst their siblings. When they were no longer visible she flew to her special tree and crawled into a crack

8

between two thick pieces of bark. Circling several times, she nestled down, tucking her legs under her. The Queen closed her eyes. Her body ached, but for the first time in many cycles, sleep came easily.

CHAPTER 3

THE RAYS PEEKED into the dark crevice, warming the Queen and rousing her from her slumber. Stretching, she flexed each leg several times, testing for the stiffness that was coming more often from long periods of stillness. Once assured all were functioning properly, she stood and crept toward the narrow opening. Cautiously she surveyed the outside world, searching for potential threats. Today, there were none. Most of the swarm were asleep; the few that weren't moved sluggishly. Sunlight hadn't yet reached them so their bodies still suffered from the chill of the night. Shenara launched herself into the air. With the new day came the continued responsibilities of preparing her daughters for the final test; a journey from which only one would return.

Daughters! Shenara called out. From the heart of the swarming mass crawled two white butterflies. Each flexed its wings before springing upward.

Mother, Rojani and Fenari called out simultaneously. Without responding, the Queen turned and flew toward a clearing. Her daughters followed, each at her own pace. Once in the meadow, Shenara circled the clearing several times. Occasionally she landed on a brightly colored flower to rest or to sample the sweet pollen. Some plants she avoided. One, however, she approached cautiously.

You must never touch the blue ones, Shenara warned, diving into the shadows beneath several large blossoms. When Rojani and Fenari followed, they saw the decaying remains of butterflies scattered around the base of the plant. Many belonged to other colonies that shared their territory. A few the sisters recognized as being from their own.

What happened? Rojani asked, clearly terrified at the horrific sight.

The flower happened. This is the Deceiver. Stay away from it, no matter how much it tempts you. There are many flowers and plants to feed from, but none as sweet as this one.

How do you know this, Mother? Fenari asked, shuddering.

Look around you, daughters. This is but one plant and yet hundreds of bodies lie dead beneath its beauty. Fly closer and the scent becomes irresistible. Feed and you want nothing else. Death is slow and painful. The nectar feeds only the cravings. The body dies of starvation. Even ground feeders will not touch those who have died from the nectar of the Deceiver.

We will remember, Mother, Fenari and Rojani promised.

The lessons continued throughout the day and for many weeks afterward. Shenara taught each to recognize the dangers of their world and the secrets that could save them. They gained confidence in their strengths and appreciated their weaknesses. Aerial maneuvers were perfected, the best places to hide revealed, and they were constantly reminded to be vigilant. Danger came from every direction.

Trust what you feel and the memories of those who came before you, Shenara said.

Memories? I have no memories of anyone, Rojani said.

Neither do I, Fenari agreed.

One of you will, Shenara promised cryptically.

11

The Queen continued her lessons. She taught them to sense danger before it appeared. The sisters were intelligent and learned quickly. Shenara was pleased. Either would make an excellent Queen.

CHAPTER 4

ROJANI AND FENARI were now fully grown, no longer able to hide amongst their siblings. Their white wings glistened in the light, making them highly visible even at nighttime if the moon's beams were bright enough. It didn't help that their brothers and sisters moved aside when they moved amongst them.

The late afternoon sun was still hours from settling when Shenara led them home.

Now you must seek a special place, she said. One that is safe and comfortable, but small enough to stay warm. The entrance must be narrow. Choose wisely. The air grows cooler on the journey to our summer home, and the predators more fierce. Every night, your life and those of the colony will depend on whether you have chosen wisely. If you die, they die.

Having sent the two butterflies on their way, Shenara returned to her own special place to rest. Tomorrow she would send her daughters on a mission; one that could end in their deaths and that of the collective. With luck and skill, a new Queen would return.

* * *

Fenari! Rojani! The sun was still well below the horizon when the Queen called to them. She hadn't seen her daughters since the evening before, although she knew exactly where each was sleeping. Both had chosen their safe places well.

Rojani appeared first but only seconds before Fenari.

Yes, Mother, they said in unison.

You have worked hard, daughters. Your knowledge and skills are complete. I can teach you nothing else. Now you will test all that you have learned. For three days, you must follow the sun as it travels across the sky, each of you flying a different path. On the third day you will search for something special, something unique. Remember it and bring that memory home.

I don't understand, Fenari said. *How will we know what you want?*

It is not what I want. It is what you find.

This seems too simple, Mother, Rojani said.

Staying alive is never simple. The journey will challenge your stamina, your sense of danger and your ability to find safe places. On your return trip, all that you see will appear different than all that you remember. The world changes around us as we change around it. Now go. The sun awakens.

Obeying their Queen, Rojani and Fenari flew away, afraid but confident Shenara would not send them into the wilderness if she didn't believe in them.

CHAPTER 5

Day 1

ROJANI FLEW FOR ALMOST a full day without stopping, knowing her progress was slow. Hungry and weak, she realized she had made a potentially fatal error but had also learned a valuable lesson. Distance meant nothing if she failed along the way. Although the sun was not yet setting, Rojani decided to stop. Her first priority was to find food. Fortunately, several flowers and milk plants flourished in the area. Darting from blossoms to milkweeds, she filled her belly and then set out to locate a safe place. A crevice between two thick, scaly plates of bark provided the perfect sanctuary. It was small and compact, but comfortable. Most important, it provided the security she needed for the night.

* * *

Fatigue weighed heavily on Fenari, but her energy level was still high enough to keep her safe if she needed to outmaneuver predators. She had stopped several times during the day to feed on the sweet juices of the abundant milkweeds, carefully avoiding the tantalizing smell of the Deceiver. The decaying bodies alone would have been warning enough, even if Mother hadn't told them about the addictiveness of the plant.

Today she was both lucky and diligent. The few predators that crossed her path were either already well-fed or she sensed them before they saw her. Mother had taught her well. Fenari's growing confidence didn't blind her to the realization that she needed to stay alert day and night. Stopping before the sun disappeared behind the horizon, she found her safe place. Nestled between the narrow fissures of the bark of a giant tree, she settled down for a good night's rest. Tomorrow was only the second day of her test.

Day 2

Darting between limbs, Rojani frantically dipped and turned in an effort to escape the long, snapping beak. She had allowed herself to be distracted by a rainbow above a pool at the base of a miniature waterfall. The dancing colors were like flowers swaying in a breeze. They reminded her of home. She missed her brothers and sisters. Had she not seen the reflection on the surface of the water, Rojani would be rotting in the belly of the bird now chasing her. That could still happen if she didn't escape its relentless pursuit.

Mother would be ashamed of me. Rojani quickly discarded the thought. Mother would simply tell her there was a lesson in the experience. *That is if I live long enough to learn it.*

Snap! Snap!

* * *

Petals shaped like wings, the flowers provided Fenari with the cover she needed. Frightened, she nestled amongst the blooms hoping she wouldn't be noticed by

16

the flock of small birds frantically circling overhead. Their shrill screeches rang through the forest, blocking out the usual sounds.

Not every predator feasted on butterflies. Fenari wasn't taking any chances. Mother had taught her and Rojani many things; the flowers and plants that provided nourishment, the ones to avoid, enemies that came from the sky and those that slithered or scurried across the ground. Not everything was a threat.

But nothing must be taken for granted. Fenari remembered that day and its lesson well.

It was a day that had started like the others. Mother had summoned Fenari and Rojani from their safe places. Then a high-pitched wail broke the early morning silence. It was painfully loud and scary. Instead of flying away, Mother led them toward the sound. A large cat lay writhing on the forest floor. Huge paws slapped at its eyes as it shook its massive head. The ears were filled with small crawling creatures. The animal was covered in ants, millions of them.

Learn well, daughters, Mother said. Size does not determine the degree of danger. These animals are insignificant as individuals. One is only an irritant, but many become formidable. Nothing can withstand their ferocity.

How can I protect myself from such numbers? Rojani asked.

Be vigilante at all times. These are ants. They sleep at night like us and thus pose no immediate threat but there are things that move through the darkness. Rest with your eyes shut but your ears open... and remember, danger comes from all directions.

They are awful, Mother, Fenari said and shuddered.

They are what they are. We do not judge others, Fenari. We, too, feed off the living. Can we know for sure that we aren't causing pain when we sip the lifeblood of a flower or milk of the plant? Shenara asked. *Do not assume they cannot feel. We may think we are different, but we are all the same.*

I understand, Mother.

I also understand, Mother. Why cannot our family use our numbers to defend us? We have as many brothers and sisters as these ants.

Defend with what, Fenari? What weapon could we use? We are fragile, our wings and legs delicate. Only our numbers and a Queen's wisdom ensure that the colony will survive another season. That is all we have, all we need. The sun will be setting soon. We must return home. You have much to think about.

The three returned to the colony, each seeking out her safe place.

Shaking her head, Fenari returned to the present. Fortunately her temporary lapse had not endangered her. The normal sounds were comforting. Inhaling deeply to release some tension, Fenari scanned the area for predators. Seeing none, she crawled from her hiding place and tested her wings. All was well. Launching into the air she continued her journey. She still had several hours of flying time ahead of her.

Day 3

The sun was peeking over the horizon, spreading its pink rays across the meadow of wildflowers. As the safe place warmed, Rojani stirred, flexing each leg. One had been slightly injured the day before in her efforts to escape a predator but had healed overnight. Pressing her wings together over her body she squeezed through the narrow

18

crack into the light. This was the last day of her forward journey. Tomorrow she would head back to the colony.

Mother said I would find something unique. Rojani scanned her surroundings. There was nothing that she would describe as **unique**. Some of the plants were unusual but the meadow was like many others she had seen. Large animals grazed on the lush grass. Smaller ones stood near the edge of the forest looking fearfully in one direction and then another. The meadow teemed with life, but nothing she could honestly say was unique. *Have I failed her?* The thought was depressing.

* * *

Fenari watched the grazers move around the clearing, cropping and tugging at the thick grass. Occasionally one would raise its head to check some unknown scent or sound. Once assured there were no threats it returned to its grazing. Other animals and insects scurried around intent on their own business.

Nothing! Fenari was disappointed. *There is nothing here. I have failed Mother.*

Reluctantly she raised her wings, lifting her body into the air. A gust of wind blew her sideways. Frantically she struggled to regain control. Twisting her body she grabbed at the limb of a nearby tree. Adrenalin gave her the strength to hold on. After the wind died she relaxed, feeling drained. Fenari knew she was now too weak to safely begin her journey home. She needed to rest. Shifting to a more comfortable position, she checked for predators and saw movement on the trunk of the tree she clung to. Could it be?

Rojani?

Fenari? Is that really you? her sister called out. *How did you get here?*

19

I flew! How did you?

I flew, Rojani said.

How is this possible? Fenari asked. *We travelled different paths. Is our world so small?*

I don't know. We flew only three days. Mother says the journey north is long. She wouldn't lie to us. Could we have taken wrong paths?

We must have, Fenari said. Each sister felt the other's disappointment and was saddened. They had spent weeks training together, learning Mother's lessons and selflessly sharing their thoughts and ideas. Only one could be Queen but both wanted the same thing, to make Mother proud.

Rojani raised and lowered her wings before folding them above her head in a more relaxed position. Her eyes searched the horizon for anything that might be unique and again found nothing.

We need to feed and then find a safe place for the night, she finally said.

Perhaps we can find one big enough for the both of us, Fenari suggested shyly.

I would like that.

The sisters soared into the air, flapping their wings slowly, each to her own rhythm. An abundance of flowers and milkweed provided them with plenty of nourishment and a variety of sweet, tasty nectar and pollens. When their bellies were full, they searched the nearby trees for a safe place large enough to accommodate them. As the sun vanished beyond the tree line they settled comfortably near each other, wings and cheeks touching. For hours they talked about what they had seen on their journeys and the lessons they had learned.

I wish we had found something unique, Rojani said, feeling depressed.

Me too, Fenari agreed. *Maybe Mother is wrong. Maybe neither of us is meant to be Queen.*

Maybe.

Shifting slightly, the two butterflies closed their eyes and slept and dreamt of forests and meadows filled with lush plants. Colorful blooms and tall, thin-leafed plants covered the earth as far as the eye could see, and in the distance they watched an enormous white butterfly coming toward them.

Mother?

Mother!

No, I am Lenila, Mother of your Mother, Queen of your Queen, the butterfly said. *You have done well, children. Your task is almost completed. In two days you will be home. Tell me, what have you learned?*

I have learned to be vigilant. That danger comes from all directions, Rojani said.

And I that it comes in all sizes, Fenari added.

That is good. What else?

Fenari and Rojani continued to tell Lenila about their experiences and the lessons learned from each. The Queen nodded her head approvingly as she listened.

You will make fine Queens, she said. *There is but one more challenge left for you. Have you not found it yet?*

No, Rojani said. *I have seen many wonderful and frightening things — animals, plants — but nothing unique.*

Nor I, Fenari added. *Have we missed something?*

Lenila nodded. *Yes, the most important thing you will ever encounter.*

How will we know what we are looking for if we do not know what it is? Fenari asked.

You will know. When you awaken, do not look so far ahead that you do not see what is beside you. Now, morning comes. I must leave.

21

Will we ever see you again? Rojani asked.

A Queen is never without her Queens, children, nor a daughter without her Mother. Raising her wings high, Lenila pushed downward, lifting her body into the air. Circling twice above the two sisters, she then flew away, disappearing into the pink rays of the rising sun.

* * *

Opening her eyes, Fenari felt Rojani stirring against her.

Good morning.

Good morning, Rojani said, shifting away so they could stretch their legs.

I dreamt about you... us... last night, Fenari said. *We were in a beautiful place and Mother's Mother was there.*

I dreamt the same thing. She asked about our journeys. Rojani rotated her body to get a better look at her sister.

And said we were not to look so far ahead... Fenari began.

...that we did not see what is beside us, Rojani finished.

Fenari and Rojani stared into the others' eyes, each widening in surprise.

We are what Mother was talking about, they said simultaneously. *We are unique!*

You have learned well, daughters. Come! a familiar voice commanded from outside the safe place. Peeking through the opening, Fenari and Rojani saw Mother hovering a short distance away. *Today you are Queens,* Shenara announced.

That can't be! The colony has only one Queen. That is you, Mother, Rojani said.

The colony has grown too large. It needs two Queens. Today we begin the journey north so you can learn the path. Your brothers and sisters will soon follow. Eventually one of you must take half of the colony and find a new home, but only when the time is right.

What about you, Mother? Fenari asked.

This is my last journey. Once you know the way, I will join my Mother and those before her. The sisters gasped. The thought of Mother not being with them was frightening and sad. *Queens are never without their Queens,* Shenara said. *Come, your real journey begins today.*

* * *

Before Shenara had left to find Fenari and Rojani, she called all of her children together.

Children, soon you travel north. As I have led the many generations before you, I will lead you, your children and your children's children to their final homes. This is your final journey. So will it be mine. None of us will return here. It is our way of life. Telling you this was not necessary. All of you will be gone before me. Shenara hesitated, looking at the thousands of butterflies that surrounded her. No wing moved, no eyes strayed from hers. *I have loved each generation equally. Each child the same. Every death I mourned, every life I cherished. You are the first of my children to take this final journey with me even though you won't be the last. Know, though, your faces, these memories I will carry with me when I am with my Queens.*

Mother? A small voice called out timidly.

Without hesitation Shenara turned to gaze at one butterfly amongst the mass surrounding her. Queens were able to identify all of their children by patterns and voices.

23

Yes, Sorilia.

Will we see you after we die?

I don't know. I have only been visited in my dreams by my Queen. Shenara's eyes swept over the colony. *Have any of you been visited by a brother or sister?*

Oroni came to me after he disappeared, Sorilia said.

And Pilara came to me after she was seduced by the Deceiver, another exclaimed. Soon other voices joined in until none were silent.

Pleased, Shenara raised and lowered her wings several times.

That is your answer, then. We will see each other again beyond this life. It will be a joyous reunion. Come now. Let me touch each of you so I may take your essence with me.

One by one each butterfly moved forward and rubbed his or her forehead against Shenara's. Afterward it flew away, making room for the next. The ceremony lasted half the day. When the last flew off, the Queen gave their southern home one final glance. Then, lifting her body into the air, she started her own journey. There were two daughters who needed her.

Several grazers lifted their heads to watch a large white butterfly soar across the meadow toward the rising sun. As it disappeared into the growing light, the grazers lost interest and returned to their morning routine of feeding. They had just arrived from their northern migration. The lush growth would provide them with the nutrients necessary for the trip home in the fall.

CHAPTER 6

FIVE ROUND TRIPS were completed before the Queens felt confident they could each lead half the colony on their own. Four had been made without Mother. Their sisters and brothers knew it was unusual having more than one Queen. When born, they were taught the history of their species. Knowledge of the past was important if they were to understand the importance of their role in the future of the colony.

The time has come, hasn't it? Fenari asked, already knowing the answer. *How will we do this?*

Each brother and sister will make their own choice. It is beyond our control, Rojani said. *When we leave, we will keep to the main routes but take different smaller paths as we move north. Those who follow yours will be yours.*

What about the nurseries? They have become crowded. Who will look for new ones?

I will look for a new one for the first generation. You must look for one for the next. The third and final are still large enough to sustain two colonies. While our children feed and grow strong we will scout other places for next year.

Fenari circled the broad leaf they were resting on. Their family was prospering under their reign. The numbers had increased.

I will miss those who follow you, Rojani, but you are a great Queen. They are lucky.

25

As I will those who choose you, sister. They too are lucky. I think Mother would be proud of us.

I still miss her, Fenari said.

We will see her again. Until then, we have responsibilities. Shall we begin?

Rising slowly into the air, the Queens started their journey north, their iridescent white wings fluttering at their own pace.

* * *

Winter was still several cycles away. Millions of wings fluttered through the forests and across meadows. The young butterflies enjoyed playing together, forming strong bonds. Although now two colonies, they acted as one. Family was family. Only when they started the return journey to the south would they divide back into separate groups.

Fenari and Rojani had stayed with the arriving generation through their final life cycle. Butterflies sought partners, mated, laid their eggs and then flew away amongst the tall trees, disappearing into the dark forests. When the last were gone, the Queens felt the loneliness of the empty land. It quickly vanished once the eggs hatched. The plants covered with the ravenous caterpillars were quickly consumed until, fat and bloated, the larvae could eat no more. They then metamorphosed into pupae and eventually transformed into butterflies.

* * *

It was time for the Queens to begin their search for new nurseries. Their children were old enough to be left on their own for days at a time. Fenari and Rojani followed the southern route for half the morning, unaware they were being followed.

Do you smell that? Rojani asked, catching a strange scent.

It smells sweet, sweeter than normal, but not in the way of the Deceiver, Fenari said. *Could it be another variety?*

Maybe. We must be careful. Mother warned us about the addiction of excessive sweetness. If it smells too good —

— then it is probably bad, Fenari finished.

Yes, she also said there are plants that mimic the Deceiver but are harmless, Rojani said.

I remember. She told us we would know the difference. We must have faith in Mother's trust of us. We should investigate this smell. If it is another Deceiver, we can warn the colonies. If not, it may be another food source.

The sisters followed the scent trail through a dense forest, across several hills until they finally located the source, a large meadow filled with a thick carpet of grasses and wildflowers. Fenari and Rojani didn't recognize any of the floras. It was if they had flown into an entirely new world. Surveying the area, they found several more clearings. One, in particular, had an unusual rock in the middle. Its shape and color didn't blend with its surroundings. The object obviously didn't **belong**. Sunlight reflected off the smooth, shiny surface. Cautiously Fenari and Rojani approached it, staying far enough away that they could flee if they needed to. When a strange animal suddenly appeared, they realized there was a cave entrance on one side. Two similar creatures followed.

What are they? Fenari asked

I don't know.

Fenari and Rojani watched the things moving around the rock, picking up smaller ones and carrying them back into the cave. It was obvious they could communicate, which meant they were intelligent.

Mother would know what they are, Fenari said confidently.

Rojani agreed, but Mother was not there to tell them. *I think we should leave now. It will take a half-day to get back to the colony. Come, sister.* Turning, she caught a slight breeze and soared upward. Fenari followed. Neither looked back. If they had, they would have seen the creatures staring in their direction and a dozen small, curious butterflies flitting carelessly behind them toward the rock. Trailing behind the group was a tiny white one. Too young to be afraid and too hungry to resist the sweet smell coming from the cave, they disappeared into darkness. Neither creature seemed to notice the intruders as they too went inside. Moments later, the entrance sealed itself. The ground shook as the strangely shaped rock rose higher and higher into the air before finally vanishing into the clouds.

Fran Heckrotte

Touch

Of the Butterfly

PROLOGUE

SIP968X WAS DISCOVERED more than thirteen-thousand velyars ago. The life forms were now more diverse and evolved than many worlds presently under Lieran observation. Xplor Corporation had designated the planet a Category SIP, meaning of special interest. Three evolving species exhibited unusually high degrees of intelligence. One in particular was on the verge of space travel. They had primitive crafts with propulsion engines powerful enough to push them into orbit. Their progress was monitored every two hundred velyars by an unmanned research vessel. If the inhabitants perfected a drive efficient enough to carry them beyond their solar system, the Lieran would initiate contact. Until then, computers gathered valuable data and transmitted it to Xplor.

Planets approved for physical exploration were normally very primitive. They were EVWs, evolving worlds. Before receiving an assignment to one, Xplor researchers received extensive indoctrination in contact protocols with plant and animal life. Fear of cross-contamination between Lierans and indigenous species was a major concern. One planet had an entire eco-system destroyed because of the careless behavior of a research technician. Other worlds had suffered less severe damage but had been irreparably altered. The Lierans vowed to never repeat those mistakes.

Unfortunately, even the best of intentions is often sacrificed for profit. Screening and training didn't guarantee researchers would adhere to every regulation. Explorers were naturally curious, a strength that, occasionally, exposed weaknesses. Xplor chose their brightest people for their research teams. Sometimes they overlooked minor infractions if person showed exceptional potential. Progress always came with risk, and profits came from progress.

CHAPTER 1

EVW984L

THE LUMINESCENT WHITE butterfly was exquisite. Light reflected off the wings, creating a faint glowing halo around an elongated golden body. Louai watched it flutter aimlessly from flower to flower, settling on one and then moving to another. The size of a small plate, it was the largest Louai had ever seen on any of the EVWs she had explored. Without thinking, she held up her left hand, palm upward, wiggling her fingers in hopes of enticing the beautiful creature closer. It worked. As if drawn by an invisible string, the butterfly launched itself off a red-and-yellow blossom straight toward her, settling lightly on her fingertips. Louai shifted the animal to her right hand, barely able to contain her excitement. She could easily make out the intricate patterns on each wing.

"You're gorgeous," Louai whispered, not wanting to startle the insect. "I know touching you is forbidden but, technically, you came to me, didn't you?" Lifting her hand higher, she raised it to eye level for a closer inspection. The butterfly adjusted its position to face Louai. Glistening dark purple eyes stared at her. Louai felt herself being drawn into their depths. The world around her momentarily disappeared, replaced by swirling ghostly images from her past; memories she had long forgotten and wished had remained that way. Then scenes of lush, tranquil forests and flowers flashed by, bringing with them a sense of calm and wonder. Suddenly the vision vanished in an explosion of colors, bringing her back to reality.

What the helvin happened? she thought, shaking her head to clear the lingering memories and disorientation. Not wanting to risk a repeat of the experience, Louai tossed the butterfly into the air and watched it flap slowly away, unconsciously rubbing her hands together in an attempt to wipe all evidence of having handled the creature. A loud crack of thunder reminded her that a storm was moving in. From previous experiences, Louai didn't want to be caught outside when it arrived. They were usually short, but often violent.

"That wasn't very smart," she muttered, regretting her impulsive behavior, a character trait she had battled all of her life. Lylia wasn't going to be happy when she learned Louai had violated a critical Xplor regulation, especially since they had recently reinstated her after a similar infraction. Restricted to lab work for six velmons had felt like an eternity. Fortunately, Lylia, one of the top researchers in the company, agreed to team up with her if she promised to behave.

"Behave! It makes me sound like a child. What's the use of being a scientist if I can't examine specimens up close?" She sighed and then flinched as lightning flashed closer in the distance. If lucky, she had thirty velmins before the rain started, more than enough time to reach base camp. *I'd better go and tell her what I've done.* Dreading the impending lecture, Louai gathered her equipment and trudged quickly but reluctantly toward the ship. Hopefully Lylia wouldn't report her to Xplor. She doubted if they'd be so forgiving this time.

* * *

Crouching, Lylia studied the data scrolling across the datavid in her right hand. The soil contained interesting minerals and elements but nothing to get excited about, not that she usually got excited about anything anymore. Well, other than the thought of seeing Ariana soon. Velyars of exploration had a way of tempering youthful exuberance and Lylia felt she had seen just about everything there was to see. It was true every planet was unique. The chemical composition of life on habitable EVWs was less so. In the infinite worlds of possibilities, only a small window of variables existed that could sustain complex species. EVW984L was beautiful.

But boring, Lylia thought and then looked at the sky as thunder rolled ominously just beyond the tree line. *Looks like a bad one coming in. I hope Louai gets back soon.*

The sound of something thrashing through the underbrush snapped Lylia back to her surroundings. Slipping the datavid into her pocket she glanced around, attempting to locate the direction of the noise. To her right, the tops of bushes were being slammed aside. Whatever was moving toward her was big. Her hand moved to rest on the weapon strapped to her left hip. EVW984L wasn't a hostile world, but plenty of animals were capable of killing her or, at the very least, inflicting serious harm. Lylia had already destroyed a large-horned herbivore after it tried to gore Louai. They had inadvertently stumbled onto it while it was resting. Startled, the frightened animal attacked them, leaving Lylia no choice but to kill it. The researchers were saddened at the taking of a life.

* * *

A bush in front of Lylia shook violently. Gripping her plazgun tightly, she partially slid it from her belt but shoved it back in place when Louai's head and shoulders pushed through the thick foliage. Her left hand was cupped in her right. Both were clutched tightly against her chest. Whether the expression on her face was fear or pain, Lylia couldn't tell, not that it mattered. Louai was in serious trouble.

"What have you done?" Lylia shouted, racing forward but barely reaching Louai in time to cushion her assistant's fall as she collapsed to her knees.

"I'm sor —"

"It's alright. I've got you," Lylia said, lowering her to the ground. "Louai! Louai! What happened?" Receiving no response, Lylia checked for a pulse. She exhaled slowly when she felt the faint beat near the right ear. Her relief was short lived. Her assistant was clearly unresponsive but her eyes were wide open. Blue bruise-like blotches began appearing on her face, followed by webs of dark green streaks. Fearing Louai was infected with an unknown organism, Lylia jumped to her feet and backed away.

Felk! What happened? What do I do now? she thought, staring in horror at her companion. Her mind raced through all the possibilities and came up empty. *Think! Antivere!* Yanking open the small pouch on her right hip, she grabbed a small vial. The pink solution glowed under the red rays of the sun peeking between rapidly moving clouds. Lylia snapped the tip off. Cautiously she stepped forward. Although they had been on assignment less than six velmons, she and Louai had grown close, a necessity for the mental stability required to complete the long, isolated research assignments.

I can do this. I can do this. Lylia repeated the mantra over and over in a useless attempt to control the underlying fear that Louai had contracted a transmittable disease. *I'm probably already infected.* Unconsciously, she wiped her free hand on her pant leg then examined it for evidence of contamination. *Maybe it's something she inhaled. No, the nasal screens would prevent that.* Facemasks weren't practical for long-term explorations; all offworld researchers were implanted with micro-filters, preventing airborne contaminants from entering the lungs. Feeling panicky, she slowed her breathing. *This is ridiculous. Whatever happened doesn't matter now.* Kneeling, she reluctantly leaned forward and plunged the needle into Louai's neck.

* * *

Louai's face was swelling. Her eyes appeared to be closing. Lylia felt nauseous when she realized the growing puffiness of the lids was forcing them together. *How much more can skin stretch?* she wondered in morbid fascination. Touching Louai was no longer a possibility. Whatever was causing the bizarre reaction had progressed beyond Lylia's capability to handle. The antivere proved useless. All that was left was to watch and hope she didn't suffer the same fate. *I need to record this,* Lylia thought and then grimaced. *Scientist to the end.*

Sliding the datavid from her pocket, she activated the vidcord and swept it along the length of Louai's body. Images streamed across the screen as the instrument transmitted the recorded data to the main computer in their spaceship. At least, Lylia hoped it was being transmitted. Something in the atmosphere of EVW984L had proven problematic for any transmission when storms were present or even nearby. Lylia wasn't sure if the approaching front would have the same effect.

Because Lylia had also pressed the emergency button, two events were automatically triggered. The information received by Comm, the onboard communication system, would be relayed to Xplor to be analyzed. What the corporation did after that was up to them. Then the research vessel's launch thrusters were locked down, preventing the ship from taking off. Xplor wasn't going to chance an epidemic outbreak on the home world. Vessel decontamination would be necessary before it could leave the planet.

Right now, Lylia needed to identify the source of Louai's illness, or at least if it was contagious before any rescue mission received authorization to land. *It will probably take a good velmon before they get here,* she thought. *And that's the least of my problems.*

Turning her attention back to Louai, Lylia was horrified to see the body had swollen to more than twice its normal size. The gray one-piece uniform was stretched to its limit. The suit would probably withstand the stress of the bloating body awhile longer but Lylia knew the exposed skin around the hands, neck and head did not have the same strength or elasticity.

"I'm sorry," Lylia murmured. As a friend she felt she had failed Louai. As a scientist, the rapidly developing symptoms were intriguing. Being so close, however, was a foolish risk. Lylia stood up and backed away, her eyes never leaving Louai's distorted face — that is, until a butterfly with white wings landed on the swollen, bulbous nose.

"What the..." Slowly the butterfly raised each wing, lowered them and repeated the movement four times. A golden halo surrounded the insect's body, causing it to glow. As gently as it had landed, it lifted into the air and flew away. Mesmerized, Lylia watched it disappear into the forest. Louai had mentioned the day before that she had seen one, but Lylia didn't really believe her. That species of insect was conspicuously absent on this particular world. She thought it was wishful thinking on her associate's part, perhaps mistaking a small bird for something she hoped to see. As a scientist, Lylia knew better than to assume anything. She should have asked more questions, not that it made any difference now. They wouldn't be sharing this experience. "A butterfly," Lylia murmured, looking down at Louai, hoping beyond reason she had seen it too.

What Lylia saw paralyzed her. Gasping, she gagged, trying to suppress the urge to vomit.

Eyeballs protruded, extending outward beyond horribly swollen cheeks. Instinctively, Lylia raised her hands up to block what she knew was about to happen. She was barely able to shield her eyes before the head exploded, spewing greenish-blue ooze over the surrounding area.

"Felk!"

Dropping the datavid, she frantically wiped at the thick, warm goo covering her face, inadvertently smearing some into her eyes. If she wasn't infected before, she had to be now. Going home was no longer a possibility. Considering the rapid advancement of Louai's symptoms, Lylia probably had velmins left before the same thing happened to her.

* * *

The datavid seemed so close... agonizingly close and yet unreachable.

Lylia's legs felt heavy, almost as heavy as her arms. Her uniform was designed to be comfortably formfitting, capable of stretching and adapting to the type of physical work required for exploratory expeditions. Even it, though, had limitations. Looking down at her thighs she saw they had doubled in size. Her hands and wrists were puffy, more than twice their normal size. Unable to flex her fingers, Lylia knew she would be dead in velsecs. Still, she wasn't going down without a fight. Xplor needed to know what happened. If a rescue team arrived, it could suffer the same fate, especially if the transmission hadn't gotten through.

Shuffling awkwardly forward, she tried to nudge the datavid with her toe.

I... can... do...

A butterfly flitted near her foot.

"You... a... gain," Lylia gasped. The pressure on her chest was making it difficult to breathe.

Wings flapping slowly, it moved delicately over the surface of her boot and then launched itself in the air directly toward Lylia's face, fluttering frantically. Lylia wanted to blink so badly but her lids wouldn't move. She stared helplessly at the creature, overwhelming curiosity replacing the horror of everything else.

The butterfly soared upward to eye level. Purple eyes stared into Lylia's. The world around her disappeared, replaced by a swirling colorful mass of kaleidoscopic images — shifting patterns of trees, plants, flowers constantly changing shapes until they finally morphed into a single mosaic of —

The image disappeared and with it the return of reality. Lylia's lifeless body crumpled to the ground.

CHAPTER 2

ARIANA PEERED AT THE organism swimming in the crystal globe. The specimen had been delivered to her from one of the eleven research vessels monitoring the twenty-six SIP planets that had been discovered in the Kalgar Quadrant. This specimen was particularly interesting. It had the ability to alter its surface colors and patterns, making it almost invisible. Were it not for the Similor energy beams reacting with the Sustainer fluid, the casual observer would see nothing more than a globe filled with a clear liquid.

"Have you discovered its secret?" Sorelle asked, walking up to peer over Ariana's shoulder.

"I just received this specimen yesterday," Ariana said, sounding a bit exasperated. "And would you please quit looking over my shoulder like that? You know how I hate people doing that."

"Sorry." Sorelle shifted slightly to Ariana's left and motioned toward the globe. "It doesn't look like much, does it."

"Maybe not, but if we can discover how it blends so perfectly with its background, we might be able to replicate the process. We could physically explore the SIPs. Can you imagine living amongst other intelligent life forms undetected?" Ariana asked and immediately regretted her words.

Sorelle would never get that opportunity. He was an excellent scientist but incapable of controlling his

40

curiosity, often taking unnecessary risks in the rush to find answers. His requests to be assigned to a research vessel were always refused.

Xplor wanted quick results, but not at the cost of lives or equipment, especially equipment. Over-exuberance could prove disastrous, financially and politically. The corporation spent a fortune screening research applicants, identifying character flaws and weaknesses. Enthusiasm was welcomed, within reason.

"I'll never have that opportunity," Sorelle said, his voice tinged with suppressed anger. "It's not fair. I'm one of the brightest brains at Xplor. My record is impeccable and they have profited considerably from my work. If I'm passed over again, I might as well put in for retirement."

Ariana didn't know what to say. She understood Sorelle's disappointment. He was eighty-five and had never been spaceside. At forty-three, she was one of the brightest scientists at Xplor. Her credentials were impressive, seven expeditions to EV1s, three to the more advanced EV2s. With fifty-six patentable discoveries, multiple degrees in plant and microbial life forms, both primitive and advanced, Ariana was a valuable asset to Xplor. One EV2 was being upgraded to SIP thanks to Ariana and Lylia's excellent observations and research. The corporation was rewarding them with a new assignment to another Special Interest Planet once Lylia returned from her present assignment.

CHAPTER 3

Two years earlier

ARIANA AND LYLIA had been on the waiting list for five velmons when they were notified of their next assignment. EVW788L was scheduled for an update evaluation. The evolving world had not been visited in almost five-hundred velyars. The last exploration team had made a few interesting observations about peculiar plant behavior but was unable to establish the cause. Xplor had flagged the planet as a 'to watch' and scheduled it for a follow-up visit.

They had spent almost four velmons categorizing the flora and fauna on EVW788L. Plants were lush and abundant; the animals that fed on them numerous and diversified. Predators existed but were rare. For the most part the planet was a vegetarian's dream.

The research team spent most of their time cataloguing plant and animal life, assigning each species a genus and epithet based on characteristics such as color, shape, size and molecular make-up. The discovery of a handful of grasses that had developed a rudimentary form of communication was more than Lylia and Ariana could have hoped for.

"Did you ever imagine we'd find something like this?" Ariana asked excitedly, barely able to keep from jumping up and down like a schoolgirl. "Intelligent plants! It's amazing!"

"There's no reason to think plants can't evolve into intelligent life forms," Lylia reasoned, amused at her assistant's childlike enthusiasm. "Statistically, it was only a matter of time before one of our teams found one."

"Maybe, but **we're** that team. How can you be so calm about this? Others would kill to be in our boots right now."

"I doubt that." Lylia gave Ariana a wry grin and patted her on the shoulder. "Let's review everything one more time. We need to make sure our conclusions are irrefutable before we report to Xplor. You know the rules: verify, verify, verify. Now, let's go over the logs. You're the plant expert. Read to me what you have in your notes. They have to be precise."

Ariana pulled the datavid from her hip pocket and tapped the screen several times.

"Where are you?" she mumbled, unaware of Lylia's faint, knowing smile. It wasn't a secret Ariana hated the newest prototype to their data-gathering arsenal. Xplor had incorporated more functions than any single Lieran could remember. "Ah, here we go," Ariana said and proceeded to read what she had written. "Completed categorization of animal and plant life on the four major continents and seven islands. We decided to investigate small volcanic island in Sector 5, Quadrant 33, Southern pole, Region 101. Three active volcanoes present. Two dormants. Identified several unique plant species unrelated to any on the other sites. Possible deviation may be evolutionary changes due to extreme volcanic activity, isolation from nearest Continents Seisa and Segma, or unusually high latitudinal temperatures. Plants of interest —"

"Ari, just read what you have on this particular plant," Lylia said. "The other stuff isn't important right now."

43

"Oh, sorry. Let's see..." Arian scrolled further down. "Okay... Spidorous Rizonel... a short, wide-bladed grass species. Colors vary from pale green to deep purple depending on acidity and alkalinity of surrounding soils. Appears to multiply by sending rhizome-like shoots underground to surrounding areas but appears not to be aggressively invasive. They form subterranean structures similar to a spider web." Looking up at Lylia, Ariana smiled proudly. "I thought that was a pretty good name for this particular grass."

Lylia nodded but fluttered her fingers signaling for Ariana to carry on with her report.

"When threatened, Spidorous Rizonel rubs its blades together, creating a low-pitched hum that resonates at about fifty velmets. Grass within that range mimics the behavior, increasing the frequency strength to three hundred velmets. While the sound is below the audible range of Lierans, grazers apparently hear it. All feeding activity ceases." Glancing up at Lylia, Ariana tapped the screen with her finger. "This behavior was repeated only when grazers resumed eating. When animals aren't grazing on Spidorous Rizonel, no frequencies are emitted."

"What about the nearby fields?"

"Nothing happened. There was no noticeable change in the plants or the grazers' behavior in the adjacent areas as long as this particular plant wasn't under assault."

"That's certainly different, but not enough to conclude —"

"Today was different," Ariana interrupted excitedly. "Three young grazers ignored the warning — if that's what it is. They continued eating and died almost instantly. I ran a blood analysis on each and all showed high levels of trilynic acid."

"Trilynic? In a grazer?" Lylia asked, her expression reflecting her surprise. "That would inhibit the digestive system's ability to break down plant fiber."

"I know. It surprised me too, so I tested the grasses near where they were eating. Not only did it have trilynics but also phelotetona. I don't know of any complex organism that could withstand that strong a digestive acid. Still, the phelotetona may be weakening it to a tolerable level. Perhaps it's normal in these grazers."

"Not according to our earlier scans. Neither chemical was present in the adults," Lylia said. "You said they died almost immediately. Trilynic is strong but even it takes time for the acid to penetrate the guts, babies or not. This is an extremely hardy species."

Ariana unconsciously nodded her head.

"I know. That's why I performed an autopsy on them... bionetically, of course," Ariana added. "I wouldn't think of jeopardizing our futures by touching them."

"Your future," Lylia said. "Mine is never in jeopardy."

"Rub it in. Just because you received a lifetime achievement commendation doesn't make you irreplaceable."

Lylia's eyebrows shot upward. "Actually, it does," she said and motioned for Ariana to get on with it. Only seven others had received Xplor's top award. The corporation didn't present them often. Lylia had spent half her life traveling to different worlds, examining their eco-systems. She had also developed an efficient system for categorizing plants, animals, minerals and anomalies. Xplor was able to quickly consolidate data from each research team, saving the corporation time and money. As far as the company was concerned, Lylia was indispensable — and she knew it, although she never allowed it to go to her head. Too many lives depended on her judgment and decisions. "Are you finished?" Lylia asked when Ariana didn't immediately start reading.

"Almost. As I was going to say, the grazers' primary and secondary stomachs were liquefied within velmins. The surrounding organs turned into a gelatinous goo."

"Gelatinous goo? Is that some new scientific term?" Lylia teased.

"No, but it's as good a description as any technical jargon. Anyone reading the report will understand what I mean. These animals suffered a horrible death."

"Maybe the phelo is acting as a catalyst with the tri. They don't occur together naturally, so the reaction could be creating a toxic byproduct that they aren't able to metabolize. I'd put my bet on that scenario at the moment."

Ariana nodded. "It's as good a theory as any."

"We need more information. Move six of the recorders to monitor the Spidorous field around the clock. If we can prove this particular plant is sending warnings to the rest and that grazers recognize those signals as a potential threat, we should be able to convince Xplor that it's an evolving intelligence. Good job, Ari."

Ariana beamed at the compliment. Although ten velyars older, Lylia was her mentor and best friend. They had been on four expeditions together and had grown close. Not surprising, since Xplor tested every team candidate for compatibility. Exploratory missions were usually only a few months long, but some could last up to a year depending on distance, planet size and evolutionary stages. Researchers were encouraged to develop mental and emotional bonds during their voyages to minimize stress and prevent boredom. After each assignment they were put on a one velmon hiatus and then returned to normal lab duty for three velmons under the guise of 'Refreshering.' Everyone knew it was Xplor's way of monitoring their mental stability. If the probation period was completed without any serious violations, they were reinstated for new assignments and placed on rotation.

* * *

"Ari, have you sent Xplor our last report yet?" Lylia asked.

"For the third time, yes. Are you feeling alright?" Ariana walked over to her associate who was kneeling on one knee examining a small, feathery plant. "Where's your bio-mask?"

"I took it off. We've been here almost three velmons and have examined almost every square velin in this area. Nothing on this planet produces hazardous pollen or spores. The air quality is almost as good as what our ship's purification system produces. The chance of inhaling something dangerous is miniscule at best."

"Miniscule is still an unacceptable risk and you know it," Ariana chided. "You've preached that to me a thousand times."

"A thousand? You're not that slow a learner," Lydia replied, giving Ariana a cheeky grin.

"I'm serious. If you don't follow protocols, how can you expect others to?"

Lylia sighed. "You're right, of course. I'll be glad when they perfect those micro-filters." Reaching for the small mask dangling below her chin, she started to pull it over her nose and mouth when Ariana stopped her.

"It's a bit late for that isn't it?" Ariana pulled her own mask down and grinned. "We're a team so what happens to you happens to me."

"Now that's not very smart," Lylia said. "If something did happen, you could return home."

"And leave you here? All alone? Not on your life! Besides, the trip back would be unbearable. I'd be bored to death, not to mention very **frustrated**."

"Oh, so I'm just a good lay, huh?" Lylia asked, making a wry face.

"Did I ever say you were good?" Ariana teased and then relented. "Alright, you're good. In fact you're a wonderful lover. The best there ever was. Now do you feel better?"

Rising to her feet, Lylia brushed soil off her knees and then removed her gloves.

"Assuming you're not being sarcastic, yes. And to make sure you remember that, how about we take a few velmins to prove it?"

"Now?"

Lylia nodded.

"You're joking, right?" Ariana asked.

Lylia shook her head. Her copper orange eyes darkened to an almost earthy brown, a clear sign of her arousal.

Ariana grinned. "Why not?" Stepping closer, she ran her fingers down Lylia's cheek. "But I'm not about to go primitive and do anything on the ground. There may not be anything in the air but I'm not about to chance having something crawl up my butt. I'll see **you** in our cabin. Give me ten velmins, though. I have a surprise for you." Ariana turned and strolled seductively toward the spacecraft, slightly exaggerating the sway of her hips. Halfway to the ship, she turned and looked back. "Oh! And make sure you arrive naked. I don't want to waste time undressing you."

* * *

Running the back of her hand down Lylia's neck, Ariana leaned forward and pressed her right cheek against

48

Lylia's and exhaled, knowing the effect it would have on her partner. Lylia inhaled the scent of her lover's warm breath. It reminded her of povenspice, a sweet nut seasoning used to flavor frozen desserts. She could feel her heartbeat increasing with anticipation of what was to come.

Lieran cheeks were extremely sensitive. A light caress could easily arouse the passion of the recipient if the partners were compatible. Foreplay was essential and often lasted a velhor or more; anything less was usually a sign of inexperience or disinterest. Delicate strokes to cheeks, neck and shoulders excited specialized receptors under the skin, causing the skin to produce hormonal secretions designed to enhance sexual arousal. The more released, the greater the sexual experience. Lip-to-lip contact wasn't unheard of, but rarely provided enough stimulation to make it worthwhile. Only the most experienced lover dared to kiss. Lylia was that lover.

"You know we're spending way too much time doing this?" Ariana whispered as Lylia nuzzled her right ear.

"Are you complaining?"

"No, but I do have an image to uphold."

Lylia leaned slightly backward, making eye contact with Ariana.

"What image is that?" Ariana's dark eyebrows shot up and Lylia smiled. "Oh, **that** image! Well, your secret is safe with me." Lylia rolled onto her back pulling Ariana close. "You know the corporation expects their researchers to interact on assignments. Even encourages it."

"I know, and I've tried to satisfy all my partners, but it always felt more like work."

"Maybe it was," Lylia said, running her fingers through Ariana's hair. "Being compatible working doesn't mean being compatible in bed. I heard rumors..."

Ariana shifted her position to stare at Lylia.

"Rumors? What kind of rumors?"

"Nothing bad. Just that you were all business, very professional and **verrry** task oriented. At least that's what one of your team members said. All perfectly true."

"I'm a scientist! I'm supposed to be that," Ariana said. "And who's been talking about me?"

"Of course you are. No one said it was a bad thing." Lylia's lips curled up at the corners.

"You're teasing me, aren't you?" Punching her on the shoulder, Ariana resumed her previous position. "What do you think?" she asked.

"Me? I think you're professional, task oriented, aannd a terrific lover."

Smiling, Ariana wrapped her arm around Lylia's waist and squeezed.

"Only because of you. I never knew sex could be so wonderful."

Lylia grinned.

"Like everything it has to be studied, tried and perfected. I happen to believe in practice, practice, practice."

"You make it sound so clinical. Is that what it is to you?"

"No, but that's what it took to learn the skills. And now we both reap the benefits. You get the pleasure of my expertise and I get you."

"You know if we weren't —"

"Oh, but we are," Lylia said, her voice turning slightly husky. "Enough talk though. I need more practice." Ariana rolled onto her back. "As a professional, I'm sure you agree."

"Oh, by all means, practice away."

* * *

After wrapping up their research on EVW788L, the two researchers returned home. It often took velmons or even velyars for the data to be thoroughly reviewed. If their hypothesis of the intelligent plants was accepted, they would be credited with the discovery and split a substantial reward. The EV world would be re-categorized as a SIP, making a future expedition possible sooner.

CHAPTER 4

The Present

ARIANA HAD JUST FINISHED logging in the results of her day's work when Sorelle came rushing in, clearly agitated.

"Ari, have you heard?"

"Heard what?" she asked, surprised by his sudden appearance. "And why are you still here? I thought you were leaving early today."

"I was but then I heard a tech tell another that Comm-Command lost touch with one of our research vessels. When I asked him about it he said I had misunderstood and then hurried off. I knew better. It took a while but I managed to contact a friend of mine who works in communication. She said it was true."

"What ship?"

Sorelle glanced nervously at the floor and then looked up.

"The Rondal."

"Lylia and Louai's ship?"

Sorelle nodded. "They haven't filed a report in the last seventy-eight velhors and Comm-Command can't get a response from them or the emergency response system."

"It must be an equipment failure. We have too many fail-safes for it to be anything else." Ariana yanked off her lab coat and pulled on her jacket.

"Where are you going?" Sorelle asked.

"To see what I can find out."

"You can't. Command doesn't want anyone to know about this yet."

"I don't care what they want," Ariana declared. "If Lylia's involved, I —"

Sorelle grabbed her arm. "Listen, Ari, that information was given to me in confidence. If you start asking questions they'll want to know where you heard this. She'll lose her job. Wait a bit longer. They're not going to be able to keep this quiet more than a few velhors. They have to notify Sec-Central after eighty-four velhors and... well, there's really nothing you can do for now. Besides, didn't Lylia mention weather issues in her last communication to you? Maybe it's just a natural interference."

"Maybe, and maybe it's something more serious. Another six velhors of not knowing is too long. I'm not waiting —"

"Please, Ari. You know I'm right. Besides, if you appear too distressed over this they'll send you home. It's a minimum one velwek leave for anyone labeled emotionally unstable. Do you want that?"

Shaking her head, Ariana realized Sorelle was right. The corporation knew individuals developed emotional attachments that lasted well beyond their research assignments. It was to be expected and deemed acceptable, as long as it didn't interfere with their work.

"What am I supposed to do, Sorelle? If something's happened to Lylia..."

"...then you'll want to be on the rescue team. You've already been reinstated to active flight status and with your record you should get preferential consideration. Do this right and you can request the assignment. If they think you're too emotionally involved they'll refuse you." Taking Ariana by the shoulders, Sorelle pushed her down onto her stool. "You know I'm right." She did. "Wait. If or when they confirm something is wrong, **then** do what you have to."

Ariana nodded and sighed. "Thank you." Leaning her head against his shoulder she closed her eyes. Normally very independent, it felt good having someone else to lean on for a change.

* * *

Geora Moulara, Xplor's chief security officer, stared at the report on his desk. The EVW984L research team hadn't updated their status in the last eighty-six velhors. All attempts at communicating with the vessel or the crew had been unsuccessful. Corporate policy required they wait an additional twelve velhors before launching a rescue ship. That wasn't very much time to make the proper preparations. If anyone but their top scientist had been on the team, they could wait even longer. Lylia's safety was too important to ignore.

"They should never allow our best researchers on these types of missions," he grumbled. "Who do we have capable enough to lead a rescue team?" he asked his executive officer.

Jamana Rebera handed him the list. "We have seventeen experienced pilots on the active list and twenty-three navigators. Seven med-personnel are qualified for rescue but none have been off-planet. We also should include someone with a micro-bio background just in case."

"I agree. The last thing we need is another alien virus or bacteria making its way back here. The last outbreak cost the company a fortune and took velyars before we paid off all the claims."

"Not to mention our exploration program was almost legislated out of existence," Jamana added. "The public would demand it this time, especially if something —"

"Exactly! We need to make sure the members of the rescue team are discreet and trustworthy. The company's interests are the priority," Geora said.

"I understand. I'll review each one's file."

Geora nodded and dismissed Jamana.

* * *

Commander Rebera carefully examined the woman in front of him and then reviewed the data on the monitor to his left.

"Miss Colorun, I see you volunteered for this mission. Why?"

Ariana had never met Security's second-in-command but had heard a lot about him. The most important thing was that he was a company man. That meant he cared nothing about her personal relationship with Lylia, and frankly she preferred it that way.

"I believe I have the best credentials and am the most qualified to lead this expedition," she replied. "I'm an experienced pilot, navigator and hold degrees in multiple bio specialties. I'm also a trained med tech."

"You think highly of yourself, Miss Colorun," Jamana said, sounding slightly sarcastic.

"If by that you mean I recognize my worth then yes, and so does Xplor. I don't think I need to remind you that I've received several bonuses and awards from the corporation. And one planet is being upgraded to SIP because of my work. Xplor has profited enormously from my skills and knowledge."

"I'm aware of your work **and** the significance of that to Xplor. It's my understanding that Lylia Teylra was your

55

research companion on that SIP mission. Does that have anything to do with your request?"

"Of course, Commander Rebera. Lylia is a great scientist as well as my mentor. If something happened to her it would be a tremendous loss to Xplor, myself and future scientists in this company."

"Yourself, meaning from an emotional standpoint or scientific?" Jamana asked, leaning back in his chair while giving her a hard look.

"First and foremost, scientific. Although I won't deny that I like Lylia. She's intelligent, professional and competent. As for the emotional standpoint, as you put it, while we are sexually compatible I have no strong emotional attachment to her. I'm sexually compatible with many team members."

"That's good! I'd have to deny your request if I thought you were in love with her. You understand. Company policy prohibits —"

"I'm aware of company policy. I assure you, Commander, my concern is the loss to Xplor. My libido can be more than satisfied by any number of choices available."

"I can well imagine." The commander's eyes roamed up and down her body in a detached way. "Your experience means I won't need to assign more than three people to this mission. Since you'll be leading it, do you have any preferences for the navigator and bio-specialist assistant?"

"Navigator, no. As for my assistant, I'd like Sorelle Laeren. We work well together."

Jamana scrolled through the list of active personnel and frowned.

"Laeren. I don't see his name on any of my lists."

"He isn't on the active list," Ariana said.

"Miss Colorun, you know I can't approve of anyone —"

"Commander, we both know Xplor will want this mission to be carried out as discreetly as possible. Sorelle has no family members or friends that will ask questions or demand compensation if something goes wrong. He's an excellent scientist who's about to retire without having been off-planet even once. In other words, he'll do anything asked of him for this opportunity **and** keep his mouth shut afterward. Besides, he's the only one I'd trust to follow my instructions to the letter should we find it impossible to return home... if you know what I mean."

Jamana knew exactly what she meant.

"All good points. As long as he understands the complexity of the situation I'll approve him, but I'm holding you responsible if something goes wrong."

"Captains are always held responsible, Commander," Ariana said and stood to leave. "I don't care who you get for the navigator. Everyone on the list is competent. Is that all?"

"For now," Jamana said, feeling he had just been dismissed. "Be prepared to leave in seven velhors."

Ariana tipped her head slightly, acknowledging the order, and left the room without looking back. Jamana activated the vidscreen, opening a link to his boss to update him on the status of the rescue mission.

CHAPTER 5

"**I'M WHAT?**"

"You heard me. Get packed. We leave in less than seven velhors," Ariana said. The excitement on Sorelle's face was priceless.

"But I'm not even active! I'm too old..."

"Sorelle, do you want to go on this mission or not?"

"Of course I do! I've dreamed of this all my life."

"Then get packed and meet me at launch bay four in two velhors. I'll explain everything then, but keep this to yourself. No one, not even your friend in communications, is to know you're going. Is that understood?" He nodded. "And Sorelle, I told Commander Rebera you were the only one I trusted to follow my orders without question. You understand, right?"

Giving her a questioning look, he hesitated and then realized what she meant.

"We may not return home."

"That's always been a possibility on research assignments. Normally, we think it's because we'll have no choice, but there might be one. I need to know that if I say we can't, for whatever reason, you'll back me all the way."

"You have my word, Ari. And... well, thank you." Sorelle hurried from the lab, his excitement obvious by a youthful stride he hadn't exhibited in many velyars.

* * *

Ariana, Sorelle and pilot/navigator Clieron completed their pre-flight checkup. Their departure was scheduled in two-point-three velhors. The shuttle had dropped them off at the space terminal orbiting Liera. Xplor had assigned their fastest ship in the fleet, the Zayon. Larger than the standard research vessel, it provided sleeping quarters for seven as well as a small lounge and kitchen. Crew members had the choice of eating pre-prepared nutritional items or making their own meals from concentrates stored in the food lockers.

The control center was positioned in a small dome mounted in the middle of the ship. Several crystalline windows gave the crew a 360-degree upper view of their surroundings while vids and sensors monitored everything beneath the belly of the craft. The outer skin of the body was made from a dense silver mineral mined from the Lieran moons. Virtually impenetrable, it provided the protection needed to withstand high-speed particle impacts during space travel. Absorbent photon shields captured intergalactic low-level light emissions from distant stars, converting the weakened beams into energy for propulsion, ship operations and life support. Space travel was no longer restricted to fuel consumption and capacity. Millions of stars provided an unlimited source from the light spectrum.

* * *

"What do we know about EVW984L?" Ariana asked, spinning in her chair to look at her two companions.

"For one thing, it's going to take us less than a velmon to reach it, which is considerably faster than one of the regular ships. Xplor must really be concerned about something if they gave us their newest prototype," Clieron said.

"Have you any experience with this model?" Sorelle asked nervously.

"I've taken it for a few test drives. That's probably why I was assigned to the mission. There were a few glitches but I was told they were worked out."

"Glitches? Like what?"

"Relax, Sorelle," Ariana said. "New technologies always have a few problems. You can bet if it was something to worry about we wouldn't be here. The company's not going to risk losing one of their most expensive investments."

"Exactly!" Clieron agreed. "Now, back to your question. Xplor's been monitoring EVW984L's evolutionary progress for almost ten thousand velyars. They think it has the potential to be upgraded to an SIP based on data sent from the most recent UEV. Personally I'm not too hyped about the new unmanned exploratory vessels, but they do save money. Anyway, Lylia and Louai were sent to collect additional information. You know Corp policy... monitor, monitor, verify, verify, verify. Makes me wonder why they don't get rid of all the UEVs and just send the teams. All the technology in the world isn't as good as old-fashioned hands-on explorations."

"Spoken like a true navigator," Ariana said. "If you're so into **old fashioned**, why aren't you piloting one of those old buckets the supply companies use? Some of them still use compression drive systems. That's as old as it gets."

Clieron laughed.

"I'm talking science stuff not transport. Technology is great for getting us from system to system, but the vessels still need good navigators and pilots."

"And you're a good navigator I suppose," Ariana quipped.

"Absolutely, **and** a great pilot! That's why I'll get us to our destination quicker. I can plot the best gravitational pulls for slinging and how to avoid starstorms. Now do you want to take us out of here or should I?"

"You do it. I'm familiar with the system but haven't actually tested this model. Sorelle and I need to review the reports the research team transmitted. Hopefully they'll give us insight into what happened."

"Forewarned being forearmed," Clieron said and turned his attention to the control panels.

"Something like that."

* * *

Sorelle and Ariana spent most of their time reviewing all the data Lylia and Louai had forwarded to Xplor. The reports were typically uneventful, focusing on the life, topography and climate. From everything Ariana and Sorelle could determine, the EVW appeared relatively benign with few predators and mild temperatures. If the data was accurate the planet was actually boring, a researcher's worst nightmare.

"So far I've found nothing in their reports that raise serious concerns," Sorelle said. "This EV is unusually favorable for exploration."

"I know... uncomfortably so. It sounds too good to be true. Knowing Lylia, she was probably bored to death on this assignment."

"Not every planet needs to be exciting to be interesting. I think this would be a perfect place to explore, especially for a beginner. Besides, there **has** to be a few propitious planets amongst the millions of stars."

"Propitious?" Ariana laughed.

Sorelle blushed, lowering his gaze. "You know what I mean."

"Yes." Patting Sorelle on the arm, Ariana smiled fondly at her companion. He often used unusual words to describe things. "It's a good thing we stopped the colonization program. This one sounds like a prime candidate to settle. Temperate climates and an abundance of life are irresistible. Anyway, there's nothing in their reports to indicate a problem. They were scheduled to return home three veldans after the last transmission. Whatever happened, it came about suddenly."

"It could be just a communication issue," Sorelle said. "The weather or something."

Ariana knew better. The chance of that was zero. Weather could be a factor for a short time but not this long. Each Xplor vessel had multiple independently operated technologies for the transmission and reception of voice, image and data, not to mention a redundant backup system. Theoretically, a total failure could only occur if a ship was instantly destroyed, an unlikely event. Onboard sensors analyzed potential threats and automatically took evasive actions. The data was transmitted to Xplor where the information was processed, stored and uploaded to the rest of the fleet for future reference. Ariana shook her head.

"No. I have a feeling it's something worse."

* * *

"Ariana!"

Ariana swiped at the hand shaking her shoulder.

"Ariana! We're almost to 984L. Do you want primary or secondary seat?" Clieron asked. Xplor regulations required two crew members to be at the controls during landings. It was normally the most dangerous part of the flight.

"Second is fine." Ariana rubbed her eyes and sat up. "How long before we reach the planet?"

"You mean how many times have we circled it?" Clieron teased. "I thought we should do a few orbital scans to see what we're getting into."

"And?"

"And so far nothing that raises any concerns. A few storms, but nothing to worry about. Atmosphere is similar to Liera. Like the reports said, temperature and climate are moderate. I've located the Rondal. We should be able to put our ship down near enough to reach her quickly. I still have to go over the landing protocols with you and transmit the data to Xplor for final authorization."

"Great job, Clieron." Ariana pulled on her boots and went to find Sorelle. She knew he would want to be awake to experience his first off-world landing.

* * *

"Make sure your bio-grav is activated," Clieron said, glancing momentarily at Sorelle.

"It's on," Sorelle replied.

"What color is the light?"

Sorelle sighed. "Green. I know how to operate bio-gravs."

"He's just doing his job," Ariana cut in. "Anything can happen during our approach. If something goes wrong, we don't need you flying around the cabin slamming into us or the equipment or being injured. You're no use to me if you can't work."

"Sorry," Sorelle apologized.

Ariana nodded her acceptance of the apology. Her tone probably sounded a bit harsh but neither she nor Clieron would be able to assist the scientist if there was a problem. They would be locked into their own seats until touchdown.

"Repositioning for final approach, vector 103A... altitude 7545, attitude 180, rotation 2 degrees, 2 velsec intervals, slowing descent," Clieron said. "Altitude 6899 at 150... rotation 5 degrees at 4 velsecs."

"Slow rotation to 3 degrees and maintain 4 velsecs," Ariana said.

"I thought I had primary. Slowing rotation to 3 at 4 velsecs." Clieron glanced up from the controls and made eye contact with Ariana. "Are you assuming the controls?"

"Sorry," she replied. "Continue."

"Altitude 3400, attitude 90 positioned for landing. Touchdown in 13 velsecs. 10... 9... 8..."

A slight shudder shook the ship as the three anti-grav boosters activated, creating a magnetic field similar to but slightly less than the planet's own geo-magnetic energy. As the ship descended, the strength of the field decreased while the gravitational pull increased, allowing the vessel to sink until it settled softly on the surface.

"Touchdown complete. Shutdown phase initiated," Clieron announced, pressing several buttons on the console around him. "Sensors indicate atmosphere quality is good. We won't need enhancement gear."

"What's the weather like outside?" Ariana asked, turning to Sorelle.

"85 veldegres. Slightly cloudy. No unusual weather activity. The sun will be setting in about three velhors. We should wait until morning before going outside."

"I agree. Scan the area. Nothing in the reports indicate serious threats on this EV but we can't be sure. Also activate the perimeter defense. Better safe than sorry. And instruct Comm to transmit our ID and location every five velmins. If the Rondal's Comm is working, it might respond."

"Do you want me to stand watch?"

Ariana shook her head.

"The defense system should be adequate. Get some rest. Tomorrow we'll locate the Rondal and check it out."

CHAPTER 6

CLIERON HAD DONE an excellent job of setting the Zayon near the Rondal, thanks to the coordinates provided by Xplor. The vessel was resting in a small clearing only a two-point-one velhor trek from the rescue ship. Vines covered the hull while tall, waist-high grasses surrounded it. It was almost invisible to the naked eye.

"The protective shields must be deactivated. They'd have prevented that," Clieron said.

"It's protocol," Ariana. "Researchers are required to keep as small a footprint as possible. The unnecessary destruction of plant life is unacceptable. Lylia is a stickler for following regulations."

"Protocol or not, Xplor wouldn't want those things growing on their vessel like that," Clieron replied. "Where do you want to start? The ship or the surrounding area?"

"The ship. Whatever went wrong, that would be the safest place to stay."

"Ship it is." Pressing a button on his datavid, he spoke into a voice sensor. "Zayon, open main door to Rondal."

"Opening Rondal main door," a female voice responded.

"Thank you, Zayon."

Clieron, Sorelle and Ariana watched the ship's door as it lowered to the ground providing a ramp for them to walk up.

"You two stay here," Ariana said. "I'll check inside."

"Do you think that's wise?" Sorelle asked. "What if —"

"If something happens to me, Xplor has to be notified what's going on. You and Clieron get back to the Zayon at the first sign of trouble."

* * *

The lights inside the Rondal eased on as Ariana progressed toward the control room. She had checked the sleeping quarters, galley and supply rooms. Nothing appeared out of order, except for the missing crew.

Where are you, Lylia? she thought. *What happened here?*

The answer was obvious. Nothing had happened. The ship was on emergency lockdown but not because of anything occurring from within. A quick review of the last recorded data indicated an approaching storm that day but nothing else. Ariana would have to search elsewhere. The prospect of Lylia and Louai being alive was disappearing quickly. Activating her datavid, she informed Clieron and Sorelle of her findings.

"Lock her up," she said, walking over to where the two men were standing.

"Nothing?" Clieron asked.

Ariana shook her head.

"Everything inside is in order. The last log entry showed a storm approaching. Maybe they were caught outside and couldn't get back. Has Zayon picked up any life signs yet?"

"No, nothing Lieran, anyway. There are several indigenous species moving around the area but nothing that I'd call a threat. A few hundred velmets to the east is a herd of grazers, something Louai was more interested in than Lylia, according to the reports," Sorelle said.

"Anything in the other directions?"

67

"Not really. More clearings and forests. A small mountain range but that's a three veldan walk. I doubt they'd travel that far from the ship."

"Not without a rover, and this explorer model isn't big enough to carry one. Lylia wouldn't want to be that far away from home base. I don't know about Louai."

Sorelle checked the researcher's bio.

"She's been reprimanded and suspended before. If Lylia hadn't specifically asked for her she'd probably be released from her contract."

"Lylia wouldn't ask for her if she wasn't good at her job," Ariana said.

"That doesn't make her a poster child," Sorelle replied. "She had some serious infractions recently."

"Haven't we all?"

"Ari, I'm not attacking the woman's credentials. Of course she would be good at what she does, but she has an undeniable history."

Closing her eyes, Ariana took a deep breath. Sorelle was right. Why she wanted to defend someone she'd never met she didn't know.

"All right! Let's assume Louai is somewhat of a wild child. Lylia is usually a by-the-book person. Even if she goes off regs once in a while, she's wouldn't do anything to risk her companion or the mission."

"She wouldn't have to, but there's always the chance of something going wrong, including a team member being a little... overenthusiastic. Like you said, whatever happened here wasn't on the ship. That means we investigate the surrounding area," Sorelle said.

Clieron, who had been listening to the discussion, nodded in agreement.

"I suggest we base from here. The Rondal is equipped with everything we need. It'll save us about a half-veldan of travel time."

68

"Good idea," Ariana said. "Open her up again. We'll get Environ up and running, cook a meal and then take a quick look around."

"Let's wait until morning," Sorelle said. "Night's only a few velhors away. We can look over the logs to see if there's any information in Lylia's or Louai's personal files." Anticipating Ariana's objection, he held up his right hand. "I know! I don't like the idea either but we don't have a choice. It could give us some insight into what went wrong. If it makes you feel better, you check the personal stuff and I'll go over the scientific data."

* * *

Ariana spent half the night watching the two researchers' personal vids. Seeing Lylia, hearing her voice, brought memories rushing back of their expedition to EVW788L. The last recording brought tears to her eyes.

Lylia had apparently just finished her shower and was stretched out on the bed relaxing, a sheet partially concealing her nude body from the vid. Louai was sleeping next to her.

"Personal log — Lylia, ID XP4986." Lylia gave the date. It was almost three velmons ago. "Well, we'll be heading home soon. Louai and I have categorized about everything on this planet... at least it feels that way. So far I've found nothing to get too excited about. Louai disagrees. Young people have a way of seeing something in nothing. She's a good scientist. Maybe a little too enthusiastic at times but she's accurate and precise. One day she might be as good as Ariana." Lylia stopped talking for a moment. Her face took on an almost longing expression. "I miss her. If there's one person I would spend the rest of my life with it would be her. But long-

69

term relationships between researchers are frowned upon by the company. One of us would have to resign our flight status. I know it's selfish but I've decided I'm not ready for that. I'm going to turn down Xplor's offer to teach. I haven't told anyone yet. Ariana should be scheduled for a new assignment by the time we return. Maybe already gone. I hope not. I'd like to see her before she leaves. I want to ask her something." Lylia glanced at Louai's sleeping form and then at the clock. "I guess it can wait. I'm tired. Tomorrow's another day. End Personal log. Lylia, ID XP4986."

* * *

Breakfast was a quiet event. Ariana was still thinking about Lylia's last log entry. She wondered what Lylia had wanted to ask her.

"I didn't find anything in the ship's log," Clieron offered, deciding to break the silence. "Either of you?"

Sorelle shook his head.

"Nothing indicating a problem. They received authorization to terminate the research program and head home."

"Lylia said the same thing in her last entry."

"Nothing else?" Sorelle asked.

"No. They mostly talked about personal things."

"You know, when the Rondal is retrieved, Xplor is going to go through those logs," Clieron said. "If they were my personal thoughts, I wouldn't want that."

"If you were dead, it wouldn't matter," Ariana replied. "But I know what you mean. There's nothing we can do about that now. Let's set up a grid search. Configure the sensors for one hundred velmets, point-two-five width and depth. It should pick up any anomaly not natural to this planet based on existing data."

"Yeah, but what about what is natural?" Clieron asked.

"We're looking for signs of Lylia and Louai right now. Any threat we'll handle if it happens."

"You know that narrow a search parameter could take a while. If we expand it in increments of five percent after each sweep, it'll cut down the time by seventy percent and accomplish the same thing," Clieron advised. "Of course it's only going to pick up large objects. If we don't find anything then, we can always reduce the specs."

"How long will it take?"

"I'll have the data in less than two velhors."

CHAPTER 7

"**FIND ANYTHING?**" Ariana asked, leaning over Clieron's shoulder to look at the holographic image of the gridded topography around the Rondal.

"There are fifteen objects within the specified parameters. I've managed to identify all but two." Clieron pointed to each square with flashing ID codes. "Those are research equipment. Some are storage containers. Four are monitors. These two are datavids. They belong to Louai and Lylia. Both haven't been active for quite awhile... and **those** two things I can't figure out. They aren't tagged. Xplor is anal about putting trackers on its property so nothing gets left behind."

"Could they be bodies?" Sorelle asked.

"No. There's no biological readings. Even if they were dead, we'd get something."

"Lock in the coordinates and let's check it out," Ariana said, ignoring the last comment. Whatever it is, it doesn't belong here."

* * *

As they approached the unidentified objects, a swarm of black-and-golden butterflies rose into the air, creating a kaleidoscope of color and movement. The three rescuers stood mesmerized until the horde disappeared into the forests on the far side of the clearing.

"Beautiful animals," Clieron said. "I've never seen so many in one place before."

"It's actually a common occurrence," Ariana replied. "Butterflies seem to be one of those species that evolve as colony or communal creatures, no matter what planet we find them on. There's no reason to think this place would be any different."

"That's probably why the log didn't reference any," Sorelle said. "Although I'd have thought they'd have at least gotten a small honorable mention."

"And that's the problem with you scientists. You're so busy dissecting life you stop living it. If I saw this a thousand times I'd feel special. But then I'm just a pilot." Clieron shook his head and walked away.

"What's with him?" Sorelle asked.

Ariana shrugged.

"Beats me. Maybe he's never seen a cluster before. You're right, though. I didn't see anything in the logs I reviewed."

"Maybe they're mentioned in the earlier ones. It's really not important," Sorelle said.

* * *

Green and silver were the designated colors of Xplor's research department. Ariana stared at the material barely visible amongst the tall grass. Had it not been for the coordinates provided by the Rondal, they'd have never found the two uniforms.

"This doesn't make sense," Sorelle said. "Why would they take their clothes off out here?"

"They wouldn't. It'd be too risky and completely against company policy."

"Everyone breaks the regs sometimes, even the Lylias of the world." When Ariana glared at him, Sorelle held up his hands as if to ward her off. "Hey, the truth is the truth. We scientists are supposed to be open-minded. Consider all possibilities."

"Lylia may break a rule now and then but she'd never go outside naked! This is a ridiculous conversation."

"Point taken. So what explanation would you give for their uniforms being out here?"

"Maybe an animal dragged it out."

"Before or after they locked down the Rondal?" Sorelle asked. "Listen, Ariana, it's really not important how these clothes got here. The fact that they are is the problem."

Ariana knew Sorelle was right.

"I know. There has to be a logical explanation. If we run an analysis —"

"That doesn't take two people," Sorelle cut in. "I'll do that while you and Clieron continue looking around. Maybe you'll find something else that can help us determine what happened to Lylia and Louai."

Clieron, who had been standing quietly to the side listening, touched Ariana's shoulder.

"I'll go back to the Rondal and expand the search grid while you two work on separating the uniforms from the overgrowth. Personally, I'd just rip them up. It may damage some grass or bugs, but under these circumstances we don't have time to worry about Xplor's concerns for flora and fauna. As hard as it is to hear, we have to assume Lylia and Louai are dead. Now we need to know what happened to them and could it happen to us."

After Clieron left, Sorelle and Ariana examined the uniforms, trying to determine the best way to extract them from the tangled growth. As scientists they were repulsed at the thought of just **ripping** the items away from the clutches of the indigenous grasses. Eventually they decided Clieron was right.

"You grab the sleeves and I'll take the legs," Ariana said. On the count of three they yanked hard. Slowly the tenacious plants released their grip until it was finally free. "One more."

"Thankfully." Sorelle rubbed his lower back. "I'm too old for this type of work."

Laughing, Ariana shook her head.

"I thought you wanted to be an off-planet researcher."

"I just changed my mind. No one told me field techs had to do heavy lifting," he grumbled.

"Heavy lifting?"

Sorelle gave her a sheepish grin, walked over to the other uniform and grabbed the legs.

"For me. I'm the cerebral type. Come on, let's get this over with. The sooner I get them to the lab, the sooner we may have some answers. I'll send Clieron back out to help you play explorer," he teased. When Ariana frowned, Sorelle's tone turned serious. "Sorry, Ari. I know this is hard but we can't let it get to us."

"You're right. Tell Clieron I'm going to check over there," she said, pointing toward the east. "The scanner shows a large clearing. That's where Lylia and Louai would focus their research — the best possibility for finding the greatest number of diversity is in open spaces."

CHAPTER 8

FOR FIVE VELDANS, the team searched the surrounding area within a half veldan of the Rondal. Everyone agreed that an extended exploration probably wouldn't turn up any more than the sensor probes.

"Where's Clieron?" Ariana asked Sorelle after returning from another search near where the garments had been found.

"Xplor sent an update request. He's talking with Jamana."

"Did you find anything on the uniforms?"

Clieron shrugged. "Just grass, roots, seeds and primitive life forms. A lot of caterpillars. I was actually surprised at how many. I gathered the live ones up and took them outside. No reason to kill the locals."

"And nothing unusual about the clothing?"

"Nothing that tells me anything. The fibers were stressed."

"Stressed how?" Ariana asked.

"Stretched beyond design limitations."

"What would cause that?"

Sorelle shrugged.

"I don't know. Another thing. There's no DNA trace on either suit."

"Bacteria activity could account for that. Being exposed to the elements for a long time would degrade bio-matter. So basically they aren't much help."

76

"None at all," Sorelle said. "It's almost as if Lylia and Louai had never worn them or carried these clothes outside to throw away after sterilizing them."

"Which they wouldn't do unless —"

"— unless something affected their minds," Sorelle finished. "And if that happened, anything's possible. They could have removed their clothing and wandered off."

Ariana didn't like where the discussion was going, but as a scientist she had to consider all the possibilities.

"Let's say you're right. That means they were affected by the same thing. Maybe a virus or a bacteria."

"The micro-filters would prevent any inhalation."

"Theoretically! This is a new world. We can't be sure the filter works on all viruses or bacteria. Nothing's fool-proof."

"So we might be infected," Sorelle said, frowning at the thought.

"It's possible if the contaminant is airborne. On the other hand, they could have come in contact with something. The problem is there are hundreds of scenarios that we could think of and still be wrong."

"What now?"

Ariana shook her head.

"I don't know. Other than stressed fibers, we have nothing. No bodies, no anomalies, no nothing. It's like they just disappeared. I don't know...."

Clieron strode into the room looking frustrated.

"Jamana wants us to wrap this up. Xplor thinks it's a waste of their resources. It seems losing two researchers, even their top one, isn't as important as recovering the Rondal and all their equipment."

"That doesn't make sense. We could be infected and the ship contaminated. The regulations say —"

"Xplor doesn't care. I told them about that possibility. We've been ordered to fly the Rondal home. A crew is being sent to recover the Zayon. Jamana said if we're infected, we'll show symptoms before we make it back to the base station and they'll deal with it then."

"Deal with it my ass," Sorelle said. "We're as expendable as Lylia and Louai. All they want are the ships back. If we die, they'll eject us into space and try to decontaminate the Rondal."

"That's actually pretty much what Jamana told me. Of course, we'd receive posthumous recognition. Our families would receive survivor benefits and any bonuses we're due."

Ariana rolled her eyes and laughed.

"That's comforting. Any of you have family? I don't." Clieron and Sorelle shook their heads. "Good, because if I'm infected, it'll be over my dead body before Xplor gets this ship. They can't decontaminate something if they don't know what the problem is. And I don't feel the least loyal to them if they can throw us away so easily."

"You realize once we take off, Comm will take over automatically if we become incapacitated. The computers are programmed with a failsafe for that type of emergency."

"Well, you know how these systems were designed. There must be a way to deactivate the thing," Ariana said.

"Oh I know exactly what to do. I'll have to destroy a few sensors. Once that's done, they can't be repaired or bypassed. Before I do that we'd better be sure of our decision."

Ariana looked at Sorelle.

"It's all or nothing," she said.

"When you first asked me to be part of the team you said I might have to make the hard choice," he replied. "So far I haven't had to. This one isn't either. We might as well begin stowing all the equipment. Those storage containers outside will need to be sterilized before we bring them inside. No use taking any more chances than necessary."

"We should retrieve our personal stuff from the Zayon first," Clieron added. "I'm not leaving my logs or things behind for someone else to rummage through."

"That's not a good idea," Sorelle said. "If we are infected--"

Clieron shrugged indifferently.

"Not our problem. I'll prepare a final emergency transmission to be sent prior to any action we take if we have to destroy the Rondal. It'll say we're infected and are taking appropriate action in accordance with Lieran interplanetary exploration protocols and advise the Lieran Interplanetary Council to designate the Zayon and this place off-limits. They won't allow Xplor near this planet for the next five-thousand velyars."

"Let's go then. We can be back by late afternoon," Ariana said, standing. "I wish we could do more for Lylia and Louai. All the years of dedication Lylia gave to Xplor and they're only willing to spend a few veldans trying to find —" Her voice cracked from unshed tears.

Seeing her distress, Sorelle put his arm around her shoulders.

"We've always known the company is all about profit. That makes everyone dispensable."

* * *

It took the three Lierans longer than expected to get to the Zayon, gather their personal belongings and return to the Rondal. A herd of grazers had wandered into one of the meadows between them and their destination. Not wanting to disrupt the animals' routine, they waited on the perimeter of the clearing.

"I like this world," Sorelle said, resting his butt against a fallen tree. "It's peaceful, not hectic like home."

"It's all right." Clieron looked around. "But I'd go nuts having to spend velmons here. I don't know how you exploratory type don't get bored."

When a small yellow butterfly drifted past them, almost within arm's reach, they followed its slow movements with their eyes. It flitted from one flower to another, delicately sampling the different nectars.

"They're such fascinating insects," Ariana said. "One of the few species that varies little from planet to planet." Standing, she brushed off her uniform. "Looks like the grazers are moving on."

* * *

All of the containers but two had been moved into the storage areas and secured. Ariana and Sorelle volunteered to get them while Clieron examined the Rondal's exterior, making sure there were no vines covering the vessel.

"Everything's clear," he said. "Once you get that stuff inside we can leave."

Picking up one box, Ariana turned toward the ship when she heard Sorelle gasp.

"Look!" He pointed toward a spot near the edge of the forest. Two white butterflies soared into the air. The sun's rays reflected off their wings, giving them an almost golden aura. "Too bad I'm a scientist," Sorelle said wistfully. Ariana gave him a strange look. "They seem almost magical, and we both know there's no such thing."

"One of the banes of believing there's a logical explanation for everything," Ariana agreed. Hefting the container a little higher, she and the others walked up the ramp. Shortly afterward the door closed. Within velmins, the earth shook as the Rondal lifted into the air.

EPILOGUE

Commander Jamana Rebera wasn't happy. He had just received a report that the Rondal was missing. The unfortunate messenger was standing nervously at attention while the chief security officer paced back and forth in a vain attempt to calm his anger.

"Ships just don't go missing. There are too many failsafes for that."

"Our engineers said the same thing. They think it's a computer glitch and are attempting to do a manual override of the Rondal's Comm system."

"Don't you have to be in communication with the computer to do that?" Jamana demanded.

"Ummm, well, technically, yes, but..."

"Technically? Isn't **technically** all that matters? Who the hell are you, anyway?"

"I'm Comm Supervisor Faleon."

"Well Comm Supervisor Faleon, I don't want to hear about glitches or technicallys or manual overrides. I want a straight answer. Do you believe the Rondal is still out there in one piece?"

"Commander, we lost contact with the vessel while it was passing through the Wyndnor Quadrant. At the time, there were three starstorms converging at the vector pre-programmed for their return trip. When Comm tried to contact the Rondal for a reroute, we received no response. That was eighteen velhors ago.

I believe our transmissions were interrupted by the starstorms and that the Rondal was caught in the convergence and destroyed."

"That's too bad," Jamana said. "A big loss for the company. Replacing it is going to cost a fortune. How long before our recovery team reaches the Zayon?"

"Fifteen veldans."

"Good! Let me know as soon as it touches down. And Faleon, if the Council catches wind of any of this before we retrieve the Zayon, it's your ass on the line. Understand?"

"Understood, sir."

"Good! Now get back to work?"

"Yes, Commander."

After Faleon left, Jamana settled down in his chair and smiled smugly. If everything went according to plans, once the Zayon was recovered, EVW984L would be declared off limits to further exploration. It would then be eligible for colonization under a new program Xplor was developing in secrecy. The company's profits would more than double in less than five velyars and by the time word got out, the Council wouldn't be able to do anything to Xplor other than issue a reprimand.

"I might even be in charge of the new colony's Council," Jamana said, looking around his office and smiling smugly. "And it'll be goodbye to this place."

Fran Heckrotte

Kiss

of the Butterfly

PROLOGUE

SUZE MCMURPHY WAS STILL able to maintain a quality of life most elderly could only dream of. At seventy-five, she was independent, physically healthy and mentally sound; an inspiration to the people that knew and cared about her. Sadly, the same couldn't be said for her partner, Jen Stone, who was only sixty-eight. Diagnosed with early-onset Alzheimer's disease several years earlier, Jen was frail and now suffered from dementia. Suze didn't accept the neurologist's diagnosis. Doctors didn't know everything, although some thought they did; especially one in particular. When he tried to convince Suze she was too close to Jen to recognize the early warning signs, she wasted no time telling him what he could do to himself. Her suggestion wasn't nice, but it did bring a lot of smirks from the doctor's staff. Most of them secretly applauded her recommendation.

CHAPTER 1

A Day

MORNINGS WERE PERHAPS the worst part of the day. Getting Jen to wake up could be difficult because of how soundly she slept.

"Wake up, sweetie," Suze said, gently shaking Jen's shoulder. "It's time to get up."

One eye opened slowly, looked around and then closed. "Oh no!"

"Come on Jen, you have to get up." Suze picked up a small brown teddy bear that Jen liked to sleep with and put it on the stand next to the bed. When she tried to pull the comforter back, Jen clutched it tightly with both hands. For someone who looked so frail, Jen had a strong grip.

"Go away! Leave me alone!" Jen replied angrily.

It's going to be one of those days, Suze thought. "Turn loose, sweetie." She pried the fingers back, snatched the blanket away and tossed it to the side. Then she picked up a pair of lavender slippers off the floor and slipped them onto Jen's feet. "I've made your favorite breakfast, maple flavored oatmeal. It'll get cold if you don't get up right now."

"Oh all right!"

"Thank you." Suze helped Jen to her feet. "Let's go to the bathroom first. Here's your robe."

85

Breakfast was a slow, tedious process. Normally Jen could feed herself. Occasionally Suze had to help because of Jen's palsy or stubbornness, but the main reason was the terrible disease that was slowly and irrevocably destroying her life-partner's brain.

Once she finished her meal, Jen wandered into the bedroom and rifled through her dresser drawers. She would begin by taking out her stockings. Unrolling a pair she examined each sock, neatly pressed them back together and meticulously rolled them back up. Assured everything was as it should be, she checked the next drawer and the next. Every article of clothing was carefully scrutinized. The process took almost an hour.

The rest of the day Jen moved around the house picking things up, putting them down, watching television or napping. On particularly good days, she and Suze would sit and talk. Generally it was about nothing but neither cared; Jen because she couldn't and Suze because she had no choice. Nothing was better than the meaningless monologues that Jen was having with herself more and more often.

* * *

"Here you go," Suze said, placing a bowl of homemade chicken noodle soup on the table. "Do you need any help?"

Jen looked at the steaming brew for a few seconds and then reached for the spoon lying on the napkin. "I may be forgetful but I'm not an invalid," she grumped. Her hand shook from the palsy she had developed in her early 60s.

Recognizing that Jen was going through a mood swing, Suze decided discretion was the better tactic.

"Sorry. I don't know what I was thinking when I asked that."

"Neither do I. You act like I'm a damn retard or something," Jen said.

"Now that's not true and you know it. I was concerned that your palsy may be acting up a bit. I added extra noodles so you could use your fork if you wanted to."

"Well, I don't need a damn fork and my hands are as steady as they ever were." To prove her point Jen held her hands out for Suze to inspect. They trembled uncontrollably. "See! They're fine. I'm fine. Now can I just eat or do you want to chew my food for me too?"

Suze sighed.

"No. You wouldn't like the way I chewed it."

Jen glanced up at her partner of eighteen years. Her eyes narrowed suspiciously and then widened. A twinkle appeared, followed by a big grin. Wrinkled cheeks creased, exposing two linear shaped dimples on each side of her mouth.

"I can be such a bitch," she said and then began eating her soup. "Where's the pepper? You know how much I like pepper."

"Yes, and I know how you hate it when I put it on your food." Suze pointed to the small shaker a few inches away. "Let me know if that's enough."

Jen gave a soft snort. Hand shaking wildly she scattered the small black particles on her food and the table. "At least this palsy's good for something. I don't have to work hard getting the stuff out of the bottle."

Suze chuckled. "True. You go ahead and eat. I'll be back in a minute with my own bowl."

"Good. You can't eat out of mine. I don't want your cooties." Not sure if Jen had regressed back into her dementia or was joking, Suze hesitated. "Well? You just going to stand there?" Jen asked, giving her a questioning look.

It was times like this that Suze found the most frustrating — the not knowing.

"Back in a minute," she said, turning away.

"Suze?" Jen called after her.

"What, sweetie?"

"You can share my soup if you want. I don't mind your cooties." The pitiful expression on Jen's face broke Suze's heart.

"I knew you were joking, Jen. We've shared cooties too long to worry about them now. Eat yours while it's still warm." Kissing Jen on the forehead, Suze hurried off. A moment later she returned, quietly setting her bowl on the table. The dinner continued in silence as she watched Jen concentrating on lifting each spoonful, trying not to spill the contents.

Washing dishes was always a relaxing time for Suze. The warm water soothed her aching arthritic hands. Jen usually disappeared into the living room to watch television. Her attention span was normally short, often fluctuating between the program and some distant, elusive memory. The latter would cause her to become agitated. Occasionally, though, something on the screen would catch her interest, holding her spellbound for an hour or more. Suze was grateful for those moments, reprieves from her constant vigil. It provided her an opportunity to nap without worrying what Jen might get into.

This was one of those better nights. Joining Jen on the couch, Suze leaned her head back and closed her eyes. Within minutes she fell into a deep slumber, her chin resting on her chest.

* * *

"Where are you, dagnabit? I know you're here somewhere."

Jen's grumbling voice intruded on Suze's sleep. Blinking, she looked around expecting Jen to be sitting next to her. She wasn't. A rustling noise from the hallway followed by a thump caught her attention.

"Jen? What are you doing?" she asked pushing up from the couch. Her body ached from exhaustion.

"I'm looking for it," Jen said, clearly agitated.

"Looking for what?" Suze walked to stand by Jen, who was rummaging through the closet. The hall was strewn with stuff, things she had pulled from shelves and hangers in search of some unknown item.

"My book! I want my book."

"All of our books are in the library."

"Not **our** books. **My** book. I want my book." Jen was gesticulating with her shaking hands, obviously distressed.

Suze stepped closer and touched Jen's arm.

"Listen, why don't you let me help you? I'll take everything out. When we find your book you tell me, okay?" Jen nodded and stepped back, letting Suze take over. "Now, where might that book be?" One by one she picked up an object and held it up for Jen to inspect. The first was an old sweater stored in a clear plastic bag.

"That's not a book," Jen said. "Don't you know what a book is?"

"Silly me," Suze replied seriously. "I must be getting old." Sifting through a stack of old quilts and Afghans she felt something hard. A gray fireproof box with a key sticking out of the lock was buried under the pile.

"What's this?"

"Let me see." Pushing Suze aside, Jen rushed forward. "It's a box! What's in it?"

Twisting the key she lifted the lid and peered at the contents. Several legal documents lay inside but didn't completely obscure the thick glossy blue cover of the book beneath.

Jen grabbed it, turned and triumphantly waved it in the air.

"My book! You found my book! Remember this?" she asked, holding it out for Suze to see.

"Yes. How silly of me not to remember **your** book," Suze said.

"Oh!" Jen's brow wrinkled in confusion. "Did I buy it?"

"No, sweetie, you began writing it several years ago." Jen looked bewildered. She had already forgotten what had been so important just minutes before. "Look," Suze said, opening the manuscript. Jen's forehead wrinkled from confusion. "It's about you and me. And our friends, sort of an autobiography, only in story form," Suze explained. "You used to tell me about all your experiences with your business and I suggested you write a book. Don't you remember?"

"No!" Leaning closer for a better look, Jen pointed at the words on the bottom of the first page. "That's my name. Why is my name on it if it's about us? Why isn't your name here?"

"I didn't write this," Suze said patiently. "You did all the work."

"Are we still married?"

The question caught Suze by surprise. "Married? We never... oh... of course we're still married."

"Then why isn't your name on it? Married people put their names on everything."

Suze knew she was fighting a losing battle. Any attempt at an explanation would only confuse Jen more.

"You're right. I must have forgotten to put my name on it. Would you like me to do it now?"

"Yes." Jen looked at Suze worriedly. "Suze? Are you all right?"

It was Suze's turn to be confused.

"I'm fine. Why are you asking?"

"Well, you forgot to put your name on our book. That's not like you. I thought you might be getting a little forgetful."

Suze laughed.

"Maybe I am, Jen, maybe I am. Come on. Help me find a pen before I forget again."

"That's okay. I'll remind you," Jen promised.

Smiling, Suze wrapped her arms around Jen and squeezed her gently.

"Thank you. After I write my name below yours, how about we put **our** book on the table and go to bed. I'm awfully tired," Suze said.

"Why did you get it out, then?"

"I... I guess I wasn't thinking." Reminding Jen that she wanted the book served no purpose and would probably provoke an argument.

CHAPTER 2

THE NIGHTLY ROUTINE of getting Jen ready for bed was a tedious, complicated process. Jen was often rebellious when it came to showers. Suze could usually coax her into the bathroom but after that it became a battle of wills. Jen didn't like undressing, climbing over the tub edge, getting wet, and then having to climb out. The effort was exhausting for both women.

"I'm cold," Jen complained and shivered. Her hands shook violently. Suze wrapped a towel around Jen's shoulders and grabbed another to dry the rest of her body.

"I know. I'm almost done. Let's get your jammies on." Jen leaned heavily on Suze as she stepped over the rim. That was always the scariest part of showering. One slip and they could both fall down. It had already happened once, resulting in Jen splitting open her forearm on the vanity edge and Suze bruising her right knee. "Sit on the toilet and let me put your undies on." Suze pulled a pair of Depends from the stack beneath the sink. "Here you go. Lift your right foot... good girl. Now your left. Now raise your arms so I can put your top on you."

"You don't have to treat me like a child," Jen grumped. "I can put my own top on." Suze stepped back to avoid the flailing arms as Jen struggled to pull the tee shirt over her head and down her chest. "See!"

"That was great! Are you ready to go to bed?"

"I'm dressed for it, aren't I?"

"Silly me," Suze said, gently grasping Jen's elbow. "You don't mind if I hang on to you, do you? I feel a little unsteady."

Straightening proudly, Jen gave her a bright smile.

"Of course not. You'd help me, wouldn't you?"

"Absolutely!" Suze agreed and gestured toward the bedroom. "I'll just stay close to you."

"Good. Don't fall. I can't pick you up if you fall."

"I won't. Not as long as you're helping me."

Making their way to Jen's bed, Suze helped her lie down and covered her with the thick handmade quilt they had bought on a trip to Mexico. Carlton, the stuffed bear, was nestled against Jen's right cheek.

"There! Are you and Carlton comfortable?" Suze asked.

"Yes."

"Are you warm enough?"

"Yes."

"Do you need anything?"

"No."

"I love you," Suze said, bending down to give Jen a quick peck on the lips. The routine was always the same.

"I love you too. Now go away. I'm trying to sleep," Jen said, closing her eyes.

"Goodnight." Standing quietly next to the bed, Suze waited patiently until Jen's breathing slowed to small, quiet puffs. Spying several strands of errant gray hairs near Jen's right eye, she twirled them together and then positioned them behind her ear. "Dream well, sweetie," she whispered and then shuffled away, turning off the night light after crawling into her own bed.

Sleep rarely came easily to Suze. Most evenings were spent watching television or dozing in her favorite chair. Tonight, lying in bed she felt restless. Jen's manuscript had always caused mixed emotions. The detailed descriptions were bittersweet memories of their past, the last entry four years ago a sad reminder of the present. Jen had stopped writing when the effort became too much. Suze had put it away for safe keeping and also not wanting to be reminded of things past.

* * *

A loud crash startled Suze awake. For a moment she laid still, listening and wondering if she had been dreaming. A metallic clang told her she wasn't. *What now?* Sitting up slowly, she stifled a groan, not wanting to awaken Jen. *Damn arthritis!* When she heard muffled noises coming from the other room, she grabbed the baseball bat resting by her nightstand. Creeping from the bedroom and down the hall Suze peered cautiously into the darkened living room but saw no one. A pan rattled in the kitchen startling her.

Burglars! Suze gripped the wooden handle harder, raising the bat over her left shoulder. Inching along the wall she felt her heart pounding painfully in her chest. *I'm too damn old to be doing this and I can't afford a heart attack. Should have called 9-1-1,* she thought belatedly.

"Goddamnit!" a voice grumbled from inside the kitchen. "Where's that thing at?"

"Jen? Is that you?" Suze called out, peeking cautiously around the corner. Jen was rummaging through the silverware drawer. *Lord, this is going to be a long night,* she thought, rubbing her eyes tiredly.

"Who the hell else would it be? No one lives here but us," Jen mumbled. Then, as if having second thoughts about something, she stopped her search and glared suspiciously at Suze. "You haven't rented my bed out have you?"

At first Suze thought she was teasing. Jen's worried expression said otherwise.

"Now why would I do that?"

"I don't know. You've been acting strange lately."

"Strange? How have I been acting strange?" Suze asked.

"Well, look at you now. Who walks around with a bat in the house? That's for robbers and there aren't any robbers in here." Jen hesitated. Her eyes narrowed. "I'm not stealing anything. This is my stuff. You weren't going to konk me with that were you?"

"Of course not. I heard a noise and thought you —"

"You were going to kill me," Jen accused, grabbing a spatula from inside the drawer. "You come near me and I'll kill you," she threatened, her hand shaking violently.

"I was **not** going to kill you. I heard a noise and thought someone had broken in. Now put the spatula down and tell me what you're looking for."

Jen frowned, looking confused. Suze knew she had already forgotten what had been so important just minutes earlier.

"Are you hungry?" Suze asked, hoping to distract Jen. "Do you want something to eat?" Suze eased the spatula from Jen's clenched hand. Placing it and the bat on the counter, she led her to the table. "I'll warm up the soup. Would you like that?" Jen's relieved expression was its own reward. Smiling, Suze patted the hand she was holding. "You sit right here."

"I tried to be quiet," Jen said. "Did I wake you up?"

"No, I was feeling a bit peckish but I didn't want to wake you up," Suze lied. "It was very thoughtful of you not wanting to wake me."

"I'd feel bad if I woke you. I couldn't find that damn... whatchamacallit."

"Well, I'm glad you couldn't. Now we can eat something together. I'm sooo hungry." Suze's stomach growled loudly. "See!"

Jen giggled. For a moment the old twinkle reappeared but quickly faded.

Minutes later, Suze was placing two steaming bowls of leftover chicken soup on the table.

"Here you go," Suze said, handing her a spoon. "Would you like some bread or crackers?"

"No. Now shut up! I'm trying to eat." The curt order was not unusual. Mood swings were the norm when Jen was tired. "Sundowning," the doctor called it.

"Sorry."

The two women grew silent as they sipped their soup; one saddened by the reminder that her partner was slowly slipping away from her, the other focused on not spilling any of the liquid as she raised the shaking spoon toward her lips. Suze would have offered to help steady Jen's hand but knew it would make her angrier.

You don't deserve this, Jen. Suze sighed softly. *But who does? We should have had so much more.* The clattering sound of a spoon hitting the floor, followed by a short expletive from Jen, interrupted Suze's reminiscing.

"Damn thing jumped out of my hand!"

"That's okay. They do that sometimes. I'll get you another one," Suze offered.

"Don't bother. I'm tired. I want to go to bed. Can I go to bed?" Jen's voice had become pleadingly sweet, like a child.

Suze clasped Jen's hand and helped her to her feet.

"Absolutely," she said.

Tucking Jen back in bed for the second time Suze returned to her own and crawled under the thick, fluffy comforter. Yawning, she listened to Jen's labored breathing. *I hope her bronchitis isn't coming back.* When the exhales softened to quiet poofs, Suze relaxed.

Her thoughts again turned to the precious manuscript. Each page was a narrative pearl in their lives. How they met, the times they shared, good and bad. Sadly it would go unfinished.

Suze had discovered the notebook a few years ago. It was a manuscript written by Jen titled <u>Chronicles of a Property Manager</u>. At first she was reluctant to read it, believing it to be Jen's diary — her personal thoughts, things she probably didn't want anyone to know about. Eventually curiosity got the best of Suze. Opening the notebook, she imagined how Pandora must have felt when she was lifting the lid to the forbidden box. Afterward, Suze knew. The difference was that this time Hope had also escaped, leaving nothing but memories and a handwritten letter. But what a letter it was. Those few words summed up all that was Jen, all that they had.

Oh Jen, why did this have to happen to you? To us? Suze thought before finally falling asleep.

CHAPTER 3

A Week

DAYS BECAME WEEKS, each moment a repetition of the one before, only minimally worse. Sadly, even small changes added up to huge losses. Jen's memory continually deteriorated, but there were moments when she was her younger self.

"Are you going to read to me tonight?" Jen asked, "Or do I have to read the damn thing myself?" A smirky grin and twinkling eyes were clear signals that Jen was teasing, which always provided Suze a sense of relief and joy.

The day had gone exceptionally well. Jen was in a good mood. Her dementia had waned some, not uncommon for victims of mini-strokes. The brain sometimes created new pathways, trying to circumvent old injuries. Still, no matter how marvelous its recuperative powers, the doctor had warned them such moments would be temporary. He advised Suze not to get her hopes up whenever they occurred. Dementia was a downhill slope occasionally interrupted by plateaus of stability or slight improvements. Suze cherished those moments.

"That would be nice," she teased back. Jen's lower lip poked out in a mock pout. "Alright! You're going to step on that lip if it gets any longer. What do you want me to read?"

"You choose."

"Okay. Tonight it'll be from your... our book."

Suze opened the blue notebook, flipping to the first page.

Jen's handwriting was clear and precise. The words flowed easily. She could hear Jen's voice in her mind as she silently read the first lines.

"Suze? Suze?"

Suze looked up at Jen's troubled face.

"I'm sorry, sweetie. What did you say?"

"Are you okay?"

"I'm fine. I was just thinking about you and what an amazing person you are. I'm so lucky to have you."

Jen cocked her head sideways, giving Suze a thoughtful look.

"Even now?" she asked.

The question surprised Suze. Jen was rarely aware of her failing memory. Normally all that mattered was now. What she wanted, what didn't, how she was feeling. The past and the future no longer existed. That was a blessing under the circumstances. In the beginning, Jen was sure she could win her battle against the progression of the disease. She struggled to be normal. As her symptoms grew worse, Jen became creative in developing ways to overcome the problems. For a while it worked. Only those closest to her noticed the little changes. Her smartphone was exchanged for a flip cell. The small netbook was replaced with a seventeen inch laptop. Eventually she began carrying a recorder. Finally a pen and pad appeared. Jen wrote notes to herself about conversations or appointments until they turned into confusing scribbles.

Even now? Suze thought about the question. Jen was her life, for better or for worse. She could give Jen a simple yes answer and that would probably end the discussion. Tonight, well, tonight the other Jen was with her. The Jen who asked the hard questions and demanded the truth no matter how difficult or hurtful it might be. The Jen she had shared joys and sorrows with.

Before Jen's decline, their relationship had been everything they could dream of. Their love-making had been intense and at times overwhelming. Anyone who thought middle-aged women couldn't feel passion was either naïve or delusional. Both knew how to satisfy each other and themselves. Jen was the burning, concerned lover; always wanting to please Suze. Suze was the clown. Making love was a challenge, a game with constantly changing rules to keep it fun and exciting.

Eventually their sexual desires did fade some, but nothing could diminish the love they shared, nor their commitment to each other. The more Suze saw her life-partner slipping away, the tighter she held on to her, helping Jen fight her demons. Perhaps it was a losing battle, but not for Suze. She would never give up. It was important Jen know that now. Even when her mental lapses returned, and they would, somewhere deep in Jen's mind, where the real Jen dwelled, she would always know she was loved and cherished.

"Do you remember the year we went to the Festival de la Mariposa Monarca in Mexico?" Suze asked, reaching over to hold Jen's hand.

Jen nodded.

"We wanted to see the butterflies."

"**I** wanted to see the butterflies," Suze corrected squeezing the hand she was holding to let Jen know she was teasing her. "I told you about a documentary I'd seen and mentioned how much fun it would be to see a gazillion at one time. You acted sooo disinterested and then turned up with tickets and reservations three days later. I was speechless."

"I remember. Sadie got them for me. Where is Sadie?" Jen asked, looking around as if expecting her old business partner to be in the room.

"She's home, but she called yesterday to see how you were doing," Suze said.

"Oh, I'm fine," Jen replied. "Tell her I'm fine, would you?"

"I will. We were talking about the butterflies. Do you remember?"

"Of course I remember. Why wouldn't I?" Jen asked, sounding irritated. Then she smiled. "We had fun, didn't we?"

"Fun? It was more than fun. You gave me this," Suze said, holding her left hand out to proudly display the ring on her third finger.

"The butterflies were beautiful, weren't they?"

"Yes, they were." Suze tried to ignore an overwhelming sadness. Jen wasn't to blame for her lack of interest in the ring. Dementia destroyed more than memories. It robbed the person of the emotions that accompanied them.

"There were gazillions. One even kissed me." Jen's face glowed. "On the cheek!"

You haven't stolen everything, Suze thought, referring to the dementia. She considered the illness more a thief than a disease. *No matter how hard you try, you won't get all of my Jen.*

Suze remembered the moment as if it was yesterday and still wondered if they had made a terrible mistake going to Mexico. Jen's symptoms first appeared on that trip, although Suze didn't make the connection until years later.

* * *

The Festival of the Monarch Butterflies was a huge event, attracting people from around the world. Surrounding villages participated in the celebration. Dances, parties and exhibitions were everywhere. The reserve designated walking trails to minimize damage to the ecosystem and disruptions to the Monarch's daily routines. Jen had hired a local named Joaquin to take them on a tour of the countryside and the protected areas. The guide's knowledge of the butterfly's life cycle and migration from Mexico to Canada and back was impressive; his willingness to prove it almost exhausting as he proudly chattered non-stop.

While watching a swarm resting in the trees, Jen noticed a white speck amongst the horde of orange fluttering wings and pointed it out to Joaquin.

"Ask Joaquin what that one is," Jen said to Suze.

"Sure," Suze said and asked Joaquin.

"La Madre de todas las Mariposas Monarcas," he replied.

"¿La madre?"

"Este es nuestro día de suerte, Señoritas. Ella es la Señora Blanca, La Dama Blanca."

"He said it was our lucky day. They believe the white butterfly is the Mother of the others," Suze translated.

"Si. Estas..." He said raising his arms upwards to symbolically embrace everything around them. "Estas son su hijas. Ella las guiará al norte y luego las traerá de vuelta sanas y salvas. Siempre está con ellas."

"These are all her children. She leads them north but leaves about a week in advance."

"I thought Monarchs only live a few weeks," Jen said. Suze again translated to Joaquin.

"La Madre no. Ella regresa cada año siempre el mismo día. ¡Mira!" Joaquin exclaimed pointing toward the moving mass. "Ella las ha despertado. Ahora volarán pero no harán el viaje. Ella se va primero. Ellas la seguirán dentro de siete dias. Creo que están practicando."

"Not the Mother. She comes back here every year on the same day. The others arrive shortly afterward." The swarm rose into the air.

"No se muevan, Señoritas. Vienen hacia aquí," Joaquin said excitedly pointing to the colony.

"What?" Jen whispered.

"Don't move. Joaquin said they're doing a practice flight."

Suze and Jen held their breaths, tense; afraid they would interfere with the butterflies as they launched themselves from the trees, turning the sky into a moving mosaic of black and orange. A soft breeze fanned the leaves around them. Suddenly the white butterfly fluttered to within inches of Jen's face. Large purple eyes stared into Jen's. Mesmerized, she exhaled slowly. Something in the dark unblinking gaze made her uneasy.

What do you want? Jen thought and felt foolish for asking the question. The butterfly continued to hover, never breaking eye contact. I don't understand. Visions of lush green forests and meadows flooded her mind. Every plant was covered by undulating rivers of orange, black and gold, constantly changing their shape and directions, slowly, hypnotically drawing Jen closer and closer. A small white spot appeared in the center of the shifting mosaic. First it stayed stationary but then began circling clockwise. Changing direction it walked counter-clockwise, clearing an area around it. Suddenly it sprang into the air, directly at Jen's face, or at least that's how the vision felt. Startled, she jerked her hands upward to protect her face.

"Jen? Jen! Are you alright?" A hand shook her right arm. Jen blinked, feeling disoriented and slightly nauseous.

"I... I'm fine," she said shaking her head slightly.

Suze gave her a curious look.

"Are you sure? You look a little pale."

"I'm fine, really. Just a bit overwhelmed I think."

"I know. All those butterflies taking off like that. It's impressive. They're so beautiful."

"As beautiful as this?" Holding out her right hand, Jen uncurled her fingers. In her palm was a silver and gold band. Two small bars held six diamond chips. Between them was an embedded diamond.

"Oh!" Suze gasped.

"Oh? Is that it? Just oh?"

Tears slid down Suze's cheek.

"It's... it's beautiful."

"No, you're beautiful. And well, I... I was hoping you'd... well, you know..."

Suze looked at Jen's face, giggled, and then took pity on her.

"Are you asking me to be your wife?"

Jen nodded and then blushed. "Yes. I mean... I know we can't get married, but..."

Putting her finger to Jen's lips, Suze silenced her. "I'd love to," she whispered. "Thank you."

Jen slipped the ring on Suze's finger.

"Uh hmmm. Señoritas," Joaquin interrupted nervously looking around. "Por favor, no todo el mundo aqui se siente cómodo con una relación como la vuestra. Para mí está bien que dos mujeres se amen, pero debeís tener cuidado en público. ¿Entendeis?"

"Sorry, Joaquin," Suze apologized. "He's worried that some people might not like what we are," she explained. Jen nodded.

"Gracias, Señorita. Ahora debemos irnos. El parque cierra pronto."

Unclasping hands, Jen and Suze followed him back to the visitor's center, the butterflies temporarily forgotten. Not even the cloud of prejudice could dampen their happiness.

* * *

Back at the hotel, Jen remembered the butterfly incident and told Suze, half-expecting a playful razzing.

"I know it sounds crazy."

"Not crazy but certainly strange," Suze said. "You zoned out for a few seconds. At least that explains why. Joaquin told me you were under its spell and warned me not to break it. He said the blessing would become a curse. I hope shaking you didn't —"

Jen laughed. "I seriously doubt a butterfly can put a curse on anyone, but I don't think I was imagining what happened either. It hovered so close I could almost feel it. And those eyes... I've never seen anything that color."

Suze gave Jen a strange look.

"It did land on your left cheek. Don't you remember?"

"No... no, I guess I did zone out."

"Maybe you discovered an intelligent life form," Suze teased, secretly wondering if it was possible. "That would explain how they can make such an

105

amazing journey year after year. Besides, I like the thought of a matriarchal Monarchal Monarchy."

"You really didn't say that," Jen said shaking her head. "That was pitiful. Pitiful."

"You're just jealous because you didn't come up with it," Suze replied smugly.

"Right! Let's go eat before you think of another witty remark."

"And where shall we go tonight?"

"McD's," Jen replied. "I feel like a quarter pounder with cheese."

Suze laughed.

"Very funny. Seriously, where do you want to eat?"

A curious expression crossed Jen's face. Her forehead crinkled with consternation.

"I wasn't joking. I want a quarter pounder."

Confused, Suze shook her head slowly.

"This is Mexico. There aren't any McD's here. I'm sure we can find a hamburger place though."

"I don't want —" Jen stopped and then lifted a shaking hand to her right temple and began to massage it.

"Maybe we should just order in. I feel a little tired now."

Stunned, Suze was speechless as Jen walked over to the bed and lay down.

* * *

Two days later, Jen and Suze flew home. Suze, who was an English-to-French translator, picked up three new contracts and Jen returned to work. Several months later, Sadie called Suze, concerned about changes in Jen's behavior.

Sadie watched as Jen sat staring at the computer screen with some consternation.

"Shit!" Jen muttered. "Damn company needs to get the bugs out of this program."

"Having trouble?" Sadie asked.

"I can't get into the management program. It won't accept my password," Jen explained, massaging her right temple with her fingers.

"Let me see," Sadie offered and moved to stand by Jen. Leaning down, Sadie entered the password. Instantly the screen changed and the program opened revealing the options page. "There you go," she said and returned to her desk.

"How did you do that? I spent ten minutes trying to get into it."

"Probably a computer glitch," Sadie replied. "Maybe it's about time you bought a new laptop. That one's at least four years old."

"I guess. Maybe I was just hitting the wrong keys. I feel a bit tired today."

"Well go home and get some rest. Jackson and I can deal with anything that comes up."

"Oh, so I'm not needed anymore, huh?" Jen asked, grumpily.

"Needed? Yes. Today? No! And since I am the office manager, I'm sending you home."

Jen sighed.

"Maybe you're right. Ever since our trip to Mexico, Suze's been nagging me to take another vacation, this time up north. I keep telling her it's too soon. Perhaps I should think a little more about us. I don't want to screw this up like I did with Lindsey... and we're not getting younger, you know."

"You didn't screw anything up and you know it," Sadie replied. "Lindsey and you just weren't meant to be. I think your problem is you're afraid of letting go of things. It's time you trusted people a little bit more."

"Meaning you? I guess I haven't been fair to you, have I?"

Sadie knew what Jen meant. Even though Jen had made Sadie her business partner years ago, she hadn't been able to hand over the reins except when she took time off... and Jen rarely took time off. Two vacations in one year would be a record. Before Suze had come into her life, Jen rarely took time off. That was one of the reasons her relationship with Lindsey had failed.

"You've always been fair, Jen, just never trusting enough."

"I'm sorry," Jen said.

"Listen, Jen. You've changed. Suze's good for you. Take another trip. Have fun. Relax! Where does she want to go? I'll make the arrangements and call you with the information."

"Mt. Saint... Saint... I don't remember. Saint somewhere or other. I'll have to ask her," Jen said.

"How about you get out of here and I'll call her. By the time you're home, everything will be set. You and Suze can leave the day after tomorrow."

Jen smiled.

"You're not trying to get rid of me, are you?"

"Of course. How else am I going to get real managerial experience? Now get!" Sadie ordered and dramatically pointed her finger at the door.

"Aye, Aye. Oh, how long am I supposed to stay away, boss?" Jen asked.

"At least two weeks. Three would be better. If I see you back here before then, you're fired."

The two women laughed. Sadie had started out as a part-time assistant when Jen started the company and was now a full partner, owning thirty-three percent of the company.

"See you in a couple of weeks," Jen said, saluting. Sliding her laptop into her briefcase, she grabbed her jacket and left, giving Sadie a goodbye wave.

Sadie immediately picked up the phone and dialed Suze.

"Hello."

"Suze? This is Sadie."

"Hey, Sadie, how're you doing?" Suze asked.

"Fine, thanks. Listen, I just sent Jen home. She should be there in about thirty minutes."

"Is she okay?" Suze's voice sounded slightly panicky.

"She's fine, but... Well, she couldn't remember the password to our management software today. She's used the same word for ten years... and I've noticed a few other things that aren't like her."

The silence that followed was telling.

"Suze?"

"I'm here. Sorry. I didn't want to say anything but I noticed a change when we were in Mexico. I was hoping it was my imagination. I'm worried about her, Sadie."

"I know. Any chance of getting her to go to a specialist for a check-up?"

"Jen hates doctors and I wouldn't know how to broach the subject. Physically, she's as healthy as a horse, but she hasn't been very good to herself over the years."

"I know, at least not until she met you. You're the best thing that ever happened to her. I guess we'll just have to make sure she doesn't backtrack. I told her to take a couple weeks off. She mentioned a place up north you two had been talking about. Maybe with a little rest she'll be back to her old self. Anyway, I told her I'd call you for the information and make the arrangements."

"What a great idea! Thanks, Sadie." Suze gave Sadie the name of a ski resort near Montreal. "Jen said she used to ski before she met Lindsey."

"She did. How's Lindsey, by the way? I haven't seen her for a few months."

"Enjoying her honeymoon," Suze answered. "Her second, actually. She and Becky are in Cancun, supposedly taking surfing lessons."

"Surfing! At their age?" Sadie asked.

"Exactly! The only thing they're probably surfing is each other."

Sadie chuckled. Lindsey hadn't wasted any time moving on after her breakup with Jen. As a player she bounced from woman to woman, rarely staying in a relationship for more than a few months. Then Becky entered her life. Young, wild Becky, who loved sampling everything that life had to offer, and Lindsey could offer her sexual experiences beyond her wildest imagination. No one thought the relationship would last. The age difference of fifteen years, by itself, was reason enough to expect failure. Often life had a way of proving people wrong.

* * *

"Suze!" Jen's voice again shook Suze from her reverie.

"I'm sorry, sweetie. What were you saying?"

"I said a butterfly kissed me."

"Yes, a white butterfly landed on your cheek," Suze said. "Joaquin called it a kiss, a special blessing by The White Lady. He was right. I still have you. How could I not feel lucky?" *So why do I still feel your memory loss had something to do with that damn butterfly? You were fine until that happened.*

"I have to poop!" Jen said suddenly, a look of desperation crossing her face. "I have to **poop!**" she repeated, struggling to stand up.

Suze sighed. Like the Monarchs of Mexico, the old Jen had vanished, leaving only the memories of what had been and an emptiness of what now was.

I wish we'd never gone on that trip. Instantly she regretted the thought. Blaming an insect for Jen's problem was ridiculous.

"Come on, sweetie. It's almost bedtime anyway. I'll read to you tomorrow." Holding Jen's hand, she led her to the bathroom. A sour smell filled the air. Suze's night had just gotten a little longer.

CHAPTER 4

Months were like years

EVERY DAY WAS A Groundhog Day, rarely changing. Routines provided balance to the unstable minds of dementia sufferers. The occasional surprises were normally unpleasant, but Suze was an expert at adapting. Jen always took an afternoon nap at two o'clock. Today was no different. Suze had just finished putting Jen to bed when the doorbell rang.

"I wonder who that is," she mumbled, looking at her watch and grimacing. The arthritis in her back had flared up, making walking painful. Shuffling to the front door she peeked through the peephole and then unlocked the deadbolt and entry lock. "Dr. Henry, what are you doing here? Is it Tuesday already?"

The tall, thin man smiled warmly, extending his right hand to shake Suze's. Although only in his mid-forties, he was already balding and walked with a stoop. His suit was slightly wrinkled and a size or two larger than necessary.

"I came to check on my two favorite people," he said. "How are you doing, Miss Suze?"

"As well as can be expected," she replied, motioning him into the living room. "When are you going to get some clothes that fit? You look like a hobo."

Dr. Henry laughed.

"Surely I don't look that bad."

Suze eyed him speculatively and then relented. "Well, maybe more like you slept in that thing." Limping slightly, she pressed on her back and groaned.

"Your back bothering you again?"

"A tad. Dadburn weather always makes it act up."

"Would you like me to prescribe something? A mild painkiller might take the edge off."

"Naw, I don't like taking medication. I'd appreciate it though if you'd look in on Jen."

"Of course," Dr. Henry said. "That's why I'm here. How is she?"

"About the same as the last time you came. Well, maybe a little worse, but she's had some real good days too."

"Wonderful! That's what I like to hear. Shall I go and examine her now?"

"You know the way. I'll fix us a cup of tea."

Dr. Henry came every other week to check on Jen and Suze. He checked Jen's heart, lungs and blood pressure. Then he and Suze would enjoy a few cups of tea and discuss everything from the weather to politics. Often the conversations turned a bit feisty over the latter. Suze suspected it was his way of making sure she still had her mental faculties. She enjoyed the visits and was always sad when they ended.

* * *

"I guess I should head on to the hospital," Dr. Henry said, glancing at his watch. "I need to check on a few patients."

"It was nice of you to come," Suze said. "I still think you should bill us."

"Miss Suze, it's an honor to be able to come here. And besides, you make the best tea in town. That's payment enough." When Suze started to stand, he put his hand on her shoulder. "No need to show me out. I know the way. I'll lock the entry lock when I leave and you can do the deadbolt later."

"Thank you. I think I'll catch up on some reading since Jen's asleep. Good brain exercise."

"Indeed it is. Have a good afternoon and I'll see you in two weeks. You call me if your back gets worse."

Suze promised she would. Once the doctor was gone, she picked up Jen's manuscript. For almost two weeks it had lain abandoned on the coffee table. Jen had shown no further interest in it.

An hour later, Suze closed the notebook and clutched it against her breast. Leaning back she thought about their first meeting. Neither had guessed where it would lead. She used to question if she had caused the breakup between Jen and her former girlfriend, Lindsey. The two had been together for over three years. Eventually, though, they grew apart, each unable to provide what the other needed. From the way Jen's friends talked about Lindsey, Suze couldn't understand why Jen had stayed with the woman so long. After meeting her several years later, Suze had her answer. Lindsey wasn't the ogre some people painted her out to be. She and Jen were just too driven by their own agendas. They would never have been compatible. Their breakup was painful, but not the end of their relationship.

Time always had a way of changing people. Sometimes it also opened doors to new opportunities, even in the most clichéd of ways. Girl leaves girl, girl meets new girl, and they live happily ever after — except they didn't. The final pages in Jen's book epitomized what Jen and Suze's lives had become; words painfully misspelled; sentences jumbled until the story's ending was as chaotic as Jen's thoughts. Sighing, Suze set the notebook on the end table. Pushing painfully to her feet, she headed for the kitchen. It was almost dinner time.

CHAPTER 5

A Lifetime

MUMBLINGS FROM THE bedroom, especially at nighttime, had become commonplace. Standing in the doorway, Suze listened. She knew Jen's dementia was getting worse. The meaningless words and frequent arguments with herself attested to her deteriorating condition.

"Come here!"

"No you come here."

"No, **you** come here."

"Okay. I'll come there but you take my hand."

"No, you take my hand."

"Okay."

Moving quietly to stand next to the bed Suze saw Jen's eyes were closed.

"Are you okay," Suze asked.

"Yes," Jen said, opening her eyes. A vacant stare turned into recognition. "Go away!"

"Who are you talking to?"

"That man!" Jen pointed toward the ceiling.

Suze looked up. **That man** came almost every night now. She wasn't sure who Jen was seeing but knew that telling her no one was there was futile and only caused Jen to grow more agitated.

"Well, tell him to go away. It's bedtime," Suze said.

"He doesn't listen to me."

"He'll listen to me. GO AWAY!" Suze made shooing motions with her arm. "It's bedtime. You don't need to be here." Turning to Jen, she leaned slightly toward her. "Is he gone?"

Jen nodded.

"Good." Leaning all the way down, Suze gave Jen a quick kiss on the lips. "I love you." Jen closed her eyes, a clear sign she intended to ignore Suze. "I love you," Suze repeated.

Opening one eye, Jen looked up and then closed it again.

"I love you," she mumbled grudgingly.

Suze knew the moment she left the room Jen would begin her argument with herself again. It was a scene that played over and over again every night, often going on for hours.

CHAPTER 6

STEPHANIE CAME TWICE a week. A local dementia support group provided her as an aide to give Suze some relief on Monday and Thursdays so she could do the shopping or just relax. The first few times, Jen had been resistant to the stranger's attention, quickly making it clear the aide was not going to give her a bath. Nor would she allow Stephanie to change her Depends™. After a while, though, Stephanie's southern charm eased her suspicions and Jen accepted the gentle attention and affection offered.

"Miss Jen, I do believe you're gaining weight," Stephanie said, tugging Jen's slacks up over her client's slender hips. "Miss Suze's gonna hafta go buy you a bigger size if you keep this up."

"Stop that!" Jen said, slapping at the hands.

"Now don't you go actin' that way. I'm tryin' to get you dressed. You can't go runnin' around in your panties. It ain't ladylike."

"Well I **ain't** a lady, so I don't have to worry about that... and I **ain't** getting fat either."

Stephanie chuckled. Feisty was good. Patting Jen on the shoulder, she leaned down and kissed her right cheek.

"Ain't no reason to be afraid of puttin' on a few pounds, Miss Jen. It's not like you're gonna get fat or anything. You're way too ornery for that. Now, let's go get something to eat. How about I fix you some warm oatmeal with honey? That sound good to you?"

"I don't want nothing to eat. I want to go to my bed," Jen grumbled.

"Only after you eat. No breakfast, no bed."

"I said I didn't want anything. You can't make me eat."

"Now why do you want to go and be difficult? You know you hafta eat."

"No I don't! You're trying to kill me. YOU'RE TRYING TO KILL ME!"

Hearing raised voices, Suze peeked around the corner. Stephanie held up her hand and motioned Suze to stay back.

"Miss Jen. I don't allow no one to talk to me like that. We don't yell at each other. You be nice to me and I'll be nice to you, okay?"

Jen glared at the caregiver for several moments and then lowered her eyes.

"Oh alright," she mumbled.

"Thank you." Turning to Suze she smiled. "You go rest now. I'll feed Miss Jen and then get her into bed. If you're asleep by then I'll just sneak on out. You need to take better care of yourself, Miss Suze. You're lookin' awfully tired these days."

"I'm fine Stephanie, but thanks for caring. And thanks for helping me with Jen. I don't say that enough."

"You say it plenty, Miss Suze."

Suze headed for her bed while Stephanie helped Jen to the table.

* * *

A loud banging on the door roused Suze from a sound sleep. *What now?* "I'm coming!" she yelled out and then looked at Jen to see if she was awake. She wasn't. *At least being a little deaf has some advantages*, she thought.

Putting on her tattered blue robe and matching slippers, she shuffled slowly to the front door and peered through the peephole. Her best friend was standing on the other side waving a brown paper bag at her. Unlocking the door, Suze opened it and motioned the woman in.

"Lindsey, what in the world are you doing here this time of the day?" Suze asked. "It's almost noontime."

"I brought you and Jen some freshly made donuts. I know how much she loves them and how hard it is for you to get out nowadays."

"And I suppose you want me to make coffee now? Well, come on into the kitchen. It's the least I can do since you brought our favorite snack."

Lindsey smiled and did as she was told, making herself comfortable on one of the chairs. A few minutes later, Suze placed two steaming cups on the table.

"Here," she said. Opening the bag she spied a chocolate covered donut amongst a variety of others. "Jen will love that one. I'll save it for her." Suze picked out a glazed one and took a bite. "Mmmm. It's been awhile since I had a glazed donut, not since you were last here. How was your trip?"

"Long! Never sign up with a travel group. The guide was boring and the sites too touristy. Then Becky caught a dose of the Johnny Quick Step. Fortunately, it was mild."

"It doesn't hurt that she's just out of the cradle," Suze said and then laughed.

"She's fifty eight. That's hardly out of the cradle," her friend replied, joining in on the laughter. "Besides, I need someone who can keep up with my sexual appetite."

Suze snorted.

"Sexual appetite. I'd have thought you'd have slowed down by now."

"Oh I slowed down alright but I'm still good for several times a week."

The sound of movement in the bedroom cut off any remark Suze was going to make.

"That's Jen. I need to make sure she's okay," Suze said.

"Do you need any help?"

"No, she doesn't like anyone in the bedroom but me or Stephanie. I'll be right back."

* * *

Jen was sitting on the side of the bed looking around the room.

"Are you alright?" Suze asked, hurrying over to Jen's side.

"I have to pee," Jen said. "Where's my robe?"

Suze pointed to the foot of the bed. Picking it up, she held it out so Jen could slip her arms into the sleeves.

"I heard voices. Who's out there?

"A surprise. Let's go to the bathroom and then I'll show you, okay?"

"Okay."

Leading Jen into the kitchen, Suze watched her partner's face to see if she recognized the woman sitting at the table. Jen stared at her for a few moments. Her forehead wrinkled, a sign that she was struggling with her thoughts. Suddenly a smile broke across her face.

"Lindsey? Is that you, Lindsey?" she asked.

"Hi Jen," Lindsey said standing up. "Come give me a hug, girlfriend."

Jen moved quickly to do just that. Both women wrapped their arms around each other and rocked back and forth for a few moments. Suze watched them with mixed emotions: sadness and happiness. Sadness because the Jen she and Lindsey knew was slowly being destroyed;

happiness because **her** Jen was still fighting to maintain what was left of the old Jen.

Her recognition of Lindsey was proof. Their breakup had been ugly and for years they didn't speak even though they often met in social circles. Eventually, time had tempered the hard feelings and they began to talk to each other. Perhaps it was because both were in stable relationships. Whatever the reason, their friendship was renewed and grew stronger with each passing year. Suze and Lindsey's wife, Becky, accepted that Jen and Lindsey had a history and were happy for the reconciliation. No one posed a threat to the other. That Suze and Lindsey also developed a strong friendship was testimony to that.

"I brought you donuts."

"I love donuts," Jen said, clapping her hands together. "Ohhh! And chocolate." She looked at Suze and smiled. "Can I have some coffee too?"

"Coming right up," Suze replied. After placing the cup in front of Jen, everyone sat back down.

Jen took a bite of the chocolate donut and chewed it slowly.

"Mmmm. This is so good. It reminds me of..." Jen hesitated. Her forehead creased and then she stared at Lindsey. "Of the time you got mad and threw a whole box at me. What a waste of good donuts."

Lindsey laughed.

"I remember that. That wasn't one of our finer moments."

"No, you were mean. Why were you mad? All those broken donuts lying on the floor. I could have eaten them." For a moment Jen seemed sad, but then her expression lightened. "I looked funny with all that chocolate on my face and clothes. It looked like poop."

"You know, Jen, I don't remember what it was about either," Lindsey lied. The reason was no longer important.

"But it sure did. And I had to clean the mess up since you refused to. They'd have stayed on the floor forever."

"We were both pretty stubborn, weren't we." Jen looked at Suze. "We were, you know? Maybe I was more so. Such a waste. Donuts shouldn't be wasted. You shouldn't have thrown them like that."

"No, I shouldn't have," Lindsey agreed.

"I guess all of us can be hard-headed at times. Even now," Suze teased.

"Oh yeah," Lindsey said. "Becky is always calling me that."

"Becky?" Jen asked. "Oh, I remember. She's that woman you married." Jen shook her head. "I never thought it would last, you and Becky. She's awfully young. Guess I was wrong. I'm glad you found someone, Lindsey. You're nice now. You deserve someone nice. We weren't good for one another, were we?"

Lindsey patted Jen's hand and then squeezed it.

"We were always good for each other. We just couldn't live together. Our needs were too different, that's all."

"I suppose. That's a good thing, isn't it Suze? I mean that Lindsey and I couldn't get along? Otherwise we wouldn't have each other, would we? And Lindsey wouldn't have Becky? Becky's nice. I like her a lot."

Suze nodded.

"Definitely! A very good thing. And you still have Lindsey. She's your best friend."

"Oh! I thought you were my best friend," Jen said, looking confused.

"We're all best friends, Jen," Lindsey said. "Suze's your best partner friend and I'm your best friend friend. Understand?"

Jen looked at the partially eaten donut in her hand and frowned.

"I think so. Sometimes I don't understand things as clearly as I used to. Suze tries to explain or help me remember, but I just can't. One day I think I'm not going to understand anything at all. Then Suze will have to leave me somewhere. That makes me sad."

Tears welled up in Suze's eyes. Lindsey gave her an empathetic look and leaned toward Jen. Lifting Jen's chin with her hand, she smiled.

"Listen, Jen, you know I've never lied to you, right?"

Jen nodded slowly.

"Well, I'm not going to start now. Maybe the day will come when you can't remember anything. Maybe not, but Suze's never going to leave you, and I'll always be here too. You're a strong woman. The Jen I know and love will never go down without a fight. Okay?"

"But what if —"

"You once told me there are no what ifs. Don't start them now. We're going to take one day at a time. And yes, there will be times when you won't understand something or remember things, but that happens to all of us."

"And you remembered the donut fight, sweetie," Suze added. "That had to be a long time ago."

Jen perked up.

"I did, didn't I," she said, straightening up and smiling. "That's something."

"That's a lot," Lindsey said. "Even I didn't remember it until you mentioned it."

"And... and I remember what the fight was about now. I forgot our anniversary and brought them home hoping to cover it up. I wasn't very good at trying to fool you."

"There you go! You were forgetting things even back then, especially those types of things. So what if you forget a few things now and then. I'd say you haven't changed at all," Lindsey teased.

"No... no, I haven't. I guess I've always been a little absented-minded, huh?"

"Well, I wouldn't say that. Maybe just preoccupied. "

"Preoccupied. I like that word. It sounds... important." Jen looked longingly at another donut. "We ought to finish these off. I wouldn't want them to spoil because I got preoccupied with something else," Jen replied, giving a wry grin. During the next two hours, the three friends reminisced about the old days. For Suze and Lindsey, the Jen of yesteryears had returned.

After Lindsey left, Suze helped Jen into the living room and lit the gas fireplace.

"I'm going to do the dishes and then I'll be right back," Suze said.

"Suzeque?" Jen said hesitantly.

Startled at being addressed by her online name, Suze sat down next to Jen and reached for her hand.

"What, sweetie?" she asked.

"Why do you put up with me like you do?"

"Oh Jen, I don't put up with you. I love you."

Jen didn't say anything for a few moments and then sighed.

"There's something wrong with me and I don't know what to do. It's like I'm somewhere else... or... I don't know. I'm afraid. What if I forget who you are like I forget who I am? What happens to me if you die? Or get sick? No one will care for me."

"Sweetie, let's not worry about that now. One day at a time, okay? You and I... well, we're like a pair of old shoes. What good would we be without each other?"

"I think I'm the one with the hole in the sole," Jen said.

Suze didn't know whether to laugh or cry at the comment. It was only after Jen looked into her eyes that she realized she was being teased. Jen's twinkled with a humor she hadn't seen in a long time.

"I guess that makes me the one with the worn out tongue, huh?" Suze replied and leaned in to give Jen a hug.

"I guess it does." The twinkle faded. Jen's expression changed to concern. "There was something I wanted to tell you, but... I forgot what it is."

"Don't worry about it. When you remember, you can tell me then."

Jen's forehead crinkled. She looked down at the hand holding hers and squeezed it.

"You're a good person, Suzeque. I never told you that enough, did I?"

"Now what makes you say that?" Suze asked.

"I don't know. Just a feeling I guess, but I think you've always known I thought so."

Suze smiled. Seeing it, Jen's lips curled up at the corners.

"Sweetie, there wasn't a day that went by that you didn't tell me or show me you loved me."

"You know something, Suze?"

"What?"

"You're getting a little forgetful yourself. I didn't say anything about loving you. I said you were a good person." Jen laughed at the surprised expression on Suze's face. "Gotcha, didn't I?"

"You sure did. Here you're worried about being forgetful. Hey! I have an idea. We haven't been outside in several weeks and there's some fresh snow on the ground. Let's go make a couple of snowballs."

"I'd like that," Jen said. "Do we have to go far? I can't walk far, you know."

"No, there's enough snow on the porch. And we won't be out long. I get cold easily. Old bones, you know."

"Yeah, you are older than me. I forgot about that. We should change. I don't think it's proper to wear robes outside." Jen stood up and looked around the room. "You'll have to show me where my coat is. I don't remember where I put it."

"How about I help you get dressed and then I'll get the jackets and gloves?" Suze asked.

Jen straightened from the slightly stooped posture she normally had and gave Suze and indignant look.

"I may be getting old, Suze McMurphy, but I'm still able to put my clothes on." Stalking away, she hesitated at the living room entrance and turned around. "No matter what happens to me you'll remember I've always loved you, won't you?"

"I've never doubted it, Jen. And you remember that I'll always be here for you."

Jen nodded. Tears streaming down her cheeks, Suze went in search of their winter coats. She still had to change her own clothes but didn't want Jen to think she was checking on her.

* * *

Lindsey brought Jen and Suze donuts every Saturday. Occasionally Becky would join them and then have to put up with the good natured teasing about her youthful age. One day they decided to take Jen outside. Becky had borrowed a wheelchair. She insisted on being the operator. The early spring air was crisp and filled with the faint scent of lilacs.

"Are you warm enough?" Suze asked, checking Jen's hands. When Jen didn't respond, Suze leaned closer. "Sweetie, are you —"

"Look!" Jen exclaimed pointing excitedly at a patch of ground recently landscaped with colorful flowers. "I want to go there."

"Sure," Becky said and pushed the wheelchair next to the area. Bees and butterflies flitted from bloom to bloom, sampling the pollen. Jen sat entranced by all the activity.

"Look, Suze, butterflies! I love butterflies! Can I touch them?"

"I don't think they'll let you."

"They'll let me. Please? They'll let me. One kissed me, remember?" Jen touched her left cheek.

Although Suze dreaded the thought of Jen being disappointed, she didn't have the heart to say no.

"Can you stand up? We can't take your chair on the grass."

"I can stand... if you help me." Placing her hands on the arm rests, Jen pushed upward. Her arms trembled.

"Let me help," Lindsey and Becky said, simultaneously moving to each side of the wheelchair. Gently taking her by her arms, they lifted Jen up. Suze stepped in and Becky stepped aside, taking the chair with her. Tentatively Jen shuffled onto the thick grass.

"Aren't they beautiful? Just like the one that kissed me. No, like the others. The one that kissed me was different. She was different, wasn't she, Suze?" Before Suze could answer, Jen began clapping her hands excitedly. "She's here! My butterfly is here!" she exclaimed gleefully.

The small group watched curiously as a white butterfly flitted back and forth, up and down several few feet away. Unlike the others, it showed no interest in the flowers, only in Jen.

It does look like her, Suze thought, remembering Joaquin's words. "This is our lucky day." When Lindsey and Becky gave her a strange look, she gave them a brief narrative about the trip to Mexico.

"You don't believe this is the same one, do you?" Lindsey asked incredulously.

"No. She'd be ancient in butterfly years. Jen believes it, though. That's what counts," Suze said keeping her voice low. "Isn't she beautiful, Jen?"

"It's The White Lady. She flew all this way to see me."

"Yes, she did. Wasn't that nice of her?"

Jen nodded, holding her hand up. Immediately, and to everyone's surprise, the butterfly floated toward it and landed on the palm. After circling several times it stopped and then stared into Jen's eyes. Jen's head bobbed up and down.

"Yes," she said. "Yes, she's the same one. I don't remember things so well anymore... No... I wish we could... I know. Children? No... Okay... I wish you didn't have to go.... Next year?" Jen smiled. "Oh yes, we'll be here. Be careful... Goodbye." The butterfly flapped its wings. Slowly The White Lady lifted into the air and then drifted toward Jen's face. Landing on her left cheek it spun around once and launched itself into the air, aiming for Suze.

It is you! Suze thought, stunned. Large purple eyes stared into hers. Visions of lush green forests and meadows flooded her mind. Every plant was covered by undulating rivers of orange, black and gold, constantly changing their shape and directions, slowly, hypnotically drawing Suze deeper and deeper into a kaleidoscope of shifting images. *I... I don't understand.* When the images morphed into one picture Suze gasped and then smiled. *Yes, of course. How silly of me. She **is** innocent... like your children. Yes, I will. Have a safe journey... and... and thank you.* La Señora Blanca flew away but not before she was joined by three smaller white butterflies.

"It's time to go home, Jen," Suze said, placing her hand on Jen's arm. "The Mother has a long journey ahead of her." Turning to her friends, she motioned for Becky to bring up the wheelchair. "I'll tell you once I get her settled in," she whispered.

Neither woman doubted what they were later told. They'd have never believed it if they hadn't seen it for themselves.

EPILOGUE

"Dagnabit!"

Drying her hands, Suze hurried into the living room. Jen was on her knees peering under the sofa.

"What in the world are you doing?" Suze asked.

"I dropped the damn thing," Jen said.

"What thing?"

"You know, the thing for the television. I dropped it."

"Oh, let me look." Within seconds Suze had recovered the remote and handed it to Jen. "Here you go. Anything else you need while we're down here?"

Forehead wrinkling, Jen appeared to be giving the question serious consideration.

"You could help me up. I'm not as young as I used to be."

"Neither am I," Suze said. "Maybe we should just help each other. You push, I'll pull." Both laughed as they awkwardly tugged themselves upward.

"You must be getting fat," Jen grumped, huffing and puffing.

"Must be? I've been fat for over ten years. You used to tell me you liked me with meat on my bones."

Jen's eyes twinkled. "That was before I had to help you up."

* * *

Over the next several months, Jen's memory and mood seemed to improve. At first Suze thought it was her imagination and kept the thought to herself. Lindsey came to visit twice a week, sometimes accompanied by Becky. During one of the visits, after an animated debate over who made the best donuts, Jen announced she was going to bed. When Suze got up to help, Jen motioned for her to stay where she was.

"I can do it myself," she declared proudly, surprising everyone. "I'm not that far gone." Shuffling down the hallway she stopped and turned stiffly. Raising her hand, she moved her fingers up and down. "Toodles."

"Toodles," everyone called back simultaneously. After she disappeared into the bedroom, Lindsey shook her head in wonder.

"I can't believe she's doing so well. It's like... I don't know... I can't explain it," Lindsey said. "I mean I don't believe in magic or anything but..."

Becky shook her head in agreement. She and Lindsey had spent many hours discussing what they had seen the day they had all gone to the park.

"I think what Lindsey is saying is... maybe your guide was right. Maybe that white butterfly is good luck."

"Maybe she is," Suze said. "Maybe she is."

Although Jen continued to have memory lapses, her self-awareness improved, and with it, pride in her ability to dress herself without Suze's help. One of her proudest moments was the day she graduated from Depends™ back into regular underwear.

"I can go panty shopping," she declared. "These old things I'm wearing must be a hundred years old."

"More like five or six," Suze said. "And hardly worn... but if you want new then new it'll be."

* * *

Two days later, they went panty shopping. Becky picked them up in her car and drove them to a nearby clothing store where Jen oohed and ahhhed over the latest styles.

"I'm sticking with flagships," she declared. "They look awful but they cover my entire butt. You better do that too, Suze. You're sagging."

"Jenetica Stone, how dare you talk about my butt that way."

Giggling, Jen went back to inspecting the latest 'flagships.' Suze surreptitiously slipped off to inspect her own butt in the mirror near the changing room.

My butt doesn't sag. Besides, I'm an old woman. What does she expect?

* * *

A month later, the twin beds were sold and a queen-size was moved into the bedroom. It took a while for them to adjust to sleeping together again but they did.

Spring came earlier than usual the next year. When warm weather arrived, the four friends ventured into the park looking for The White Lady. Jen still needed a wheelchair and Becky was more than willing to push it.

"Do you think she'll come this year?" Jen asked.

"If she can," Suze said. "It's a long way from Mexico, and she must be very old."

"Like us."

"Like us," Suze agreed. "I imagine she moves more slowly nowadays."

"I imagine."

Becky and Lindsay looked at each other and smiled.

* * *

One day the butterfly did appear, flying directly to Jen's outstretched hand. After moving to Jen's cheek, The White Lady approached Suze, hovering a few inches away. Large purple eyes stared into Suze's again, drawing her deep into a world of lush forests and plants, an unknown, mysterious world filled with millions of butterflies. Seconds later she fluttered away. This time no butterfly accompanied her. She would make her final journey alone.

Suze knew The White Lady would never return, but Joaquin had been right. Their strange encounter those many years ago had been the luckiest day of their lives. They had been given a precious gift... a kiss... a kiss of the butterfly... and the memories of two lifetimes.

Author's Note

This story is dedicated to my father, who suffered from dementia, and my mother, who also suffers from the disease. It is a small window into different realities we will never understand. A world filled with confusion, anger, fear and terror. A world where loved ones become strangers and we, the strangers, become wardens of dementia's victims. We become the caregivers.

Caregivers! 'Those who give selflessly of themselves to care for those in need.' Most of the experiences described in this story are real. Those that aren't are composites of the many people who make up a support network that is invaluable. The ending was created for the reader's comfort. The truth is that dementia steals the memories, the lives and the futures of those who suffer from it, as well as those who care for its victims. At the moment, there are no happy endings for those who suffer from this disease, but there is hope. As science learns more and more about dementia, new treatments will be available and in time, possibly a cure. Until then, thanks to everyone who takes the time to care.

To Kill

a Butterfly

PROLOGUE

NO ONE KNEW HOW the first victims became infected. There were several theories. One thing everyone agreed on was that the pandemic started in the jungles of Argentina, and would probably have stayed there if not for the arrogance of an ambitious bastard. The Argentinean province was called Jujuy. Lithium was in high demand. The salt flats of Jujuy provided a wealth of minerals for mining companies looking to increase profits for their shareholders. Exploration led to development, and development to more exploration. Pharmaceutical companies became interested in the jungles, sending botanist teams in search of plants that might have medicinal qualities. Once a region few people had ever heard of, it became a nightmare for the local tribes. Little attention was paid to them or the lands.

* * *

Franklin Jamison Langley was from old wealth; a highly intelligent, well-educated, arrogant bastard who, to humanity's detriment, had PhDs in entomology and microbiology. His one great ambition was to become a household name in the most respected scientific journals. He did.

When the CEO of Pharmaceutical Horizons asked him to examine two of their researchers who had come down with a strange affliction, he jumped at the opportunity. An all-expenses paid trip to Jujuy, Argentina, not to mention the opportunity to collect a sizeable paycheck, was irresistible. Both were guaranteed whether or not he was successful in discovering the cause of the men's illness. Unfortunately, his desire to become famous overrode all the precautions and ethics that had been drilled into him during his studies twenty years earlier; not that ethics or morals had ever been a part of his nature.

* * *

"This is wonderful!" Professor Langley exclaimed, overjoyed at the bizarre behavior of the two men pacing back and forth in the cage. "They're actually exhibiting some zombie-like traits, blue-white corneas, grunts, pale skin. Their movement isn't as rigid as I'd have thought and I don't see any signs of necrosis. That's troubling. True zombie-ism is expected to have those symptoms... not that there's ever been an actual case of it, so it's all speculation at this point. How long have they been like that?"

"About two weeks," Dr. Victor Doarte replied.

"Two weeks? And you say they haven't eaten anything since then?"

"Nothing. We tried meat, vegetables, fruits... everything we could think of. They ignore it. The only thing that excites them is us."

"What about water?"

"Nope. They aren't interested in that either."

Langley moved closer, stopping about six feet away. Immediately the two men strained against the bars, their arms stretched out to grab at him.

"They should be dead by now, yet I see no signs of necrosis or decay. Except for their bizarre behavior and eye discoloration, they appear fairly normal. Maybe a little pale."

"I wouldn't get too close, professor," Dr. Doarte warned.

"They certainly are interested in us. Have they managed to get hold of anyone?"

"While we were trying to cage them, they attacked two workers. They were ripped apart before we could do anything."

"I imagine that was a bit of a bother," Langley replied. "Where are their bodies?"

"Buried. It didn't seem wise to put them in the refrigeration unit. We keep our food in there."

"Too bad! Examining the corpses might have been beneficial. This could be an advanced case of rabies. The symptoms are consistent with the disease. I hope I haven't been dragged all the way down here for something so mundane."

"I doubt it. Even if the men were infected, they were killed so quickly it wouldn't have shown up in the blood work. What now?" Dr. Doarte asked.

Professor Langley yawned.

"Well, the first thing I need to do is study the patient records, especially their medical histories. Then find out what they were doing prior to the onset of the symptoms."

"I'll have their files delivered to your room within the hour. It'll take us a couple of days to line up the carriers and supplies needed to get to the base camp. The Land Rovers can take us most of the way, but we're still going to have to hike a few kilometers. If we leave early we should be there before sunset."

"I enjoy adventures." *It'll look good in my bio, hiking dangerous jungles teeming with poisonous insects and snakes, predators stalking us as we struggle through the thick undergrowth to the site of the first verified case of zombie-ism.* "What about them?" he asked, nodding toward the cage.

"I have guards stationed around the compound and this building 24/7. They'll make sure no one gets in here. And it's not like we have to feed or water them."

"Well done, doctor. Just tell me when we leave and I'll be there. Now if you don't mind, I'm going to go to my room. Make sure I get the files as soon as possible," Langley said. "If I'm going to solve this problem, I need to do my homework." The scientist smiled smugly, already imagining the accolades he'd be receiving from his colleagues. *If this isn't rabies, it could be something new. I might even submit a thesis to* The Journal of Nature and Science*. I'll call it Langley's Disease. Not a bad name! Not bad at all.*

* * *

Dr. Doarte watched the scientist walk toward the small group of people gathered for the journey to Base Camp Three. *God help us,* he thought. Professor Langley was wearing a starched, neatly pressed short-sleeved khaki shirt with matching shorts. At his side was a 9mm Beretta pistol. A safari hat was perched on his head. Hiking shoes and knee-high socks finished up the picture. He looked like someone from an old Tarzan movie. *The bugs are going to tear him up.*

"How do I look?" Professor Langley asked, stopping to show off his outfit. Clearly he expected the admiration of the locals, as well as the company personnel.

"Very nice, Professor," Doarte said, literally biting his tongue to keep from laughing. *I hope you're smarter than you look.* "You should be quite comfortable during the ride. Once we start walking, I'd recommend you switch to

140

long sleeves and pants. We'll be trekking through some dense brush. Not to mention the insects are vicious."

"Well," Professor Langley paused and then straightened his shoulders. "Of course I'll change. I'm not a novice. No reason to get hot in the jeep now, is there?"

"No reason at all." Turning his attention to the men gathered around him, the doctor addressed the local guide contracted to coordinate men and supplies. "Everything ready, Paolo?"

"Si, doctor."

Slapping him on the shoulder, Doarte signaled for everyone to load up.

"Ready, Professor?"

"Let's do it!"

Three Land Rovers pulled out of the compound.

* * *

Damn bugs, Langley thought, swatting at the swarm circling him. "Doesn't anyone have some type of repellent?" he asked angrily.

"Sorry, I thought you knew to put it on back at the compound. There's a bottle in the glove compartment."

"Really, Doctor, you can't expect me to drag a bunch of that stuff with me when I'm travelling. It's up to employers to furnish insect deterrents specific to the environments I'm expected to work in. Just because I'm an entomologist doesn't mean I carry repellents everywhere I go." Opening the glove compartment he grabbed a bottle of clear liquid. When he removed the cap he sniffed it suspiciously and made a face. "Deet!" he said disgustedly. "Anyone ever hear of picaridin? It smells a lot better."

"The company buys the repellents. We use what they send."

Splashing the liquid in his palms, Langley spread it on his arms, legs and face.

"When we get back to the base camp I want you to phone whoever's running your department and tell them to send me something with picaridin. I don't intend to walk around smelling like this while I'm down here."

"Certainly, Professor." Dr. Doarte had orders to accommodate Professor Langley no matter what the cost. He didn't realize he'd be working with such a spoiled, self-absorbed person.

* * *

Base Camp Three was actually more modern than Langley had expected. Seven buildings were scattered in an area cleared of trees along the bank of a small stream. Each structure had windows and doors. Mosquito netting covered all the openings. Four of the buildings were sleeping quarters. Three of them had four bunk beds that could accommodate eight people. The fourth had three cots, each separated by a curtain. The central building held the supplies. Next to it was an infirmary/laboratory. The last had makeshift tables, obviously the office. Two generators and several small barrels of fuel sat next to it. Several locals were moving about, tending to their duties.

"Not bad," he said. "I've seen a lot worse. Who runs this place when you're not here, Doctor?"

"I do," a female voice said from inside the office. "I'm Zoie. Zoie Morales."

"You're in charge?" Langley said, unable to hide his surprise and disgust. If a woman was able to live out here, especially such a petite one, it wasn't going to look very impressive in his bio.

"Of course. You must be Professor Langley. Thank you for putting yourself out by coming here. I know there must

142

be more important things you could be doing." The sarcasm was hardly noticeable. Langley missed it. Dr. Doarte didn't and smirked.

"Well, when Henry called, I couldn't refuse him."

"Henry?"

"Henry Wilkinson, Horizon's CEO. Oh, sorry, of course you wouldn't know him by his first name," Langley said, puffing up like a little peacock.

"Ummm," Doarte said.

"That's okay, Victor," Zoie said. "Professor Langley's right. There's no reason I would know **Henry**. If you'll show him where he'll be staying, I'd appreciate it. We can talk about John and Terry later. Paolo, please put the supplies in the tent and tell the guys to call it a day."

* * *

Zoie Morales shook her head as she watched Professor Langley wander around the camp site. From what she had heard and read about the man, he wasn't someone she really wanted to meet. Too bad she hadn't been consulted by her stepfather before he had contacted the scientist. She could have named a dozen others just as competent and a lot more personable. Herman was going to get a big surprise for his birthday. All she needed to do was figure out what would be appropriate.

"He certainly is full of himself," Victor said, sipping a hot cup of tea.

"His reputation precedes him. According to the people I've talked to, he's ambitious and cuts corners. We need to keep an eye on him. I don't want anyone else coming down with whatever John and Terry have. Speaking of which, how are they doing?"

"The same. I don't get it. Both of them should be dead. They don't eat, they don't drink. They don't do anything

143

but pace back and forth trying to grab anyone that gets too close... which they managed to do twice. You wouldn't believe what they did to them."

"Don't tell me," Zoie said. "More brains, right? Sorry, bad joke, but all the talk about zombies is getting a little irritating."

"I know you don't believe in that stuff, but if you saw them now, Zoie, you'd change your mind. There's no life in them. No... humanness."

"Well, hopefully the professor can figure out what's going on."

"I certainly intend to," Langley said, walking into the office. "Sorry I didn't knock but I didn't want to interrupt your discussion."

"No problem," Doarte said. "Grab a chair. We're just talking."

"So I heard. I get the impression, Ms. Morales, you don't believe in the living dead."

"You mean zombies, Professor, and no I don't. Our guys are still walking, so they're still alive. If we can find out what caused the problem, we might find a cure."

"I agree. That's why I'm here. I've read their files. Nothing in their backgrounds is unusual. I was surprised to see that John was a botanist with only a minor in entomology when he was at the university. He seemed to be particularly interested in Lepidoptera. I called one of his professors after looking over his files. He was just an average student. Nothing special, she said. Why a company would hire someone like him for such an important assignment is beyond me. I thought Horizons was serious about finding new medicinal agents for their company."

"We are," Zoie said. "That's why Corporate's interests have been represented here for the last six months.

144

Horizons' CFO sits on the board of a company that mines the salt flats."

"I'm sure that must be convenient," Langley said, mildly sarcastic.

"More like good business. When he was informed of the rumors about zombies in this area, he naturally told my... Mr. Wilkinson. I was sent to investigate."

Langley's clinical gaze slid up and down Zoie's body.

"You don't look like someone who belongs in the jungle. I mean you're... well..."

"What, Professor? Short? Too skinny? Or a woman!"

"I certainly don't mean anything personal, Ms. Morales," Langley said, his face flushing a bright red. "I'm sure you're quite competent at whatever you do. Women are good at organizing, tracking supplies, documenting issues. That sort of thing."

Zoie wanted so badly to bitch slap the condescending expression off the professor's face but decided it wouldn't change anything.

"Yes, we are," was all she said.

Satisfied that he had established his position, Langley decided he could be generous by showing some interest in this woman's role with Horizons.

"So, what do you do here? This certainly isn't a place for a woman, no insult intended."

"I'm part of their security division, but thank you for your concern. My job was to secure, investigate and contain without raising any alarms. Not exactly a job for a woman though, is it?" Zoie asked. She waited several seconds and then added, "Especially a woman like me. That is what you're thinking, isn't it?" The startled expression on Langley's face was priceless.

"Well, naturally, you certainly aren't what I'd expect. I don't know what Henry was thinking assigning any female to such a difficult task, but he's the boss."

"He is that, so, pleasantries aside, we might as well get down to business. When I saw John and Terry I suspected the cause was a virus or bacteria. That's why I asked Horizons to send a microbiologist."

"A smart move," Langley said. "But why me? This could be a simple case of rabies."

Zoie decided to ignore the question. No use stirring things up.

"I thought about that," she said. "If it's not, though..." She let the sentence drop.

"Something new could be advantageous to a pharmaceutical company," Langley finished. "Makes good sense."

"Yes. When the word **zombie** was mentioned, Corporate's ears perked up. Whatever created those symptoms? Well, you're a scientist. You know the potential value of new discoveries. Finding the chemicals —"

"Chemicals, Ms. Morales? You've watched too much television. Radiation, chemicals, all that crap is pure fiction. If this isn't rabies, my next guess is a new virus or bacteria. Maybe both."

"Both?" Doarte asked. "You mean a bacteriophage?"

Zoie looked from Victor to the professor, her expression clearly indicating she didn't know the term. Langley gave her a pained look.

"It's a bacteria infected by a virus," he explained. "Even the most benign bacteria can become deadly if the right virus invades it. The two can form quite a symbiotic relationship with the host. In layman's terms, they all receive some benefit from the relationship."

"So you've seen or heard about something like this before?"

"Not like this, but that doesn't mean it doesn't exist. We just haven't discovered them yet. Of course, as said I

146

before, this could simply be advanced cases of rabies. The not drinking, inability to communicate, and especially the rage are all symptomatic of the Lyssavirus."

"Okay, let's say you're right. What now?" Zoie asked.

"Why, investigate! Look for the source. That is your job, isn't it? We find out exactly where they were the last few months. Did either ever report being bitten by an animal? Vampire bats are common in this area. Maybe one of them complained about a wound that couldn't be explained."

"We don't track our employees' movements every minute of the night and day, Professor," Zoie said. "Terry interviewed the locals about remedies they used for sicknesses and diseases. John searched for the plants or minerals they described. The two men were rarely together in the field. Nothing in their medical history indicates issues with bites or wounds while they were here."

"Well, rabies has been known to have longer incubation periods, but it's highly unlikely they would have contracted it elsewhere. I'm sure they were infected around the same time. That makes this the place. Or the main compound."

"What if we don't find anything here?" Doarte asked.

Langley shrugged indifferently.

"We always have your patients, Doctor."

"You have to examine the brain for the virus," Doarte said. "How —"

"Well, thankfully, we're here and not in the States. It'll make your job a lot easier. Fewer regulations to deal with."

"You can't seriously mean cutting off their heads!" the doctor exclaimed.

Professor Langley laughed.

"Don't be ridiculous! I only need one brain." Standing, Langley stretched and left before the doctor or Zoie could respond.

"He is joking, isn't he?" Zoie asked.

"Professor Langley doesn't strike me as a man with a normal sense of humor, but even he can't be that crazy."

Zoie yawned. The conversation had taken a bizarre turn and she was too tired to think clearly.

"I'm not so sure. I don't like him."

"Neither do I, but he's right. If this was the States, the red tape would be horrendous. CDC would be all over the place. If it's rabies, it would simplify things. It's a better alternative than not knowing the cause and it would put a kibosh on all the rumors. Corporate would be disappointed, but I don't give a rat's ass about the big wigs... ummm, your stepdad excluded."

"I know what you mean. He can be a royal pain too," Zoie said. "Go on. Get some rest."

"You're not coming?"

She shook her head.

"I think I'll stay in the office while the professor's here. I don't relish the thought of sleeping in the same tent with him. See you in the morning, Victor."

"Okay. I'll have one of the boys bring the cot over. Have a good night."

"You too."

* * *

After spending three days at Base Camp Three, Professor Langley was ready to call it quits. No one could provide a reasonable accounting of the two employees' time. As far as he was concerned, it was another indication of the ineptitude of putting a woman in charge.

A couple of local guides did remember Señor John taking numerous treks to a small clearing about two hours from the encampment. Discovering his interest in butterflies, they told him about a local species that appeared in that particular area every spring and disappeared in mid-to-late fall.

"Sounds like the Southern Monarch," Langley said. "Danaus Erippus. An interesting species much like the Northern Monarch."

"I remember him mentioning them. He was quite excited when he heard a cluster was nearby," Zoie said. "On his days off he'd head into the jungle with one of the guides and his camera. He was hoping to get an article published with an international butterfly magazine."

"Every amateur's dream," Langley scoffed. "A professional would do a scientific study. Dedicate months or even years to a subject, not a few days off. Still, I think I'd like to see them myself. Maybe take a few specimens back home. I have several live butterfly collections, you know. Nothing from South America though."

"I thought you wanted to go back to the compound."

"A slight delay isn't going to hurt anything. At least I'll have gotten something out of this trip. You **did** say nothing had changed with John and Terry, so it's not like one day's going to make much of a difference. Now, I'm going to need some supplies — jars, a butterfly net..."

"Butterfly net? Professor, we're in the mid —"

Langley shook his head.

"Ms. Morales, since John was a purported entomologist, I'm sure you'll find exactly what I need in his belongings. I doubt if he'll need them anymore so I might as well make use of them, don't you think?" *Not that you do think much,* he thought. *I wonder who you slept with to get this job.* Unaware his expression gave his thoughts away, he gave her what was supposed to look like

149

a fatherly smile and left to prepare his backpack for the next day's trip.

"Asshole!" Zoie mumbled under her breath.

Victor, who was just outside the office, walked in and plopped down on a chair.

"That man's an arrogant bastard. If we're lucky, he'll fall off a cliff somewhere."

"Yeah. Too bad there aren't any around. Thankfully I'll be done with him after tomorrow."

"Lucky you! My time's just beginning." Sighing, Victor put his hands on his knees and pushed upward. "At least I don't have to listen to him if he's out trekking in the jungles."

"Lucky us!" she agreed.

* * *

It took more than two hours to reach the clearing. Halfway through the journey, the professor began complaining.

"I thought you said two hours. How much farther?" he demanded, wiping the sweat from his forehead.

"Si, dos," the guide said, holding up two fingers.

"It's almost dos now. How much longer?"

"Diez quizá quince minutos."

"Speak English. Only illiterates don't speak English nowadays."

"Lo siento, Señor." The guide held up ten fingers. "Diez minutos."

"Jesus Christ! Sign language now."

"Si Señor," the guide agreed, smiling broadly. "Sign lan... gu... age."

Langley glared at the man, wondering if he was being made fun of and then dismissed the idea.

* * *

"This is magnificent," Langley said, holding the camera to his eye to snap another shot. There must be a couple thousand Monarchs clustering here." As he moved closer, some of the butterflies launched themselves into the air giving him an opportunity to catch them in flight and a better view of their resting place. Thick vines and growth covered what appeared to be an odd-shaped structure that appeared somewhat triangular. *Probably an old snake-infested Inca temple,* he thought. Perhaps one day he'd come back and check it out, but archeology wasn't his thing — too much work and a dirty job at best. Clicking play on his camera, he examined the photos. "Perfect! Hey you," he called to the guide. "See if you can stir a few more up. I want some action shots of the group flying." When the guide just looked at him, the professor waved his free arm and pointed to the cluster. "Go over there."

"Si, Señor."

Walking toward the mass of moving bodies, the guide started to raise his arms when Langley spotted something pale amongst the orange and black butterflies. Zooming in, he stared in awe at a single white butterfly, almost a third larger than the ones around it.

"A mutation!" he exclaimed excitedly. "Stop!" he whispered loudly to the guide. "Don't move!" Slowly, Langley knelt to pick up the net he had laid on the ground and then stealthily approached the cluster. When he was within striking distance, he swung the net, caring little about the butterflies surrounding his target. They were dispensable as long as he caught the white one. "Got it!" he yelled, gathering the net so it and the others trapped inside couldn't escape. Ignoring the bodies on the ground and the rest of the butterflies that had taken to the air, he walked back to his pack and gently coaxed them into the jar. What didn't fit in the first, he put in a second jar. The damaged he tossed aside.

"Aren't you something!" he said, holding the container up to better examine his prize. Large purple eyes stared back at him as the white butterfly moved along the transparent wall of the glass. Professor Langley frowned. He'd never seen purple eyes on an insect before, let alone ones that seemed —

"Señor," the guide said, interrupting his thoughts. "Go now, si?"

Langley stared blankly at the man for a moment and then shook his head.

"Uhh... sure... right. Get my pack. I'll carry this. I don't want anything happening to her," he said, tapping lightly on the glass.

* * *

Their arrival back at the main compound filled Dr. Doarte with both relief and dread. The short time he had spent with Professor Langley confirmed his initial first impression — the man was an arrogant son of a bitch who cared for nothing but himself. Hopefully his research would confirm John and Terry had contracted rabies and he'd be gone.

* * *

"If it hadn't been for these butterflies," Langley said. "I'd have nothing to show for my time. I need to get them home as soon as possible."

"What about your research?" Doarte asked.

"My opinion — those men have rabies. Get me some brain samples of one of them and I'll take them back with me."

"You mean you're leaving? Just like that?"

"Please, Doctor. We both know I'm right."

"And just how am I supposed to get brain tissue?"

"Put them out of their misery. There's no cure for rabies. You'll be doing them a favor."

"I'm not about to kill them on speculation. It could be something else."

Langley stopped looking at the jar and stared disbelievingly at the doctor.

"Doctor Doarte, my recommendation is we get brain samples. Now, if you don't want to do your job then I'll contact Henry and have him assign someone that will. Those are walking dead, as far as I'm concerned. Horizon will want to know more. Consider this a mercy killing if you want. If they were dogs you wouldn't hesitate."

"But they're not dogs..."

"Exactly. So why give them less consideration? Or their families? No one wants them to suffer any longer."

The doctor knew Professor Langley's reasoning was logical. Whether it was rabies or something else, John and Terry couldn't be saved. Keeping them in cages and prolonging their lives was crueler than killing them.

"I'll need at least six vials to take back with me," Langley said, sensing victory. "Identify the patient they come from and pack the samples in dry ice. Send his medical records to my address."

"I know how to prepare bio-materials for transport." Irritated, the doctor turned to leave when a hand grabbed his shoulder.

"Of course you do. That's why you'll handle the preparations. I'll let Henry know how cooperative you've been. Oh, I'm going home tomorrow." Taking a small tablet from his shirt pocket, Langley scribbled some information on a piece of paper and handed it to the doctor. "If you think of anything after I leave, let me know. Now I must take care of my friends here and pack. Contact Corporate and have them send a jet to pick me up at ten tomorrow. It's been nice knowing you." The professor walked away, holding the jar at eye level as he examined the captured Monarchs.

Just like that, Doarte thought. *I do the dirty work while you go play with butterflies.*

* * *

Working for large corporations had its advantage. Pharmaceutical Horizons spent a lot of money greasing the right palms to keep the wheels moving smoothly when they needed to expedite things. The corporate jet, crew and occupants were cleared through Customs within thirty minutes of their arrival in the States. An hour-and-a-half later, Professor Langley was home. The cab driver carried his luggage and the cooler into the house and left, tipless.

"I hope nothing has happened to my babies," he said, referring to his butterfly collection while ignoring any form of greeting to his housekeeper.

"They're fine," she said. Elizabeth was a middle-aged woman who had worked for the scientist for six years. The pay was good, plus she had the added bonus that he was away from the place most of the time. She had the five-bedroom home to herself and the doctor's bugs. Elizabeth took special care to make sure the animals were well-cared for. Her job counted on it.

"Good. I need you to prepare another butterfly habitat. I found these beauties on my trip." Holding up the jar, Langley proudly displayed his prize. The white butterfly had stopped roaming around the glass sides and had settled on the bottom. Her orange companions surrounded her, but didn't touch her. "Let me know when it's ready. I'll be in my lab." Picking up the small cooler, he clamped it between his elbow and ribs so he could carry the jars in his hands. His mind was back to his new acquisitions, especially the female Monarch. He was certain she was a mutation. If he could successfully breed her and reproduce a white cluster he could name them after him.

What's taking Elizabeth so long? he thought. I need to get them into the habitat soon. Irritated, he loosened the lid on the jars. There! That'll give you some air. Now for those vials. A quick look under the microscope will confirm my suspicions and I'll be done with Horizons.

Opening the cooler, he pulled out the six vials and laughed. The labels said John. Butterfly man. *Dr. Doarte has a sense of humor.* Langley set five vials in a rack. The sixth he uncorked. From it, he removed a small piece of brain matter with tweezers and placed it on a slide. *Now, let's see...*

"Professor?" A hand touched his right forearm, startling him. Spinning around, the scientist bumped into Elizabeth, knocking her off balance and the vial from his hand. Her forearm hit the jars, tipping them over. "Oh, I'm so sorry."

"You stupid bitch!" Langley yelled. Without thinking, he grabbed a paper towel and knelt to pick up the spilled specimen. A shard of glass nicked his middle finger. Neither saw the butterflies crawling out of the jars until they took flight. "Don't move," Langley whispered.

The white Monarch fluttered near his face, her purple eyes staring unblinkingly into his. Moments later, Langley collapsed against the countertop, his arm hitting the other vials, knocking them over. They rolled off the counter, crashing to the floor.

Elizabeth screamed and ran from the room. Although conscious, the scientist couldn't move. He watched in horror as the butterflies walked through the brain samples and then moved to where he was lying. Slowly, almost deliberately, they climbed up his neck and onto his face. Then they fluttered their wings and lifted into the air. The last he saw was the white female leaving through the door, followed by the others.

Justice is often quirky. Professor Langley had lost his collection but gained the notoriety he craved so zealously. Unfortunately, his name would forever be associated with the greatest pandemic humanity had ever experienced.

CHAPTER 1

THE TOWN WAS CALLED Destiny, not an original name but appropriate. Humanity's future lay within the walls of the thousands of scattered communities across the different continents; walled towns and villages filled with people too frightened to go beyond the security of the barriers between them and the outside world. With good reason: Madness ran rampant everywhere! Only it wasn't really madness. It was an unstoppable plague.

Before the breakdown of communications, scientists estimated that ninety percent of the human population had been infected or killed by the infected. Those who weren't lived in fear, terrified of catching the sickness; of becoming Phageian.

Phageian! For some reason people felt better calling them that rather than zombies. Zombies brought to mind rotting, vacant-eyed corpses shuffling aimlessly around, attacking and eating humans. They didn't sleep, they didn't feel. The ultimate killing machine, they existed for only one thing — to consume human flesh. How they digested it, no one knew or really cared. Then again, zombies were monsters created from man's imagination. Phageian were real!

There were theoretical and real differences between the two creatures. Phageian didn't rot. The flesh didn't fall from their bodies. Wounds remained wounds, almost like a form of stasis. There was no blood, no oozing pus, no anything; not even an odor. If an arm was severed, the

157

rest of the body continued to function. The lost limb eventually succumbed to natural decay but the process took longer. An even bigger distinction was that they slept, or appeared to when night came. They could also move quickly. Unfortunately, no matter how many were destroyed, more came. The world had become a limitless source of Phageian.

The similarities, in addition to the differences, made Phageian more terrifying than any zombie, real or imagined. They had the same insatiable hunger for human flesh, live human flesh. They weren't, however, the mindless zombies portrayed in the old, popular 'living dead' movies. Capable of working in small groups, circling their prey and trapping it, they quickly moved in for the kill, and kill they did. Little was left of the person who fell victim to a horde. Anyone fortunate enough to escape eventually became Phageian if they were exposed to bodily fluids; bites and eye splatters were the most common causes. How long the transformation took depended on the individual's immune system. At least that was the theory. Science never discovered the cause of the pandemic and the laboratories were long gone. Most scientists were either dead or taking refuge in the sanctuaries scattered across the continents.

Occasionally someone did survive an attack, but only if bitten around the hand or foot that was amputated quickly. The most fortunate lost a finger or two. Sometimes it was a hand, arm or leg. Bites to the body were automatically considered fatal. The victim was immediately killed and the head decapitated. In the past, bodies were burned but fuel had become scarce. Sanctuaries eventually disposed of corpses by throwing them off the town ramparts, which were always surrounded by the hordes. People learned to take advantage of Phageian cravings. They could sneak out of their protected villages to search for food. If they could kill a Phageian or two while hunting, all the better. Head decapitation was the preferred method.

Now, twenty-eight years after the pandemic began, survivors had another problem. Natural food sources around the walled communities were disappearing. Animals were scarce, making hunting difficult. Villagers were being forced to make a difficult choice: Feed the humans inside the walls or Phageian outside.

CHAPTER 2

THE MEETING HAD BEEN in session for almost two hours. Tempers flared. Jordan, one of the youngest on the Council, was the most vocal.

"You can't be serious!" she exclaimed, slamming her hand hard on the table. She was a small woman. Her slender, androgynous physique belied her strength and strong will. Some even dared to accuse her of being hardheaded, not that she was bothered by that. Jordan rarely wavered once she took a stand on something. Now wasn't any different. "No one in their right mind would agree to that."

"They'll have no choice," Eli replied, his voice as old and tired sounding as he looked. At seventy-two, it was almost a miracle he had survived the pandemic, but not necessarily unexpected considering his history. Eli Walker was a survivalist. He understood the land. He knew what plants were edible and which ones to avoid. Tracking and trapping were as natural to him as growing crops was to a farmer. They both knew how to make use of the land, but Eli knew how to make use of everything that grew or lived on it. His knowledge and skills made him a natural choice as leader.

"I don't like the thought any more than any of you," Eli said, "but what choice do we have? Our food storage is low. There's hardly any game within acceptable hunting distances and more Phageian are showing up every day.

No matter how many we destroy at night, twice as many arrive by the next day."

"Too bad we can't eat them," Raoul muttered under his breath. "We'd never run out of food."

"That's a disgusting thought," one of the Council members said, his face turning a ghastly pale.

"Exactly!" Eli agreed. "We have enough food to last a few more months. I've called this meeting now because if we are to survive, we need to make the difficult choices now."

"But storing bodies for us to eat is even more disgusting, let alone immoral. We aren't cannibals," Jordan said.

"Do you have any other solution?"

"We'll expand our hunting area. I'll take the younger hunters. We're quicker and can cover more distance."

"Jordan, one hunting party isn't going to find enough to feed the village, especially with winter coming. Even if you did manage, you wouldn't be able to transport it in large enough quantities without attracting Phageian."

"We can search for another home, an abandoned village or town. Surely there are others out there that might have stores of food. If we find one, we can move our people."

"Move the entire population? Two hundred and fifty-three people? Half of us are over fifty."

"We can do it. It won't be easy but it's not impossible. We can go in small groups."

"That would still take months," Eli said. "If you're lucky enough to find a place within a six-day march, that's twelve days round trip. Twenty-five people would be ten trips, one every two weeks. That's five months to move everyone **if** we could keep on schedule."

"I think we could do it quicker. Once we find a new sanctuary, the original team can split up, each member leading a new group. One group could leave every night. It could be done in less than two weeks if things went right."

"That's a big if, not to mention ambitious. Everything never goes right."

"Eli..."

"Listen, Jordan. You were a child when your aunt brought you here. Do you remember what happened to your mom and dad?"

"They died defending me against the Phageian," Jordan replied. The memories still hurt. Three other children had been travelling with her. Eleven people total. The night had been cool and clear. A new moon made it almost impossible to see but her dad insisted everyone keep moving. Still, everything was going fine until a noise scared one of the children. Her screams pierced the night, awakening several Phageian who had been in a normal nightly sleep-state. The inability to quiet her immediately attracted their attention. The attack came so quickly only a few adults and Jordan escaped. Although Jordan never saw her parents go down under the horde, they never found their way to Destiny. It took a long time before Jordan's aunt eventually convinced her they had to be dead. That was easier to live with than believing her parents were Phageian.

"Exactly. So you, better than anyone, know how difficult it is to move children. They're unpredictable at best. At night they'll be tired, cranky and terrified. Are you willing to put them through what you went through?"

"If it gives them a chance for a future? Yes, I would! What other choice is there? They don't have much of one here."

"Maybe not, but neither do they out there. Right now we're just speculating, hoping there's someplace else we can call home. Think about it." Eli made eye contact with each Council member. "It would have to already be a walled community. How many of those do you think exist? And if it has an existing population, they would have to agree to take us in. Do you really think anyone would want that? Share what little they may have to save us? I wouldn't," Eli added. "Even if I had a warehouse filled with food, I'd horde it and defend it. You are my people. We may have arrived separately but we built Destiny together. Almost everyone follows the rules and contributes. There hasn't been a new human arrival in three years. That says a lot as far as I'm concerned."

"What if the new sanctuary was empty but had stores of food? Enough to feed everyone for a long time?"

Eli smiled, his leathery cheeks crinkling.

"What if the food fairy flew in tomorrow with her magic wand, or a helicopter landed with news that a cure had been found that would bring the Phageian back to life. There're a million what ifs we could theorize about, but not one will solve the immediate problem. So, my question to you is not what if, but how? How do we transport all of our people, the young, the weak, the old, to another home, days away, without jeopardizing their lives? Phageian may become somewhat dormant at night, but they can be awakened. Do we gag the children? Do we abandon the elderly? Even I couldn't walk all night and I'm healthier than some twenty years younger. How would we move them?"

Jordan shook her head.

"I don't have all the answers, Eli, but we have to do something. I'm not willing to consider what you're proposing. Eating one of our own! Even starving, I wouldn't!"

"You'd be surprised what you'll do when you don't have a choice."

"There's always a choice. I'd kill myself before doing that."

"You'd be a bit tough, but I'd prefer you to those things walking around outside," Raoul piped in. Every head in the room turned to stare in horror at the young man. He was new to the Council and had a difficult time following the established rules of order. "I'm joking," he said, holding up his hands defensively. "Sort of."

A few Council members chuckled. Others gave him a disgusted look. Eli rapped the table with a rock that was kept for solely that purpose.

"I think we need to call it an evening. Think about what I've suggested. Tomorrow morning we'll reconvene and decide what we'll do. For now we need to keep this to ourselves. Meeting is adjourned."

CHAPTER 3

JORDAN PACED BACK and forth, trying to think of a solution to Destiny's food problem. She hated to admit it but Eli, possibly, had the only viable solution. The problem was she wasn't willing to go to the extreme he had suggested — eating their own dead. They would be no better than the soulless creatures scratching on the village walls to get in.

Felicia watched her lover with a sense of helplessness. Jordan had just arrived from the Council meeting and was in a foul mood. She looked exhausted.

"Eli actually proposed we eat each other," Jordan said, slamming her hat on the small make-shift table next to an old couch. "We're not animals!"

"That's exactly what we are, Jordie," Felicia replied. She was always the voice of reason when it came to tough decisions. "But he could be right, you know." Jordan gave her lover a startled look. Felicia held up her hand, preventing her from responding. "Look, I don't like the thought, but why keep those things fed when we're starving. It's only a matter of time before we turn on each other once we run out of food. Humans have eaten each other before."

"I know that!" Jordan ran her left hand through her short hair. "Would you?"

"Depends on who it is. Some of these people I wouldn't touch if my life depended on it. Others..." Felicia shrugged. "There are worse things than cannibalism."

"Maybe, but I'm not going to be the one to keep **that** tradition alive." Jordan's sarcasm was unmistakable. "At least not in the way you mean." Grinning, she plopped down on Felicia's lap and wrapped her arms around her lover's neck. "Of course, I suppose I could be convinced to give you a try. You're quite a tasty nibble, you know."

Returning the embrace, Felicia pulled Jordan closer and gave her a playful nip on the right earlobe. Then she pushed Jordan away. "You're not so bad yourself, but I think you may be spoiling. You stink!"

"Well thanks a lot!" Jordan said, jumping up. "Maybe you should get used to the smell. It'll be good practice for what's to come if Eli gets his way." Grabbing her hat, she stomped out of the room.

"Hey, I was only joking," Felicia called after her. "Damn! It's going to be a cold night."

* * *

Jordan lay awake for hours arguing with herself about the proposal. There was no question Eli was right. With their reserves getting low and no game in the surrounding areas, Destiny's future looked bleak. Rolling on her side, she stared at the face only inches from hers. Felicia was almost forty-three, ten years older than Jordan. She looked more like fifty, even in sleep. Fine lines creased her forehead. Crows' feet spidered outward from the corners of her eyes. Her skin was deeply tanned from hours spent in the community gardens.

Felicia was twenty when she and seven fellow students stumbled onto the sanctuary. The epidemic was in its fifth year. The military had been stationed around safe-havens, cities that could be fortified with walls and electric barriers. These were usually near major water sources

166

which provided power that could supply the cities' needs. Anyone entering was quarantined for ten days. Those who came down with the plague were destroyed; the others were accepted into the community and assigned duties. Life within the walls took on an artificial normalcy.

Felicia was in her third year at a university, majoring in agricultural and microbial sciences. Education was considered a top priority as long as it pertained to specific subjects. The arts were no longer important. If humans were to survive, the world needed more experts in the sciences, not entertainment.

How the breach in the militarily secured perimeter occurred, no one knew. Once Phageian gained access to her city, the infection and fear ravaged the population. Innocent people became targets. Anyone who looked faintly sick was killed, their bodies burned. People eyed each other with suspicion. Within a month, the city was a ghost town for the living and a feeding ground for Phageian.

Even now, twenty-three years later, Jordan remembered clearly the day Felicia had arrived. The commotion near the northern gate could be heard blocks away. People ran excitedly in the direction of the noise, some calling out to each other that there were new arrivals outside the walls. In those times, Phageian hadn't made it to the more isolated villages.

Those were the good old days, Jordan thought and then silently laughed. She was too young to know what the 'good old days' really were. To her, it was being able to go beyond the walls in daylight. With lookouts stationed on the ramparts and a few armed guards accompanying them, there was a time when people could venture outside of the sanctuary for a few hours, sit in a meadow watching birds or just lie on the grass and daydream of possibilities.

* * *

Felicia was tall, scrawny and exhausted. Her clothes were stained from months of traveling and stank from an inability to clean them regularly or take baths. One sleeve was missing. The other had several tears. At some point she had shaved her head, more a defense against lice than anything else. Now, dark red stubbles were growing back. Her blue eyes glistened with tears of relief when her group was allowed into Destiny. After being interviewed by Eli and examined by the village doctor, they were invited to join the community—if they cleared ten days of quarantine. They did.

She and her companions, with their education, became invaluable to the survival of the residents. Her knowledge of botany improved fruit and vegetable production. Another student who was pre-med became the doctor's assistant. The others students had studied engineering, art, history and pharmaceuticals. The pharmaceutical student, Rosie, had excelled in botany and minored in geology. She worked with Felicia to create natural remedies for ailments and ways to enrich the soils.

Unfortunately, all the knowledge and science in the world couldn't keep even the best land productive forever. Now, like its people, the earth was tired, becoming less fertile with each growing season. Soon only weeds would survive the nutrient-depleted gardens. When that happened, there would be nothing for the villagers to eat.

Jordan turned on her back and stared at the ceiling, her mind made up. No matter what the others decided, she wasn't going to stay and watch them become living versions of the Phageian.

CHAPTER 4

THE RAPPING OF THE ROCK quickly silenced the bevy of voices reverberating through the room.

"Everyone, please take a seat," Eli called out. "We have a lot of things before us today. Thank you," he said once the sound of scraping chairs subsided. "Last night I made a proposal. Normally, the Council makes policies by majority votes and then the people are informed. They accept or reject everything by referendum. This will be no different. It can't be."

"Then why call us together now?" Mary Beth asked. She was a middle-aged housewife whose husband had died of a heart attack shortly after the pandemic started. Tenacious and resourceful, she abandoned their home, leading her two children and eighteen neighbors into the wilderness in search of a safe place to live. Fourteen survived the journey. Her two children were now adults. "We could simply put this before the people."

"They would reject my proposal, just as you did last night. If, however, there's a consensus amongst us, most will see reason. They may then be able to convince others."

"Eli," Jordan said. "What about those who can't be convinced? This may irreparably split the community. Possibly even cause a riot."

"If the Council is in unanimous agreement we'll have a better chance of bringing the rest on board."

"I'm sorry, Eli, I can't —"

169

Eli held up his hand, stopping Jordan from continuing.

"I know you don't like this. None of us do, but how will we make it through the winter without protein? The hunters aren't bringing in enough to feed twenty people, let alone more than two-hundred." Turning to face the other Council members, he held out his hands in a pleading gesture. "My friends, we've come this far because we've made the hard decisions when they were needed. Would you have some of us die of starvation in a few months after all we have done to live this long? Who here will stand by and watch our children, our elderly, our people slowly waste away when we have the means to save them? I know this goes against everything we believe in. It's repugnant, but do we really have a choice? Do we die for the sake of principle, or live with the hope that one day all of this will end?" As Jordan again started to speak, Eli silenced her once more. "Please, Jordan, hear me out for a few more minutes and then you may say whatever is on your mind." When Jordan nodded, Eli patted her shoulder and smiled. "Thank you. I've been thinking about what you said last night. Searching for a new sanctuary is a good idea, but it's going to take time. More and more Phageian arrive at our walls every day. I think it's because they too are running out of food and we're the only source left in this area. When Destiny was first built, we ransacked every abandoned village or town we could find. There weren't very many Phageian in this area back then. We could travel freely, day or night. That's no longer possible, except in winter."

"That's true," Raoul agreed. "At least the cold makes them more sluggish and easier to destroy. Cutting even a leg off makes it almost impossible for them to follow us."

"True, but there are hundreds, maybe thousands of Phageian out there. Who knows how many more in the woods," Chin Lee said. Chin was the chief baker. His job was to oversee the rationing of grain to other bakers as well as train younger people how to make the coarse bread distributed to everyone every third day.

"Finding a new home is still a possibility," Raoul argued. Several heads nodded in agreement.

"I agree," Eli said, turning back to Jordan. "What I'm proposing is a sort of two-fold solution. The first is that the Council, everyone here, agrees to the concept of... of utilizing the opportunities afforded us —"

"Opportunities?" Jordan cut in. "Just say it, Eli. If we agree to eat our dead! That's what you really mean."

"All right! If we eat those who die, we may just have a chance. The second part of the proposal is that you and three other master hunters lead four small teams to search for a new home, one we can move our people to with minimal effort. Sarazon, Martin and Sheila would be my recommendation to lead the groups."

"And what if no one finds anything?" Mary Beth asked. "What then?"

"Then we pray," another councilman answered. "Not that that has done us much good."

"What do you say, Jordan," Eli asked. "This will only work if the Council stands united."

"I don't like taking that many teams out," Jordan said. "It will leave the village worse off. We'll need extra rations."

"It can't be much worse. Besides, it's only moving the inevitable forward a few weeks if we do nothing. This was your idea. The hunters are our only hope. Look, we have supplies to carry us awhile longer without taking drastic steps. Nothing's going to happen this week or this month.

171

Find us another home and my proposal becomes moot. Support me now and we'll at least have hope."

"I don't like this," Jordan repeated, shaking her head. In the end, though, she knew she didn't have a choice. She would never agree to eating human flesh. "But I'll back you."

"Good! Is everyone else on board?" When the other Council members nodded, Eli sighed with relief. "We'll call a meeting in two days, an hour before sunset. Jordan, you make the necessary preparations to leave immediately after the announcement. There's going to be a lot of unrest and discussion. Some aren't going to want us to waste our food and resources. Others will object to the hunters being gone. Plan to be gone before they have time to think about it too much." Eli made eye contact with each Council member. "One last thing. People are going to want to know why we've had two meetings in two days. Tell them we'll be making an important announcement day after tomorrow. They'll have to wait until then for more information. It's crucial nothing we've discussed leave this room except for those hunters chosen to be on the teams." Eli banged the rock on the table. "This meeting is over."

CHAPTER 5

"WHO'S GOING with you?" Felicia asked, tucking a shirt in the backpack. She always made sure Jordan had at least one change of clothes whenever she was away from the village.

Although Eli had instructed them not to tell anyone, Jordan wasn't going to keep her partner in the dark. Felicia was the most important person in her life. What first started out as a crush on a worldly college student grew to a deep love. It had taken perseverance by Jordan and a lot of years before Felicia was able accept that the young teenager she had befriended was a grown woman with all the emotions that came with maturity. When she finally did, their relationship grew strong, as did their passion. Ten years later, nothing had changed.

"Teisha said she would go. She'll make a great second. Carlos, Marco, Kanji and Thomas have also volunteered. I'm waiting to hear from a couple others."

"All good people," Felicia said, feeling better knowing Jordan had made good choices.

"And..." Jordan hesitated.

"And?" Felicia hated Jordan's 'ands.' 'Ands' usually meant her partner was going to do something Felicia wasn't going to like.

"Well, I was thinking of taking Belle."

"Belle! She's too young. A child, Jordie."

"There's no such thing anymore, at least once you're old enough to pick up a weapon or tool. I know you hoped she'd take an interest in agriculture, but she wants to be a hunter. She's applied to the guild for training. She's thirteen. It's her right."

"But why take her now? She knows nothing about being a hunter and this is probably going to be a long mission."

"It's as good a time to learn as any. Look, I can teach her the right way. Show her how to defend herself and live off the land. How to hide during the day or move without being seen. She'll learn more in a few weeks with me than anyone else and be a lot safer. I'm good at what I do, probably the best in Destiny."

"I can't argue that," Felicia said. "It's just that —"

"I know, but would you prefer Belle learn from me or someone else? And hands-on experience is always better than a classroom. She'll learn what hunting is really about."

"That's a hell of a way to learn, sink or swim. What happens if she decides she doesn't want to be a hunter while you're out there? It's not like you can bring or send her back."

"She'll learn a hard lesson. We don't always get what we want, but we do have to live with our choices. At least she'll have the survival skills to get by."

"I don't know..." Felicia still didn't like the idea.

Walking up to her partner, Jordan wrapped her arms around Felicia's waist and pulled her close. Felicia returned the embrace. They stood leaning against each other for several minutes, neither knowing what else to say. Eventually, Felicia pulled away and leaned down, pressing her lips firmly against Jordan's.

"You're right, of course. Someone has to teach her. Better you than anyone else."

"Thanks, Fels," Jordan said.

174

"Fels! You haven't called me that in a long time... and then only when you're worried. Something you're not telling me?"

Jordan chuckled.

"No... Well, yes. I'm probably going to be away for quite a while and..." Jordan's eyes teared up. "And there's always a chance something might happen. If it does, you need to move on."

Jordan never saw the slap coming. Surprised, she stepped back, her hand pressed to her burning cheek.

"What the —"

"Don't you **ever** think like that, Jordie. How dare you try to put such a thought in my head."

"I didn't mean —"

"I don't care what you meant. You're coming back! And if —" Felicia's voice choked. "If you don't, then... then you'd better not come back because I'll ring your neck."

"Ummm, okay, I think I know what you mean." Jordan started to laugh. "Although that made no sense whatsoever."

Felicia thought about what she had just said and grinned sheepishly.

"I'm sorry." Pulling Jordan's hand away from her inflamed cheek, Felicia pressed her lips against the red mark.

"You should be! Now what are you going to do to make up for it?"

"Well, I did say I was sorry, but if you think you need something more..." Felicia wiggled her eyebrows up and down.

"That'll work."

Their lovemaking started slow, each wanting to prolong the other's pleasure and build memories to sustain them through the next few weeks. Neither had any doubt about how long Jordan might be gone, nor did they fool themselves into believing nothing could happen to her. As their passions built, thoughts of what could be vanished. Now was all they had, and that was enough. It had to be.

* * *

Jordan sent word to each team member to meet her at the east gate immediately after the Council made the announcement. Six hunters agreed to go, counting Belle. Jordan made her promise not to tell anyone, stressing the importance of keeping her word. If she betrayed Jordan or the Council, she would never be trusted again. A hunter that couldn't be trusted wasn't allowed on any team.

As Eli predicted, many of the villagers were appalled at his proposal, at least in the beginning. When he informed them they only had a few months of food in storage, some began to waver, pissing off those more adamant about the sanctity of the human body.

"Stop!" Eli yelled when physical fights broke out. Motioning for security to intervene, he waited until calm was restored. "Now isn't the time for fighting. No one is going to make anyone do anything. When the time comes, each of you will make your own decision, but..." Some people grumbled. "But under no circumstances will you be allowed to interfere with another's choice. In the end we live with our own conscience. Go home and talk with yours." Taking a deep breath, Eli made eye contact with each of the team leaders. "Go!" he said "And good luck!"

Thinking he was talking to them, the villagers dispersed, some heading toward their homes, others forming small groups. Pushing past one, Jordan felt her arm grabbed. She was yanked sideways amongst a crowd of about a dozen people. Jordan shrugged the hand off angrily.

"What the hell are you doing, Larry?" she demanded, glaring at her assailant.

"We want to talk to you," the man replied. "It's not right you taking off and leaving us like this. If our supplies are that low you should be out getting us more meat, not wasting your time on some pipedream."

Jordan looked at the angry faces surrounding her.

"Are you that stupid? Have you seen any of the hunters coming back with game lately? Know why? Because there isn't any. We've killed everything but those Phageian out there. Either we find a new supply or another place to live. You don't like the Council's proposal? Fine!" Jordan turned to leave.

"We ain't done with you yet," Larry said, grabbing her arm again. Seconds later he found a knife point pressed against his belly.

"You touch me one more time and I'll gut you like a wild pig and throw your body over the wall."

Stepping back, Larry raised his hands in the air, his eyes fixated on the blade.

"No reason for you to be pulling that on me. We're just saying..."

"Nothing! You're saying nothing that I want to hear. I suggest all of you do what Eli said. Go home and think about all of this. If you want to talk about this tomorrow, look me up." Sheathing her knife, Jordan walked away. Her team was probably already waiting for her.

* * *

The first person Jordan saw near the team's meeting point was Felicia standing in the shadows talking to Belle. The teenager's head was bobbing slowly up and down. Then Belle wrapped her arms around the tall woman's waist. Felicia returned the embrace, her head dipping to rest on the top of Belle's. It was a touching scene, one Jordan would never forget.

"You trying to seduce my woman?" Jordan asked, ruffling Belle's hair.

"Maybe," Belle replied cheekily. "I happen like older women."

"You're too young to like anyone," Felicia said. "Besides, didn't I see you snuggling up to Connor Melvin yesterday afternoon?"

Belle blushed.

"Uh huh," Felicia teased. "Go on over and gear up. Don't forget everything Jordie showed you. I need to talk to her." After Belle left, she turned to the hunter. "Be safe out there. Don't do anything stupid or heroic."

Jordan pulled Felicia into a warm embrace, holding her tight and inhaling deeply.

"I won't. I know telling you not to worry won't do much good, but... well, try not to. I have no intention of getting myself killed, if for no other reason than to keep from pissing you off."

Felicia chuckled.

"I love you, Jordie."

"You too, Fels." Jordan tipped her head up, meeting the warm lips of her lover. It would be a long time before she tasted them again.

When they finally separated, Felicia grabbed Jordan's hand, dragging her into the shadows.

"Come on. I put your stuff over here."

Next to the wall was a small backpack. A water bottle was tucked into a snug fitting pocket. Two bandoliers, a small handheld hand bow, a quiver filled with bolts and a .22 rifle lay next to it. On top of the pack was a utility belt holding several woven pouches and three pistol clip cases. A machete was attached to the left side and a .22 semiautomatic revolver with a silencer holstered on the right. Every item was standard hunter issue.

The most important piece of equipment was the night goggles. Crudely made from welder's glasses, 35 mm film, LED lights, watch batteries and a few strands of wire, each hunter was instructed on how to build and repair his or her own set. Fortunately, the inhabitants of Destiny had stored vast supplies of the necessary items needed to make the goggles. As a survivalist, Eli knew the value of night travel long before Phageian ever appeared. When his raiding parties found abandoned stores that carried small hearing aid or watch batteries and Christmas LED lights, he ordered them to be taken. Everyone grumbled, at least until Eli showed them what a little ingenuity could accomplish.

Cutting the film, he glued it to the lenses of the welder's goggles. Then he cut a string of Christmas lights into strips, each contain an LED light at one end and a bare wire at the other. Wrapping the wire snuggly around the goggles' head strap, he placed the LED so it would shine forward. The wire was connected to a plastic switch made from whatever source he could make or find. Normally it was the guts from small stuffed talking animals or mini-vibrators. The latter was the better choice, although harder to find. The battery case was better constructed. Once everything was attached, a simple flip of the switch would light the film turning everything in front of it shades of gray and white. The hunters could see what Phageian couldn't.

As Jordan strapped on her utility belt and shifted it into place, Felicia picked up the backpack and held the straps apart for Jordan to slip her arms through.

"I've given everyone thirty days of purification powder. If you can boil water you can stretch it out even longer. Also, I prepared some nutrition bars. Two a day will provide you with enough protein and vitamins to get by. They don't taste good but they'll keep you going if you can't find anything to supplement them."

"Thanks."

Handing Jordan her rifle and hand bow, Felicia stepped behind her and positioned the quiver of bolts above the backpack within easy reach. Jordan swung the rifle strap over her left shoulder and held the bow in her right hand. Once everything felt balanced, she straightened, looking every bit the competent, efficient hunter she was.

"I guess this is it," Jordan said.

"I guess so. Be safe."

"I always am." Positioning her goggles over her eyes, she moved toward the group that was patiently waiting to get started. Everyone was in full gear.

CHAPTER 6

"OPEN IT ENOUGH for us to squeeze through and then close it quickly," Jordan instructed. The two guards nodded but said nothing. Eli had posted the most trusted guards to stand duty, informing them that four hunting teams would be leaving through each of the four gates. "Teisha, you first. The others will follow once you signal the coast is clear. Belle, I want you with me. We're the last out. Ready?" Everyone nodded. "Let's go," she instructed.

Teisha peeked through the opening into the darkness beyond the walls. The moonless night couldn't hide the stationary figures scattered around the barren rocky perimeter. Beyond was the shapeless black forest. Easing past the door, the hunter slid along the wall, her eyes searching for signs of unusual movement. Phageian often swayed back and forth but rarely walked after sundown. Some believed they couldn't see without light. The hunters knew better.

Signaling the coast was clear, Jordan never stopped scanning the area for movement. Carlos slipped out second, followed by Kanji, then Marco and Thomas. Jordan grabbed Belle by the shoulder.

"Are you sure about this?" she asked. "There's no shame in backing out. You know other hunters refused this mission."

"I... I want to do this," Belle said, unable to hide her nervousness and fear.

181

"All right, let's do it. Stay close to me but keep your eyes on Teisha. She'll signal what to do. I'll be a few feet behind so don't worry once you've passed a Phageian. And Belle... move silently. No noise! Understand?" Belle nodded. "Good girl."

Jordan followed Belle through the opening. Once outside the wall, the door closed. The hunters heard the reinforcement bars slide into place. They were now on their own.

* * *

The tree line was only a few hundred feet away but seemed miles as the small hunting party crept toward the perimeter. Occasionally, when a Phageian moved restlessly, Teisha or one of the hunters signaled for the others to stop. Sometimes they stood still for a few seconds, sometimes for minutes. It always seemed like forever.

Once Teisha made it to the edge of the forest, she knelt and peered into the shadowy darkness searching for signs of Phageian. The woods were safer but more problematic than open territory. Phageian were less likely to move amongst the trees even when disturbed, but they were harder to see. Fallen trees or rotting debris could trip both hunter and hunted. It only took one careless act to jeopardize one's self or another team member. As the forward scout, Teisha was responsible for insuring the safety of everyone behind her.

"Seeing anything?" Jordan whispered, moving stealthily to her side.

Teisha nodded and pointed to an object on their right.

"There's one over there and three more just beyond him. We should be able to destroy them before —"

182

"Not this time," Jordan interrupted. "We can't chance an injury. Besides, what difference are a few more going to make to the village right now?"

"True."

The group crept away, disappearing into the night.

CHAPTER 7

The Team

Teisha

AT FIVE-FOOT-EIGHT and muscular, Teisha was a force to reckon with. She was only twenty-one, but already one of the most proficient hunters in Destiny. Teisha was two years old when she was brought to Destiny. Her parents had heard about the community from a man and his teenaged son they had rescued. An angry, scared crowd didn't want strangers entering their staked-out territory, but Teisha's father convinced his neighbors to let the two stay one night. Sadly soon afterward, prejudices and racism reared their ugly heads.

Tyler and Estelle Jenson had lived in their community for almost ten years. When Estelle became pregnant they were ecstatic, and so were the people on their street. The Jensons were a kind couple, always willing to help those around them. When Teisha was born, the block threw a party celebrating the newest arrival. Two years later, the Jensons' lives were threatened by those same people.

Skin color had become as good a reason as any to not share diminishing resources, although nothing was actually said. Helping intruders was the excuse needed to accuse the Jensons of betraying the neighborhood's trust. Fearing for their lives, they gathered what few possessions they could carry and escaped with Sammy and Jerry Wilson in their quest to find Destiny. Six months later, four of the five arrived, tired and haggard. Sammy had died of a heart attack. Tyler and Estelle insisted Jerry stay with them. Jerry became the son they always wanted and the big brother Teisha looked up to. That he was white was never something she or her parents ever thought about; that she learned most of her hunting skills from him was evidence of his love for her and his adoptive family.

Carlos

Carlos O'Shannon was a conflicted individual caught between two worlds. His mom was Mexican, his father Irish. Short and stocky, Carlos had the physique of his grandfather on his mother's side but the flaming red hair of his Irish lineage. Unfortunately, he had also inherited the temperament of both parents — quick with words and quicker with their fists. He was ten when his family left their home to join Eli in building Destiny. Sean O'Shannon was a carpenter with forty years of experience building homes. Carlos' mother, Marguerite, had been a housewife. She loved staying at home, baking, cooking and sewing. She could turn the simplest things into works of art, whether it was food or clothing.

At forty-one, the hunter was as fit as any member of his team. Normally at his age he would have been a team leader, but no one wanted to work under his leadership. His hot temper flared with little provocation or notice, although it had mellowed some with age. Because he was an excellent hunter, Jordan overlooked the occasional flare-up as long as he didn't overreact. She had picked him because he, more than some of the other hunters, had a better reason for wanting their mission to be successful. His mother and father were in their early seventies. If Carlos' team found a new home, the odds of his parents living more than a few months were increased. Everyone knew the elderly would be the first sacrificed in a food shortage.

Kanji

No one knew much about Kanji. She was a loner that mostly kept to herself, except when on a hunt. One of the newest hunters on Jordan's team, she was quiet and reserved. Rarely did she comment or offer an opinion. Orders were orders. Like Jordan, she was short but less androgynous. There was no hiding the full breasts. From behind she looked like an adolescent boy, from the front a mature young woman.

Kanji was one of the last to arrive at Destiny, almost six years ago. After being released from quarantine, she applied for a hunter job and proved to be quite knowledgeable in tactical and survival skills. No one could sharpen a blade as well as Kanji, nor throw it with such accuracy. She often spent hours honing the edge until the metal gleamed. Only Jordan was better with the hand bow.

Thomas

Thomas was a mellow hunter who had recently married a villager he had been living with for more than three years. They had tried to keep their relationship a secret but it was impossible in such a small community. Although a few people grumbled about their homosexuality, no one dared to make an issue of it. He was too well-liked and under the circumstances, no one had the patience for blatant bigotry. His hunting skills were well above average but not exceptional. What he brought to the team was stability and common sense. Thomas was difficult to anger and quick to get over it if it happened. He considered every possibility before voicing an opinion or idea. At twenty-eight, Thomas was in his prime as a hunter. Slightly taller than Jordan, he was broad-shouldered with slim hips and long legs. His climbing skills far exceeded any of the hunters in Destiny, probably because he and Sebastian made a game of tree-climbing. The first one to the highest branch that could hold his weight won the 'prize.' They never told anyone what the 'prize' was and no one really wanted to know.

Marco
Marco was Marco. Easy going, difficult at times, living with two women who seemed quite content to share him. The father of four children, two with each woman, he spent most of his time in Destiny helping them with their studies and encouraging them to learn as much as possible about everything. Everything but hunting. Marco didn't want his children to be like him. Hunting was the most dangerous of the occupations. The survival odds were getting worse each year. Last year, Destiny had lost three hunters, too many for such a small community. Marco wasn't willing to sacrifice his children, even for the sake of Destiny.

Belle
Belle was the one of the few children born in Destiny. Her seven-month-pregnant mother, Gloria, had been found in a cave several days' trek from the sanctuary by a team of hunters. She was one of the few newcomers not quarantined. Pregnant women never survived the contagion to become Phageian.
Weakened from the hardships she had endured in her search to find a safe place for her and her unborn child, Gloria never fully recovered her health by the time Belle was born. Within hours she was dead, the strain on her heart too great. Belle was offered up for adoption, but only an elderly woman was willing to take on such a great

responsibility. Sadly, she too died when Belle was five. Eli then took over the care, but he knew little about fatherhood and most of his time was spent running the community.

Left to her own devises, Belle spent most of her time hanging around the hunters, listening to their stories and watching them practice their skills. She knew that was what she was going to be when she was old enough to join a team, preferably Jordan's.

CHAPTER 8

PROGRESS WAS SLOW, each foot precisely positioned to minimize noise. Where one hunter stepped, another followed. When Teisha stopped, everyone stopped and automatically knelt. Phageian were attracted to human settlements, probably drawn by the scent. No one knew for sure. It was impossible to know if they actually saw or smelled anything or if it was some sixth sense that drew them to people. They displayed no awareness or interest in other living creatures; a good thing. Their ravenous appetites would have eliminated animal populations in only a few years once they reached the pandemic stage.

The first night the hunters traveled about three miles because of the high number of Phageian scattered throughout the forests. With their night goggles they could see the things standing motionless everywhere. The hunters would have liked nothing more than to destroy every Phageian whose path they crossed, but risking themselves and their mission wasn't worth the few they would eliminate. Their mission was their primary concern.

Two hours before sunrise, Jordan motioned the group toward a tall stand of oaks. Broad limbed, they provided plenty of room for each hunter to pick one of the enormous branches to rest on. Their safety harnesses would keep them in place. Jordan felt she had spent half her life sleeping in trees.

Thomas pulled out his climbing spikes and strapped them on. He was the best climber. Sinking the tips of his fingers into crevices between the thick bark, he worked his way toward to the top of the tree. Once he located a suitable spot, he dropped the rope end to the others. Within minutes they were settled comfortably on fat limbs, their backs resting against the trunk.

"Make sure you take your goggles off, Belle," Jordan warned. "Sunlight will damage your eyes if you are wearing them in the light." Pulling her own off, she squinted as her eyes adjusted to normal darkness. "Everybody check your gear and then get something to eat and rest. It's going to be a long day. If someone hears something, wake me up. We may be in the canopy but they can still find us. Thankfully, they haven't figured out how to climb."

"Yet! I'll take first watch," Kanji offered. "I need to sharpen my knife anyway."

"Thanks, Kanji. Do it quietly. They may hear the rasping. Carlos, you're second. Thomas, you're next. Then Teisha, Marco, and Belle. I'll finish," Jordan said. "One hour watches only. That'll give everyone a chance to get a reasonable rest."

Shifting her backpack to a pillow position, Jordan settled down and closed her eyes. Within seconds she was asleep. The others, except Kanji, quickly followed.

* * *

The following night they made better time, traveling several more miles. There were fewer Phageian but still plenty to merit caution. A second day in the trees passed uneventfully, although a half-dozen Phageian wondered aimlessly below them.

"Are they looking for us?" Belle whispered nervously.

Jordan watched the creatures' movements closely and nodded.

"Probably, but they never look up. They'll move on in a little while. Get some sleep." Closing her eyes, Jordan dozed. Feeling trapped, Belle stayed awake another hour. Eventually the creatures wandering below left.

* * *

Well-rested, the hunters continued their trek west, entering territory they hadn't hunted in years. Two nights out from Destiny and back was the most anyone was able to travel nowadays. On the fifth night they noticed a significant decrease in Phageian... and something else. **Things** rustled in the undergrowth. Eyes glowed in the darkness, following the team's progress, then blinked out.

"What are they?" Marco asked.

"I'm not sure," Jordan replied, "But at least they're alive."

"And there are a lot of them," Belle added. "We could feed the whole village with what we've seen so far."

"For a night or two," Teisha agreed. "Then what?" Shaking her head, she patted the girl's shoulder. "We're still too close, but this gives me hope. Let's keep going a little longer before we call it a night."

* * *

Seven nights into their journey, the hunters started to relax a little. They hadn't seen Phageian in two days. They had, however, caught glimpses of animals bounding or scurrying away at their approach; some they had only read about. Perhaps complacency was why they failed to notice one Phageian standing next to a tree as it reached out and

191

grabbed Kanji by the hair. Whatever the reason, it was a fatal mistake.

Before the hunters could react, Kanji was dragged to the ground, the back of her neck ravaged by broken yellow teeth. Belle, who had been several feet behind her, screamed, unable to move. Jordan rushed past Belle, pushing her aside. Thomas spun, machete in hand. Raising it above his shoulder, he sliced downward, cutting off the Phageian's head and unknowingly severing Kanji's spine. The thing's head rolled onto the ground. Kicking it aside, Thomas knelt next to the body lying across Kanji's. He shoved it away hoping desperately that his comrade had survived the attack. Squatting next to him, Jordan stared at the sight and then spun around, vomiting. Thomas joined her. The others gathered around the bodies. Nothing in their experience had hardened them against what they now saw. Belle collapsed to the ground sobbing.

"Shit!" Marco exclaimed.

"I... I..." Tears flowed down Thomas' cheek.

"You did the right thing, Thomas," Teisha said, wrapping her arms around his head and pressing it against her chest. "She was dead already. You did the right thing."

"What the hell happened?" Carlos yelled, looking from Jordan to Thomas. Then he turned to Belle, yanking her upward. "Where were you? You were supposed to have her back!"

"I... I did... didn't see it," she cried out.

"Didn't see it? How could you —"

"Leave her alone, Carlos," Jordan said. "It was beside the tree. Even I didn't see it until it was too late. Kanji shouldn't have been so close to the trunk. It's one of the first lessons we learn."

"So you're blaming this on her?"

"I'm not blaming anyone, but if you're looking to, put it where it belongs. Now let's get out of here."

"We have to bury her. If any of those things are around —"

"— they'll find the body no matter what," Jordan finished. "Look, Carlos, Kanji was a good hunter and a great person. She'd understand and she'll be remembered for who she was, not for how she died. Besides, we don't have the tools or the time to dig a grave. Now move out!"

If looks could kill, Jordan thought when Carlos stomped off. Shaking her head, she walked over to Belle and pulled her to her feet.

"Come on."

"I didn't see —"

"And that'll get you or someone else killed," Jordan said. "Learn from your mistake and hers."

Teisha helped Thomas to his feet.

"Thomas," she said in a soft voice, coaxing him away from the body. "We have to leave. There's nothing we can do for her now." Pulling him by the arm she led him away.

* * *

The team traveled another two nights without incident. Thomas spoke very little. Carlos, who continued to sulk, mostly ignored Belle. Occasionally, though, he'd make a caustic remark about her cowardice or ignorance. Eventually the others grew tired of his grumblings and digs. Teisha was the first to lose her temper.

"If you can't say anything productive, shut up, Carlos. You sound like a petulant child."

"I'm only saying what everyone else is thinking and you know it. She should never have been allowed on this mission. This isn't the time or place for an inexperienced child."

"Whatever she was when she started, she's part of the team now and will be treated as such."

"Who the hell appointed you the boss?" Carlos demanded.

Angered beyond words, Teisha pulled her knife and threw it at Carlos' feet, barely missing them by inches. Startled, the hunter jumped back. His right heel snagged on a tree root. Losing his balance he fell backward, his arms flailing wildly. Teisha lunged forward, grabbing her knife.

"Teisha!" Jordan shouted. "Teisha, please," she said, lowering her voice to a gentler tone. "You've made your point."

"Don't worry," Teisha replied, sheathing the blade. "Just wanted to make my point." The hunter held her hand out toward Carlos, signaling with her fingers for him to take it. After a few moments he grabbed it and stood.

"You know I should whip your ass for that," he said.

"In your dreams."

"Stop it! Carlos, Teisha is second-in-command. If she gives you an order you obey it, just as you obey me. Teisha, leaders don't make their point with knives. Do you two understand me?"

"Sorry, Jordan. I'm just tired of listening to him. He needs to grow up."

"I don't need you to —"

"Carlos, shut up! She's not the only one."

Mumbling under his breath, Carlos brushed past Jordan, his shoulder bumping hers lightly. His left foot caught in the same root that had tripped him up before. In an attempt to stop from falling he grabbed at Jordan, pulling her with him. Losing her balance she tumbled over, her knee slamming into Carlos' leg, twisting it at an awkward angle.

"Fuck!" Carlos screamed. "Fuck! Fuck! Fuck!"

The next twenty minutes was spent splinting and binding a badly sprained ankle. Afterward, Jordan decided to call it a night, even though it was going to be very long.

CHAPTER 9

SUNRISE WAS ONLY about thirty minutes away but its reddish-yellow rays were already lighting the dark night sky. Jordan was worried. Carlos' injury was slowing them down. They had managed to travel a few miles. Now they needed a safe place to spend the day. Topping a hill, she saw a cluster of trees along a small creek that had potential. The problem was the team would have to cross an open meadow that was partially hidden by a stand of scrub oaks. Not having a clear view of the meadow was problematic. If any Phageian were there, they would have no choice but to fight.

"What do you want to do?" Teisha asked.

"I wish we had a better view of that clearing," Jordan said. "But we don't have a choice. We need to get to those trees." Turning to Carlos, she glanced down at the makeshift splints on each side of his ankle. "Can you keep up?"

"Do I have a choice?" Jordan shook her head slowly. "Do what you have to do to protect the team, Jordan. We all know what we signed up for."

"Thomas and I'll look after Carlos," Marco said. "You just clear the way."

* * *

The hunters moved slowly through the underbrush, carefully pushing the branches aside. Progress was slow and painful. Their clothing provided little protection against the tiny thorns of the thistle bushes.

"I think we're almost to the clearing," Jordan said, motioning for the group to sit and rest. It was too late to worry about reaching the taller trees before the sun cleared the horizon. "Carlos, you need to stay here. The rest of us will see what's up ahead." When Carlos started to object, Jordan held up her hand. "If there are Phageian ahead, we can't worry about you and fight at the same time. You rest that ankle. We'll be back once we check everything out." Turning to Belle, she told her to give the injured hunter her handgun. "Just in case trouble runs into you before we get back."

Carlos nodded and took the weapon, checking the chamber and clip to make sure it was fully loaded.

"You come running if you hear gunfire," he said.

"Count on it," Jordan said.

Signaling for the group to move out, she eased the brush apart, holding it for the next person to control.

* * *

The hunters inched forward, crawling slowly on their bellies. The clearing could be seen below the spreading branches of the bushes. As they neared the edge of the meadow, they heard what sounded like grunts. Putting her finger to her lips, Jordan motioned the others to spread out. Teisha moved next to her.

"Pigs?" she whispered.

"Maybe." Inching forward, she pushed a limb aside. "Shit!"

Several Phageian were wandering aimlessly around the meadow. A few were grouped together doing nothing, a behavior less typical of Phageian. Normally they were

197

constantly on the move, except at night. Even then they rarely stood close to each other except to feed.

"How many do you count?" Jordan asked.

"Thirteen," Teisha replied. "We should be able to handle them easily."

"Use your hand bows," Jordan instructed. "It's quieter than the rifles." The explanation was more for Belle's benefit than anything else. The rest of the team knew the reason. "If there are others in those woods we don't want to attract them." The hunters each pulled three bolts from their quivers. "Don't fire until I tell you to."

* * *

Belle levered the string back and locked it into place. She had practiced for hours every day while the hunters rested or cleaned their own equipment. Jordan and the others were constantly stressing to her the importance of caring for and knowing their weapons. Any malfunction could have fatal consequences. Nervously, she slipped the bolt into place. Her hands felt sweaty. Although she knew Phageian weren't alive, shooting one felt... wrong. Even after watching Kanji being ravaged, Belle found it difficult to accept the things moving in front of her were completely dead.

"I... I'm not sure I can ki... kill one," she said, her voice louder than she had intended. Startled, the hunters looked at Belle and then toward the Phageian, hoping they hadn't heard the girl. They had. Every Phageian stopped moving, their vacant stares directed in the hunters' direction.

"Damn it!" Thomas said, firing his bolt at the closest target, hitting it in the leg. The others picked targets and discharged their arrows. Two missed, two hit the same Phageian, knocking it off its feet. Grabbing the next round, they snapped the cocking lever onto the bows and positioned the new bolts. Unfortunately, they had to take their eyes off their target to arm the weapon. If they were lucky they'd get one more round off. Then they'd have to revert to knives and machetes.

Jordan and Marco were the first to reload. Raising their bows, they expected the creatures to be only feet away. They weren't! The two that had been shot lay on the ground. The rest were moving rapidly away, almost running, although their gait was somewhat stilted.

"What the hell!" Marco exclaimed, causing everyone to glance at him and then to where he was looking. "They're leaving!"

"I don't believe it!" Teisha pushed to her feet and straightened. "Those things never give up."

Everyone except Belle stood and stared disbelievingly at the raggedy figures disappearing into the woods. Belle rose to her knees, her eyes locked on the weapon in her left hand.

"What in the world were you thinking?" Thomas demanded angrily, snatching the weapon from her. "You almost got us killed again. If you can't do your job —" Pulling the bolt from the bow, he threw it on the ground.

"I... I'm sorry."

"Sorry doesn't bring someone back to life. Tell that to Kanji."

"Enough, Thomas," Jordan said. "No one's responsible for her death. Belle made a mistake. Kanji made a mistake. Hell, we've all done that. What's important is no one is hurt this time."

"Wrong, Jordan. What's important is that we trust each other to cover our backs. Otherwise, someone else is going to get seriously hurt or killed. If Belle can't pull her weight then it's going to put more responsibilities on the rest of us. We can't afford mistakes."

"No, we can't. And we can't change what's happened so drop it. You and Marco get Carlos. Teisha and I will make sure those two things are destroyed and retrieve whatever bolts we find."

"You're the boss. Come on," Marco said, slapping Thomas on the shoulder.

Jordan stooped down next to Belle.

"Thanks," Belle whispered.

"Don't thank me. Thomas has every right to be angry. We all have a right. That was a stupid mistake."

"I know."

"Don't do it again. There can't be a third time." Belle nodded. "All right. Gather up whatever bolts you can find. Teisha and I'll check out those two."

The hunters walked cautiously toward the Phageian lying on the ground. One had an arrow in its right leg, the other, the gut and shoulder.

"Those hits aren't enough to take those things down," Teisha said, walking around the bodies, unwilling to get closer until she had examined them from every angle.

Kneeling down on one knee at a safe distance, Jordan tilted her head trying to get a better view of the faces, not that it would do much good. Phageian were the most expressionless creatures she had ever seen.

"I don't get it," she said, picking up a small rock. Throwing it at the body, she watched for a reaction. When nothing happened she stood and brushed her hand on her pant leg.

"What do you want to do?"

"We need those bolts. Let's make sure they're —"

"I only found five," Belle said holding up her hand, running up to stand by Jordan.

"That's five more than we had two minutes ago," Teisha said. "Good job."

"Good job," Jordan agreed and glanced back at the bodies. *No better time than now,* she thought. "Load your bow, Belle." Teisha gave Jordan a curious look. "She needs to prove something to herself and to us."

Belle looked apprehensively at the bodies and then at Jordan. Unsnapping her hand bow, she cocked it and placed a bolt on the shaft.

"Shoot it." Jordan pointed at the body with the arrow in the leg.

Swallowing, Belle aimed at the torso.

"Not there," Jordan said. "The head."

Moving to get a better angle, Belle aimed at the head, her hand shaking. Just as she was about to squeeze the trigger, two eyes opened and stared at her. Screaming, Belle flinched. The bolt whizzed into the ground a foot past its target.

"It's a... alive, Jordan," she stuttered, backing away and tripping.

Pale eyes followed her movement and then shifted to look at Teisha who had walked over to help Belle to her feet. Jordan watched the eyes. Motioning for Teisha to come forward, she saw the thing's gaze switching back and forth between Belle and the hunter. Still, the head and body never moved.

"It **is** watching you," Jordan confirmed. "See what that one does."

Teisha walked toward the other Phageian. Pacing back and forth a few feet away, she tested its reaction.

"It's doing the same thing. They act like they're playing possum," she said.

"I hope to God they aren't. That would imply some type of intelligence."

"That's a creepy thought. Maybe they're just paralyzed. If their necks are broken, they wouldn't be able to move."

"Well, we're not getting close enough to find out." Turning to Belle, Jordan pointed at the hand bow. "Shoot that one! In the head! I'll take care of the other one."

"I —"

"Do it! You wanted to be a hunter! Be one!"

Belle reluctantly raised her bow. Closing her eyes, she pulled the trigger, then opened one to peek at the body. The bolt had entered the thing's mouth angling upward. She shuddered. The eyes stared vacantly at the sky.

Jordan shot the second Phageian and then walked up to retrieve her bolts from the head and body. Teisha removed the ones from Belle's target. Without saying anything, the three hunters walked away to wait for their companions to return. No one wanted to think about the possibilities of what they had seen.

Once everyone was reunited, the group made their way to the other side of the clearing. The sun was already up and they still needed to find a safe place.

An hour later, they were nestled high in the tree tops. Within minutes, the hunters were asleep.

* * *

The clearing was eerily quiet except for the natural sounds of insects and small birds. Shortly after the hunters disappeared into the woods, Phageian emerged from the shadows, some within feet of where the humans had walked. They moved cautiously across the meadow, stopping next to the two bodies on the ground. Some grunted unintelligible noises to each other not unlike the sounds pigs made when they were foraging. Forming a circle they bent over, grabbing the arms. Yanking and pulling, they lifted the wounded Phageian to their feet. Their hands groped the exposed tissue damaged by the arrows, paying particular attention to the heads.

202

Seemingly satisfied, the group dispersed. Most wandered aimlessly around the meadow as if trapped in a routine they couldn't break. The two wounded moved slowly off into the woods.

CHAPTER 1 0

THE HUNTERS HAD traveled for almost three weeks, searching for possible sites their people could relocate to. Belle had toughened up, learning the needed skills of survival. More importantly, she no longer slowed the party down. Muscles replaced excess body fat, giving her arms and legs contour. She still looked like a gangly thirteen-year-old but the journey had taught her harsh lessons. Her eyes constantly darted everywhere, checking for anything that didn't appear natural. Occasionally she mistook movement for Phageian only to find sunlit shadows or the wind playing tricks. Rattling bushes were particularly troublesome. Jordan assured her that everyone made the same mistakes at times. It was always better to be overly cautious than jeopardize the group's safety by ignoring something.

"The day you assume what you see is unimportant," Jordan explained, "might be the day you or one of us die... or worse, is wounded and becomes them. I'd kill myself and anyone else on this team if they were ever bitten by a Phageian."

Belle's eyes opened wider as she stared at Jordan.

"You'd kill me," she asked and swallowed nervously.

Jordan nodded.

"And I'd expect you to kill me, and anyone else, unless of course the bite's on an extremity. Cutting off the hand or foot might save a person." Jordan gave Belle a speculative look. "Could you do that?"

204

Belle swallowed nervously.

"I... I..."

"That's okay, Belle. It's not a decision you have to make now, but you do need to think about it. The sooner you make up your mind about what you can and can't do, the better prepared you'll be and the more confidence we'll have in you." Turning to the other hunters, Jordan motioned for them to move out. They had taken a short rest. Night was only a few hours away.

* * *

Teisha was the first to hear the noises. Signaling everyone to stop, she gestured for Jordan to join her.

"I heard something," she said, pointing toward the east.

"Like what?"

"I don't know. Noises. Listen!"

Standing still, the two hunters held their breath, straining to hear anything beyond the normal forest sounds. For a while they heard nothing, then a series of grunts and... an oink.

"That sounded like a pig!" Teisha exclaimed.

"Must be a wild boar. If so, then there could be more. Pigs are the one animal that could probably obliterate Phageian without much trouble. They're mean, temperamental and vicious." Jordan turned to the other hunters, motioning for them to spread out. Belle she signaled to follow her and Teisha. Silently they crept forward, crouching low until they came upon a ridge. Sliding onto their stomachs, they crawled up the incline and peered over the edge.

"It's a village!" Teisha said. "Without walls!"

"Shhhh," Jordan said, placing her right index finger against her lips. "Look over there! People!"

Humans could be seen moving about. Some were tending to gardens. Others carried baskets in and out of several huts. All around the area pigs, goats and chickens wandered about doing what farm animals normally did — look for food. The villagers paid little attention to them. One animal, though, they seemed to go out of their way to avoid: cats. Whenever one was nearby, the people either walked around it or backed up a few steps so it could pass. Some actually turned to head in another direction.

"Looks like they don't like cats very much," Jordan said.

"I've never seen a cat before," Belle whispered excitedly. "Except in a book. They're beautiful."

"Smart too. It seems a bit strange not to like an animal but have so many around. There must be at least twenty or thirty out there," Teisha added.

"Speaking of strange, you see anything unusual about those villagers?"

Teisha and Belle watched the different groups for several minutes.

"Well, they're awfully skinny," Belle said.

"A food shortage would explain that," Teisha replied.

"Yeah, except there doesn't appear to be a food shortage with all those animals wandering around." Jordan shook her head, emphasizing her words. "But that's not what I'm talking about. Look how they move. They're... slow."

Teisha shrugged.

"No reason to hurry doing what they're doing. If I had to dig dirt, I'd be slow too."

"I don't mean how fast they move. It's more like how they move."

Before either Teisha or Belle could comment, they noticed four new arrivals approaching the workers from a path to the left of the huts. A small, frail-looking woman wearing a sack-like garment almost to her knees raised her left arm, hailing one of the men. He was taller than the rest. When he walked over to her, he bent over, lowering his head as if listening to instructions. Everyone else stopped what they were doing to watch. Minutes later the man straightened and motioned toward the others. They went back to work.

"What do you think?" Teisha asked, looking to Jordan for guidance.

"They're human enough. Definitely not Phageian. That's the good news, but that doesn't mean they're friendly. Tell the others to stay hidden. You and I will check them out."

"I want to go, too," Belle said.

"Not this time. You stay here," Jordan ordered. "Better yet, check on Carlos. Make sure he's doing okay."

"But —"

"No buts! You're a hunter now. You follow orders. Understand?"

Belle gave her a rebellious look but quickly lowered her gaze.

"Oh, all right, "she said sullenly, her lower lip sticking out.

"Hunters don't pout, Belle."

* * *

Jordan and Teisha crawled to a location away from where the hunters lay hidden and stood up. Moving cautiously, they walked to the edge of the clearing. The villagers seemed uninterested in anything but their jobs. The man and woman appeared to be distracted by two cats that were circling around their legs. They obviously weren't bothered by the animals.

"Hello," Jordan called out. All heads turned toward her and Teisha. "My name is Jordan. My companion is Teisha. Can you tell us where we are?"

When no one moved or responded, Teisha looked at Jordan and shrugged.

"This is creepy enough," she whispered as they slowly walked forward.

"Maybe they haven't had many strangers here," Jordan said. "Are you in charge?" she asked, addressing the tall man. When he didn't answer, she looked at the woman standing next to him. "Are you?"

Neither spoke.

"They aren't very talkative," Teisha said, keeping her voice low. "Maybe they don't speak our language."

"Maybe. They're certainly not trusting," Jordan added, noticing the villagers growing restless. Some shifted nervously from one foot to the other. "If they attack, you get back to the others."

"And leave you here? Not on your life!"

"Do as I say, Teisha! What I told Belle applies to you too. You're second in —"

Before she could finish, several cats loped over to them. A large yellow-and-white female put her head against Jordan's thigh, rubbing its cheek up and down. Another imitated the behavior with Teisha. Unconsciously, the hunter reached down and scratched it behind an ear. A loud purring filled the air.

"At least they're friendly." Teisha straightened back up.

"We're not here to cause trouble," Jordan said, walking over to the couple who had been watching the cats. When they looked up, Jordan stepped backward. *Holy shit!* she thought. Milky blue-white eyes stared emotionlessly at her. They reminded her of an elderly couple in Destiny, but it didn't make it any less creepy.

She remembered the doctor telling her about cataracts when she was young. People could still see but not very well. It didn't help that Phageian eyes were similar.

Jordan was sure these two could see her but wondered if they were partially blind. The man's expressionless eyes moved up and down her body giving no hint as to what he was thinking. He then checked Teisha out the same way. The woman stared only at Jordan.

"Whaa... you... wannn?" the man finally asked, his voice as emotionless as his eyes.

"Does this place have a name?" Jordan asked.

"Name?"

Jordan nodded.

"Name. What do you call your village?" Jordan raised her arm to indicate the cleared area.

The man's gaze followed her arm movement and he frowned.

"Home," he said. "You..." Making a pushing gesture with his hands he then pointed toward the woods.

"Looks like he wants us to go," Teisha said.

"You..." he repeated more forcefully. "Go." The woman continued to stare at Jordan.

Jordan held up both hands. "Okay," she said and instantly realized she had made a mistake. Her gesture closely resembled his, which he and the villagers must have interpreted as an aggressive action. They dropped their tools and advanced toward her and Teisha. Their hands moved forward and then backward as if shoving them away.

"Uh oh, not good." Jordan said. "Let's get out of here."

More villagers appeared, some coming from between the buildings while others exited the huts. What was, at first, a few dozen people had doubled.

"I'm right behind you," Teisha whispered. The growing crowd was eerily silent as they closed in.

Taking several steps backwards, Jordan was about to apologize for intruding when she heard Belle calling to her. Then from within the woods a hunter yelled Belle's name. Spinning, she watched the young girl charging toward them, her machete raised high in the air.

"Belle, stop!" Jordan cried out, wrapping her arm around the girl's waist before she could run past. "What the hell are you doing?" she demanded angrily as the momentum spun both of them around.

"They're attacking," Belle gasped, out of breath and trying to shake off Jordan's grip. "Someone had to help you. No one listened to me so I decided to do it on my own. Hunters protect hunters."

"Hunters obey orders. I told you to stay back." Jordan glanced over her shoulder nervously to see what the villagers were doing. For the moment they were standing motionless, just staring at her and Belle. It was then that she noticed that they all had either white or blue-white eyes. Turning her attention back to Belle, she grabbed the girl's machete and tossed it to Teisha. "I warned you about making another mistake. You're not ready to be a hunter yet," she chastised.

Instantly Belle started to cry.

"I was only..."

"I appreciate you wanting to protect us but your actions put us in more danger."

Tears streamed down Belle's cheeks. Dropping to the ground on her butt, Belle put her face in her hands and sobbed.

"This isn't the place for this, Jordan," Teisha said, glancing at the villagers who still hadn't moved.

Jordan squatted down next to Belle, grabbed her shoulders and shook her.

"Stop that! Crying doesn't help. We need to leave. Now!"

"I'm... sorr... sorry. I... I just want... ed to..." Belle sobbed.

"Jordan," Teisha cut in.

Before Jordan could stand, they found themselves surrounded. Escape was no longer possible.

"Shit!" she muttered. "Don't do anything unless I say to!" she ordered Belle, slowly rising to her feet, unsure of the villagers' next move. Belle's charge onto the scene had complicated everything. The close proximity of so many people made it impossible for she and Teisha to effectively defend themselves. *We're screwed,* Jordan thought as several hands reached out, gripped her arms and pulled her away from Belle. *I hope the rest of the team doesn't do anything stupid now.*

CHAPTER 11

WATCHING JORDAN AND Teisha being dragged away from her, Belle grew frightened. Her momentary burst of courage was replaced by terror, especially when several villagers bent over her for a closer look. Their whitish eyes freaked her out. Panicking, she looked from one face to another, trying not to imagine what they were going to do to her. Her concern for Jordan and Teisha was temporarily replaced by her fear for herself. She screamed, slapping frantically at the nearest.

"Leave... me... alone."

Terrified, she wrapped her arms around her bent legs, pressing her forehead firmly against her knees. Something soft rubbed against her thigh. Afraid it was a villager, Belle shoved it away, expecting to feel hands. Instead her fingers sunk into thick, soft fur. Surprised, she opened her eyes and stared into the unblinking elliptical green eyes of a large yellow-and blue-white cat. Purring loudly it rubbed against Belle's leg, weaving back and forth contentedly. A second cat walked up to her, pressed its cheek against her back, sliding the length of its body against hers.

"Cats!" Belle exclaimed, excitedly. "Look, Jordan, cats! And they like me. Picking one up, she buried her face in its fur, completely forgetting the danger around her.

* * *

Released from their grips, Jordan watched the villagers back away from Belle. For whatever reason, they didn't want to be near the cats. Their reluctance provided her an opportunity to better assess the situation. Once everyone was a few feet away, they stopped and stood still, their eerie gazes transfixed on Belle and the cats.

"We need to leave," Teisha murmured.

"You go. I'll get Belle."

"And how are you going to do that?"

"I don't know but I'm not leaving her here," Jordan said. "I'll think of something."

"Well, maybe you should start with him," Teisha said, motioning with her head to the leader. "If we take him hostage —"

"We aren't taking any hostages, unless they're cats. These people have some type of issue with them. Maybe if we each grab one they'll stay far enough away that we can back out of here without a fight."

"At least it's a plan, even if it does sound ridiculous," Teisha said.

* * *

In a low voice Jordan called out to Belle, trying to attract her attention without disturbing the onlookers.

"Belle! Belle, look at me," Jordan said. The girl raised her head and looked around. Seeing Jordan, she smiled.

"They like me!"

"That's great! Do you think you can stand up and then pick one up?"

"Oh sure!" Belle scrambled to her feet and stooped over to grab the large yellow-and-white female. Her action startled it. Hissing, the cat's ears flattened against its head. It arched its back and struck at the offending hand, claws extended. Then it lunged forward, bit Belle on the fingers and slinked away. Belle screamed in pain. Clutching her hand against chest, she looked betrayed. Instinctively Jordan and Teisha ran forward only, again, to be blocked by villagers holding up their hands. Slipping her knife from her sheath, Teisha gripped the hilt so the blade was pressed against the inside of her forearm, concealing it from view, unaware the sharp edge had sliced the delicate skin.

"Baa-rraak!" a woman ordered, placing her hand on Jordan's chest, forcing the hunter back. "Baa-rraak!"

Belle whimpered. Blood poured from the wounds, running down her palm onto the hard-packed soil, forming a small pool.

"I need to help her," Jordan said, trying to look over the woman's shoulder at Belle. "Please!"

"Baa-rraak!" the woman insisted.

Jordan was at a loss. She could try force but knew it would probably make matters worse. They didn't stand a chance of reaching Belle without killing a lot of people. Frustrated, she searched the crowd for the leader. Her eyes beseeched him to do something, but he simply turned his back. Jordan felt helpless.

CHAPTER 12

"IT'S ALL RIGHT, BELLE," Jordan called out, not knowing what else to do.

The cats circled the girl warily. Except for the villagers guarding her and Teisha, the others seemed fixated on Belle. No one moved. Then, unexpectedly, the tall man raised his right arm. He pointed at two female villagers and motioned toward Belle. *Crap!* Jordan thought. *This isn't good.* To her surprise, one woman gently took Belle's hand and dipped it in the jug she was carrying. The other pulled several weeds from her basket and wrapped them around the wounded fingers.

"Hold," she said, pressing them firmly against the skin.

Belle looked fearfully at Jordan.

Jordan recognized the plant. *Yarrow!* It was easily identifiable in the warmer months by the tiny yellow or purple flowers. Every hunter was taught the benefits of medicinal plants and how to recognize them. Yarrow was one of the best choices.

"Go ahead," she said. "It'll stop the bleeding and ease the pain." The women turned to look at Jordan. Their eyes showed no emotion but they nodded, confirming her words. Once Belle put her hand over the compress they backed away and then looked at Teisha's right arm.

"What now?" Teisha whispered, glancing at her arm. "Fuck!" she exclaimed, seeing the blood dripping off her fingers.

"What did you do?" Spotting the knife, Jordan shook her head. "Put that away."

When Teisha slid it back into the sheath, the same women who had treated Belle walked over to her. The one with the plants leaned forward to look at the cut. Then she selected several leaves from her basket, dipped them into the water and pressed the bundle against the wound.

"Hold."

"Hold, okay," Teisha repeated and did what she was told, suddenly feeling foolish.

"You all right?" Jordan asked.

"It's just a scratch. What now?"

"Stay here. I think they'll let me check Belle now." Moving slowly she walked over and squatted down. "Let me see. Good, the bleeding's stopped. Does it still hurt?"

"A little," Belle mumbled. "I thought cats were friendly. That's what the books said."

"Maybe you scared it. Can you stand up?"

She nodded.

"Good." Helping Belle to her feet, she wrapped her arm around the girl's shoulder and guided her toward Teisha, all the while aware of the emotionless eyes following their movements.

"This place is just plain weird," Teisha said.

"Yeah, but at least they helped her, and you," Jordan said, gesturing at Belle with her head. "That's proof they aren't indifferent. Wait here, I'm going to see if I can talk to that guy. He has to be in charge." Taking a deep breath, she straightened her shoulders and walked toward the apparent leader, who was still surrounded by cats. *Cat man,* she thought. Immediately the villagers closed ranks around him, repeating the shoving gesture with their hands.

"Baa-rrack!" they chanted in unison. "Baa-rrack!"

Jordan stopped.

"I only want to talk," she said, holding her arms out and away from her sides, palms up. The voices stopped. No one moved. *Looks like we have a standoff,* Jordan thought. "Does anyone understand me?" When no one answered, she sighed. *This is a waste of time!* "I don't think they understand me," she called to Teisha and Belle. "Let's go."

"Nooo!" The voice was deep, guttural. "You staay!"

Surprised, Jordan watched the cat man squeeze between several villagers. Moving slowly, he stopped directly in front of her.

"She," he said pointing to Belle, "stay! You... stay. Bite... no good."

"You do understand," Jordan said, surprised. "My name's Jordan. That's Teisha and that's Belle." The man looked at the two women and then back at Jordan. "Do you have a name?" When he didn't answer, she again repeated her name, tapping her chest. "Jordan." She then pointed at him.

"Jor... dan," he said, poking her in the chest. When she nodded, he poked himself. "Der... reek." Then he pointed to the woman next to him. "Zee!"

"Derek... Zee, thank you for helping my companions."

Derek looked over Jordan's shoulder at Belle and Teisha. Zee continued to stare at Jordan.

What's with her? Jordan thought, feeling uneasy.

"Co... pan... en."

"Yes, Belle." Jordan gestured at her.

"Co... pan... en," Derek repeated and pointed to Teisha.

"Yes, she's also a companion. That's Teisha."

"Be... ell, Ti... shaa... co... pan... en."

Jordan nodded.

"Co... pan... en, you... stay."

"We have three more companions there," Jordan said, holding three fingers up.

Derek turned to stare in the direction of the trees.

"Co... pan... en... three?"

God, this is getting tedious, she thought but kept a neutral expression. "Three," she repeated. Before Jordan realized what Derek was up to, he pointed to a group of villagers and motioned for them to check out the woods.

"Get co... pan... en... three."

This isn't going to work. The guys don't know what's happening. "Wait!" Jordan called out. Derek looked back at her. "I need to let them know it's okay. That you're... friends." Without thinking, Jordan started to walk away.

"No... go," Derek said. "They... go. Get... co... pan... en. Bring... here."

"They won't come unless I tell them it's all right. I need to go, too."

Derek stared at her for several seconds. Then pointing to Teisha, he gestured for her to accompany the six villagers. "Ti... sha go. You lead... you stay. She follow... she stay," he said referring to Belle.

"I don't think he trusts you," Teisha said.

"And he trusts you?"

"He knows I'll come back."

"Gee, thanks. Okay. Get the guys." It was turning into a long day.

* * *

Surrounded by their people, Derek and Zee watched Ti... sha and three other humans exit the woods. Two were supporting the third. Once they were united with Jor... dan, Derek held up his hand.

"Why... here? What... want?" he asked. Strangers were rare. These weren't typical of the ones that normally appeared from the direction they had come.

"Carlos is injured." Jor... dan pointed to an injured co... pan... en who had been lowered to the ground. "We need somewhere to stay for a few days until he's better."

Walking over to Car... los, Derek motioned for a villager to remove the splints and bindings. When she pulled up his pant leg, she made a clicking sound and shook her head. Derek peered over her shoulder at the purplish, swollen ankle.

"Bad. You... stay. Three... three... day," Derek said, holding up his fingers like Jordan had done earlier, but showing the three fingers twice.

"Three days," Jordan repeated.

"No. Three... three... day."

Confused, Jordan shook her head.

"Three days," she said again.

Derek shook his head and then looked at the ground for a moment. Raising his head his expressionless eyes stared into Jordan's.

"Three," he said, raising one hand to show three fingers. "Three," he repeated, raising the other hand to show three fingers. "Three... three."

"Oh, you mean six... six days."

Derek nodded.

"Six... day."

"Thanks," Jordan said. "That'll help a lot."

CHAPTER 13

THE HUNTERS WERE LED to a hut in the center of the village. Jordan suspected the location was more about keeping an eye on them rather than a place of convenience.

"Yours," one of the female villagers said, holding back a grass curtain. When Belle started to enter, a man blocked her way, shaking his head.

"You... no... stay... here."

"She stays with us." Jordan took Belle's arm.

"You... stay. She... no... stay... here."

"She's staying with us," Jordan repeated. The villager shook his head. When several others closed in, Jordan knew she had no choice but to relent. "I'll try to find out what this is about," she said to Belle. "Go with them for now. If anything happens, scream as loud as you can. We'll be there," she promised.

"I don't —"

"I know, but for the moment you have no choice. They took care of your wound so I don't think they'll harm you. Remember what I said about being a hunter." Turning to the woman, Jordan pointed to Belle. "Where are you taking her?" When the villager pointed to the next hut, she felt better. "Okay. Go on, Belle. We're just next door." Reluctantly the girl left, surrounded by two women and a man. Jordan signaled for the rest of the team to go inside. At least they'd have a roof over their heads. Whether they were safe or not was another issue.

* * *

The interior of the hut was nothing more than a room with dirt floors. Grass mats were scattered throughout. From their size and position, they were probably intended as beds.

"They sure don't believe in furniture. Who do you think these people are?" Teisha asked once they had settled in.

"I don't know. One thing's obvious — Phageian don't come into this area. Without walls they'd be helpless," Thomas said.

"That we know of," Jordan added. "This doesn't make any sense. Just a few days' walk from here we saw several Phageian. Hell, we destroyed two. How could this place exist without some type of protection?"

"Maybe Phageian just haven't made it this far," Carlos said.

"But why not? They've made it everywhere else," Teisha said. "They can smell or sense humans from a long ways off."

"True. Maybe their numbers are declining. It's been over ten years since we heard any news from the outside world. We assumed Phageian had overrun everything," Jordan said. "What if we're wrong?"

"One could only hope." Teisha grabbed her backpack, rummaging for a nutrition bar.

"I know. At some point the plague has to end. If the scientists discovered a vaccine or cure —"

The curtain covering the entrance was pushed aside, interrupting the conversation. Two villagers carrying baskets and a jug walked in. Placing them on the floor, one turned to walk out. The other pointed to the objects.

"Food... drink," she said and then left.

"They don't talk much, do they?" Carlos leaned over to look at the contents in the basket. "Whatever that is, it looks better than anything we've eaten recently."

The hunters ate in silence. Tired and exhausted, all they could think about was sleep.

"Should one of us stand watch?" Teisha asked, wiping her hands on her pants.

"It wouldn't do much good," Jordan said. "There are too many of them to fight off. Besides, I doubt they'd waste food feeding us if they intended to kill us."

"Unless they want to fatten us up," Thomas added, half in jest. Unfortunately, the rest of the team didn't find it very funny. The thought kept them awake for several hours.

* * *

Jordan managed only an hour of sleep before noises from the outside disturbed her rest. Although it wasn't anything specific, the sounds weren't the normal ones she was accustomed to. Not wanting to wake the others, she picked up her boots and tiptoed past the sleeping forms.

The sun had not yet set. She felt like this was one of the longest days in her life. Villagers were moving around the area, each appearing to be pre-occupied with his or her particular job. After watching them for another hour, Jordan realized there was a predictable pattern to their routines, but mannerisms she found somewhat disturbing. No one spoke or even acknowledged each other. Those tending the gardens did so without out stopping to rest. Some villagers carrying jugs and buckets disappeared along a path leading into the woods, returning a short time later to dump the contents into barrels positioned near the gardens. Others harvested crops, putting the plants into baskets, which were then carried to one of the larger huts. Pigs and chickens wandered aimlessly around the village but avoided cultivated areas, as if restrained by an invisible fence. Jordan knew pigs could be boundary trained. Chickens she wasn't sure about. The animals that went wherever they wanted were the cats. Villagers moved out of their way whenever they got too close.

"They're certainly organized," Teisha said, silently moving up to stand by Jordan.

"Yeah, and don't talk much," Jordan replied.

"You mean at all. I haven't seen or heard one of them say a word since the food was dropped off, and that was short and sweet. It's almost as if they are from another country."

"They could be. Felicia once told me about immigrant communes that popped up after the pandemic was officially recognized. She said people became suspicious of foreigners and started blaming them for the plague. The only way some could protect themselves was to band together with their own kind."

"Makes sense. Birds of a feather type thing," Teisha said. "That would explain why they don't speak our language very well."

"And similar eye color and build. They have plenty of food to be so gaunt looking. Could be they ration their resources. It would be the smart thing to do, even if food is plentiful. Listen, you wait here. I'm going to see how Belle is."

"If you can, you mean," Teisha said.

"Yeah, there's that."

* * *

After checking on Belle, Jordan and Teisha made themselves comfortable next to the fire. An evening chill had set in. It had been weeks since they were able to just sit back and relax. Having a campfire was a luxury.

Marco pushed aside the curtain, stepping outdoors and stretching.

"Damn that felt good," he said. "Best sleep I've had in a long time. Anything happen while I was out of it?"

"No," Jordan replied. "We're just watching the activity. Things have slowed down a bit. Most of the villagers have disappeared so I guess they've called it a day."

"Just guards left, eh?"

Jordan shook her head.

"None we can see. There's only about a half-dozen people out and they're stacking firewood."

"Well, if they aren't afraid of Phageian, I see no reason for us to be." Marco' stomach growled. "I guess I'd better see if there's any food lying around... and an outhouse. I need to take a crap. Either of you know where the toilets are?"

"Nope! We went off into the woods over there." Jordan pointed in a direction opposite the main activity. "There's food over there. They brought it a few minutes ago." Two baskets sat next to the hut. "I didn't want to take them inside since all of you were sleeping so soundly."

"I appreciate that. A good sleep's hard to find. Heard anything about Belle?"

"Yeah," Jordan said. "I saw her for a few minutes. They're still keeping her isolated, and Derek has disappeared so I couldn't ask him about her. She's scared but doing okay. We can't do anything else until the morning."

"You mean if we can find anyone who talks," Marco mumbled. Picking up the baskets he disappeared into the hut only to come back a few minutes later, heading into

224

the woods. Teisha and Jordan decided to make one last 'nature call' trip before calling it a night. Being able to sleep without someone standing guard was going to be a treat.

* * *

Shortly after sunrise the hunters emerged from the hut. Fresh vegetables had been placed inside sometime during the night. That the villagers could move so quietly around them without waking them up was disconcerting. Accepting there was nothing they could have done anyway, no matter what the villagers' intentions were, didn't make them feel any better.

"Tonight I'm staying awake," Carlos muttered, limping toward the nearest fire. The air was cool due to a chilly breeze blowing from the north.

"And do what?" Thomas asked.

"I don't know. We're supposed to be hunters and yet these people move around so quietly we don't know they're here. It's not normal and I don't like it."

"You didn't move when I got up to take a piss. No wonder you didn't hear them."

"Go to hell," Carlos grumbled and disappeared back into the hut.

Everyone laughed. When two women walked past them into Belle's hut, the laughter stopped.

"I need to check on her," Jordan said. "Teisha, you're with me. The rest of you see if you can find out anything about this place. Make yourselves useful. Maybe you can get someone to talk."

* * *

The two women were emerging from Belle's hut when Jordan and Teisha arrived. One was carrying a water basin, the other a basket of herbs; neither glanced at Jordan but one villager walked over to Teisha and picked up her injured arm to examine the wound. She then plucked some yarrow leaves from her basket, handing them to the hunter. "Hold," she said and left.

"You might as well go take care of that now," Jordan said.

"It's almost —"

"I know, but humor them for now. It can't hurt. Go on. I'll check on Belle."

Teisha glared at the leaves as if they were the offending problem.

"Oh all right! But this is the last time." Stomping off, she reminded Jordan of a sulking child.

"Better not let the guys see you acting like that," Jordan called out, teasingly. "You'll never hear the end of it."

Pushing aside the curtain, Jordan stepped inside. Belle sat huddled against the far wall, her thighs drawn up against her chest. Her chin rested on her knees.

"Hey, you okay?" Jordan asked. Belle nodded, but didn't look up. Jordan sank down on her knees. Picking up Belle's arm, she lifted the herb compress. The uncovered windows allowed enough light for her to see the wound. "That looks pretty good. No sign of infection. Are you in any pain?" Shaking her head, Belle still didn't speak. "Did you eat anything?"

"No."

"Do you want to go for a walk?"

"No."

Jordan frowned.

"Are you sure you're okay?"

"Yes."

"Listen, Belle, I know you're probably upset about what I said yesterday, but you need to understand that your actions have consequences."

"I'm sorry."

"I know. We all make mistakes. You're young and inexperienced. Sometimes we forget what's it's like to be your age. Come on. If you stay in here you're going to get fat and lazy," Jordan teased. Taking Belle's good hand she pulled her to her feet. "Besides, the others are worried about you."

* * *

Belle walked into the bright light and blinked several times before putting her hand up to shade her eyes. The sun's rays were painful, making her eyes water, but she quickly adjusted. Her injured hand throbbed. Belle flexed her finger and grimaced.

"Let's go check on Carlos. I'm warning you though, he's grumpy today, not that that's anything new. Ignore anything he says if he decides to get ugly. Pain does that to people."

When they entered the hut, Carlos had fallen asleep again. Putting her finger to her lips Jordan motioned Belle to follow her back outside.

"That'll do him a lot more good than us ragging on him." Looking around she saw Thomas and Marco near the garden, surrounded by several villagers.

Shit! Jordan thought. *Now what?*

"Hey," she called out. "What's up?" Walking over to the group, she squeezed into the circle, looking first at the hunters and then at the people around them. "Problems?"

"Naw," Thomas said. "I wasn't watching where I was going and did something stupid. Stepped on a couple of plants. They were telling me to be more careful and showed us where we could walk."

"They're actually talking to you?"

"Well, no. At least not completely. Just short words and some hand signals."

"Yeah," Marco agreed. "You know, 'Stop... No go here... There.' That sort of thing. They're actually pretty clear about what they mean. Friendly enough."

"Friendly?"

"Well, maybe not friendly but certainly not unfriendly. This here is Will-em," he said pointing to the nearest villager. "And that's San-ra and Jul-en. Oh, and they pointed over there when I asked about toilets. Off in the woods. Will-em held up five fingers. I'm not sure what that's about. Marco and I were just about to check it out."

"We'll go with you," Jordan said. "Hey, Teisha!" she called out, motioning for her to meet them at the designated path. "Come on, Belle. I bet you're ready to explode," she teased.

"They brought me a bucket last night and took it away this morning," Belle replied in a subdued voice.

"Lucky you. Come on anyway. The walk will do you good."

The villagers who had been standing silently by seemed to lose interest in the hunters and went back to their gardening. No one noticed the cats following Belle until they were almost at the path. The animals kept their distance but they definitely were focused only on the young hunter.

"They really seem to like you," Thomas said.

"I don't like them," Belle said, glaring at the cats. "They bit me."

"Only one," Jordan corrected. "And only when you grabbed at it. It probably felt you were attacking it. Blame me for not warning you to move slowly. I forgot some cats don't like to be picked up, even if they do seem friendly."

"I still don't like them."

Jordan shrugged.

"I guess I might feel the same way. Just ignore them. They'll lose interest eventually."

* * *

Around mid-afternoon the same two villagers that had brought them baskets the night before left two more with another jug. After wandering around, the hunters returned to the huts but chose to sit around the campfire. The days were getting cooler. If they didn't find a new home soon they would have to return to Destiny. The thought of failure was depressing.

"Thank you," Jordan said to the villagers who had brought the food and water.

One woman nodded, the first time she had directly acknowledged their presence.

"I feel guilty eating their food and not doing anything to earn it," Teisha said after they left. "I wonder if there's something we can do to help them."

"We could certainly offer. Maybe gather firewood or help with the water," Jordan suggested. "It'll be a good excuse to check this place out."

"Thomas and I'll help with the water. Those jugs must be heavy," Marco offered.

"Good. Teisha and I'll see about the firewood."

"What about me?" Belle asked, rubbing her shoulder unconsciously.

"How's your hand?" Jordan asked.

"It hurts a little but I can do something to help."

"Actually, you can. Carlos needs to soak his ankle in cool water. It'll help reduce the swelling. Can you take care of that and then wrap it back up?"

"That doesn't sound like much. I want to do hunter's work, not be a nursemaid."

"Being a hunter isn't always about searching for food. Taking care of our own is part of the job. It'll give your hand more time to heal. We're going to be here for only a few more days. You need to get better as quickly as possible. Carlos too, but his injury is more serious. He's going to need all of our help."

"Are we bringing our people here?" Belle asked.

"No, it wouldn't be right encroaching on their space, but this place gives us hope. We haven't seen Phageian since we destroyed those two several days back. Maybe if it remains clear for another day or two, and we find a good spot, we'll go home. If we bring back an advance team, we can build a temporary compound to move our people to."

"I'd like that." Belle again massaged her right shoulder.

"Are you okay?" Jordan asked.

"I'm okay. It just aches."

"Let me look at your hand." Removing the compress, Jordan examined the fingers. "No infection. Put a fresh compress on it before you wake Carlos up. If he starts ragging on you, come and get me. There's no reason to put up with his bullshit."

Reluctantly Belle nodded and left.

* * *

Derek and Zee were standing at the edge of the garden with five villagers. Gesturing toward the barrels, Zee touched three on their shoulders then pointed toward the path leading to a small river. It provided the water for all their needs.

"Just in time," Thomas said. Picking up two buckets he tossed them to Marco and grabbed a large jug. Following the villagers, they disappeared into the woods.

"We'd like to help," Jordan explained. "Earn our keep. They can carry water. Teisha and I thought we might gather wood for the fires, unless there's something else we can do. We're not very good at farming."

Blue-white eyes glanced from Jordan to Teisha and then back to Jordan.

"Ti... sha wood," the man said. "Jor... dan... lead... come." He motioned for her to follow him. "Back... soon," he said to Zee. The woman turned and walked toward a hut without acknowledging him or Jordan. The cats trotted next to her, their tails held high.

"Looks like he's got something else in mind for me. Catch you later," Jordan said to Teisha.

"Yeah. He seems to have this thing about you being the leader. He really wants to keep an eye on you."

"Lucky me," Jordan said.

* * *

Jordan followed Derek to another path on the opposite side of the village. After an estimated thirty-minute hike, she smelled the distinct odor of cooking meat. Her stomach growled noisily. Derek stopped to stare at her stomach. The tall villager's head tilted slightly sideways. It was the first time she had ever seen him display any distinguishable emotional reaction. Embarrassed, she smiled sheepishly.

"Smells good," she said. The corners of Derek's mouth seemed to turn down, but she wasn't sure. Jordan had a feeling he wasn't happy.

231

The path led to a clearing. A hut stood to their left. Six large pots supported by triangular poles were scattered about. Beneath each was a small fire. One villager stirred the hot coals, while others stirred the contents of the pots: boiling meat. Surprised, Jordan inhaled deeply the tantalizing odor. Nowhere in the village had she seen or smelled cooked meat, not that she had thought much about it. Hunters mostly lived off plants. Cooking wasn't practical when you lived in trees.

"Umm... sorry," she apologized again when her stomach growled a second time.

Saying nothing, Derek turned away, walking to the nearest pot. Joining him, Jordan craned her neck to see what else might be cooking.

"You... eat... meat?" Derek asked.

"Sometimes. Not very often, though. It's hard to find where we live."

"Meat... bad."

"Then why are you cooking it?"

"Ness-sary... cook... to... eat."

Jordan was confused.

"But you don't eat meat."

"Meat... bad."

"So why have it at all?"

"Ness... sary. No... talk. You... help."

Realizing she wasn't getting anywhere, Jordan gave up.

"Okay. What do you want me to do?"

Derek pointed to the hut.

"You... cut."

"Cut? Oh, you mean butcher. I can do that," she said.

* * *

Stepping into the dimly lit interior, Jordan was surprised to see a large wooden table stretching the full length of the hut. Villagers were lined on both sides. Three pigs and several chickens were in various stages of skinning and dismemberment. Jordan unsheathed her knife and stepped between two women who were tugging on the tough hide of a pig.

"Let me show you how to do that," she said. Within seconds she was separating the hide from the fat and muscle with her knife. "You pull, I'll skin. Just keep your fingers and hands out of my way." Minutes later the pig was shoved down the table and another brought in. After skinning three more pigs and a goat, Jordan helped butcher the animals, slicing tendons and sawing through the joints. Some meat and entrails were thrown into leaf-lined baskets and carried outside to the kettles. Other portions were hauled up another path, uncooked. Nothing thrown in the boiling water was cleaned, not even the intestines. Jordan lost her appetite for meat.

While the meat was being cooked, a steaming bucket of minty smelling water was brought to Jordan. The villager motioned for her to wash.

"Thanks," Jordan said, dipping her hand in to check the temperature. Although hot, it wasn't uncomfortable, except for a burning sensation on her right index finger. Jordan pulled it from the water and examined it closely. *Damn! I can't believe I nicked myself.* She was even more grateful for the villager's thoughtful gesture as she cleaned the blood from her hands, arms and knife. Her shirt would have to wait. Thankfully, Felicia had the foresight to tuck an extra one in her backpack.

Felicia, she thought, feeling a strong ache of loneliness for her lover and partner, but not just for the physical passion they shared. Jordan missed everything that was Felicia — her wit, her intelligence, her sense of

233

humor. Their relationship had lasted because they understood each other, accepting the strengths and the weaknesses that made them who they were.

* * *

It was early evening before Jordan arrived back at the hut. Derek had disappeared once she started butchering the animals. When she had cleaned up, a woman wordlessly pointed to the path back to the village. The sun was just setting behind the tree line. Long shadows stretched across the clearing.

The other hunters had completed their tasks and were sitting around the fire snacking on plants and nuts. Carlos' foot was propped on a log. A thick pad of leaves buffered the ankle against the hard wood. A few feet away Belle sat staring at the fire. The orange glow of the flames reflected off her pale blue eyes.

Jordan frowned. She'd never really paid much attention to the color of the young girl's eyes before but would have sworn they were darker. Shaking her head she dismissed the thought.

"About time you showed up," Marco called out and then saw the blood on her shirt. "Are you okay?" he asked, jumping to his feet. "What happened?"

"I'm fine," Jordan said. "Let me get this thing off and I'll tell you all about it. Can you bring me some water? I need to wash this thing... And make it cold. Don't want the stains to set in any more than they have already."

"Not a problem."

A few minutes later, Jordan exited the hut carrying the bowl of water holding her shirt. Draining it, she poured clean water over the garment, rinsed it and drained it again. She repeated the process two more times before she was satisfied it was as clean as it would get.

After spreading the shirt across a log near the fire she sat next to it.

"Obviously you aren't hurt so where'd all the blood come from?" Marco asked.

Jordan gave them a quick outline of her day.

"They actually slaughter animals, cook the meat and don't eat it? What do they do with it?"

"I don't know, and they didn't boil all of it. Some they carried off. I'd have followed them but they made it clear I was to return here."

"Meat," Carlos said, his eyes taking on a dreamy look. "What I wouldn't give for a chunk right now."

"Me too," Thomas agreed. "I don't remember the last time I tasted pig or goat."

"I do." Everyone looked expectantly at Teisha. "Actually, it was a rabbit leg. Six months ago."

"Where did you get a rabbit?" Marco asked.

"On one of the hunts. It was the only thing we managed to kill. My team knew it would cause a problem if we took it back to Destiny so we decided to eat it ourselves."

"You aren't the only one guilty of that," Jordan admitted. "And to be honest, if one of us caught something on the way home and could cook it, I'd say go for it."

Everyone nodded in agreement.

"So, back to these people and the meat. They certainly don't bring it here. We'd have smelled it," Teisha said.

"My thoughts exactly."

"So what are we going to do about it?"

"Nothing right now. They'll probably keep a close eye on us for a couple of days. We need to gain their trust. Keep helping them with the chores. Once I think it's safe I'll —"

"We'll —" Teisha corrected.

"I'll check it out." The look Jordan gave Teisha and the group left no room for doubt that she wasn't in the mood for an argument. "I'm the only one who leaves the village. No one will be suspicious if I continue to help butcher the animals. When the time is right, I'll simply head up the path and slip away... by myself," she said, making it clear the conversation was over.

CHAPTER 14

DAY FOUR IN THE VILLAGE started out like the rest. The hunters ate the food brought to them and then split up to help with the chores. Derek gave no indication Jordan was needed for butchering, so she decided to work in the gardens, something she enjoyed doing when she was home. It allowed her more time with Felicia.

* * *

Felicia, she thought, remembering the last night they were together. They had made love twice. The first was intense, passionate, almost lustful, reminding her of their first years together. Back then neither thought they would live very long. Every day was a struggle for food and a battle against Phageian onslaughts. When Jordan decided to become a hunter, Felicia wasn't happy but didn't try to dissuade her. The choice made their time together even more precious.

Jordan smiled. Their second round was amazing. The passion was still there but the lovemaking was slow and tender. Felicia had slipped quietly out of bed, doing her best not to awaken Jordan.

"Where are you going?" Jordan asked, her voice husky from the raw emotion she had felt only moments before.

"To get some water," Felicia replied. "I'm sorry I awakened you. You looked so peaceful and you need to rest."

"You don't really think you can creep around without me hearing you?"

"Well, I've managed a few times so don't look so smug," Felicia teased. "Since you're awake, would you like a glass of water? Or juice? I'm trying a new veggie formula."

"Water's fine." Jordan was always Felicia's formula guinea pig. Generally the concoction wasn't too terribly bad. When Felicia climbed back into bed, she held the glass to Jordan's lips so she could take a sip. "Thanks," Jordan said. Taking the glass she put it to the side and pulled Felicia's head toward her. "Since we're awake," she whispered, "we might as well make good use of our time." Her moist lips captured Felicia's as she drew her lover down next to her. As her hands slid across the warm body, she couldn't help but notice the curvature of each rib. "You've lost more weight."

"Haven't we all," Felicia said, leaning slightly backward. "Isn't that what tomorrow's mission is about? Finding that land of plenty so you can fatten me up?"

"You'll never be fat, but let's not think about tomorrow. Right now I have my own land of plenty." Jordan cupped Felicia's small breasts in her palms and leaned upward to kiss each nipple. "God I'm going to miss these," she said.

"My tits? That's what you're going to miss while you're out there prowling the woods?" Felicia tried to sound indignant but couldn't pull it off. Laughing, she lowered her weight onto Jordan, pressing her hips into the hunter's and grinding slowly.

"Well, not just those, but I have to admit they one of your most endearing assets." As the hips pushed harder against hers, Jordan gasped.

"Are you sure of that?" Felicia whispered in her ear, her warm breath tickling.

"Ummm." Groaning, Jordan shifted her hands to Felicia's buttocks and squeezed. "May... maybe not."

"I didn't think so." Warm lips traveled down her neck to the pulse at the base of her throat. Jordan's heart started racing with anticipation. "Jordan..." Felicia whispered, huskily.

"Jordan! **Jordan**!" a voice called, interrupting her reveries. Looking around, she saw Thomas running toward her. "Phageian!" The other hunters were racing to the hut. Carlos had hobbled outside carrying an armful of weapons. He tossed Teisha a bow and several bolts. Marco grabbed the pistol, two hand bows and the remaining bolts. Running to Jordan, he handed her a rifle and machete.

"Where?" Jordan asked.

"Coming from the river. Two of them. They're heading this way."

"What about the water bearers? Where are they?"

"By the river. I had to leave them to warn you."

"Shit! Let's go!" she said. "We can't let them make it to the village. These people are defenseless."

The hunters moved cautiously up the path toward the river. When they reached the banks, they didn't see any villagers or Phageian.

"Spread out, but be careful. If you see anything, call out. And for Christ's sake, don't get too close to any tree trunks."

For an hour they combed the area but found nothing.

"Maybe they moved on," Marco said once they had regrouped.

"Maybe, or we missed them somehow. Let's get back to the village," Jordan said.

As they neared the village they heard a familiar chant.

"Baa-rrack! Baa-rrack!"

"Sounds like they may have caught them," Teisha said.

"Not with words," Jordan replied. "Phageian don't understand language. These people may not know that. Hurry!"

When the hunters entered the clearing, the first thing they saw was a crowd of villagers surrounding two Phageian. Everyone had their arms raised making the same pushing motion they had used the first day the hunters arrived. With each gesture they took a step forward, making the circle smaller and smaller, restricting the Phageian's movements.

"Baa-rrack! Baa-rrack!" they continued to chant.

Instead of attacking, as would be expected, the Phageian tried to avoid the hands by raising their arms as if to protect their faces.

"I'll be damned," Teisha said. "They seem afraid."

"They're something, for sure. Come on!" Jordan said.

* * *

The villagers had closed in on the Phageian, confining them to an area of less than ten feet in diameter. The people clearly provided an intimidating force with their arms moving forward and backward, accompanied by the chant.

"Wait here," Jordan ordered, but signaled for Teisha to follow her. Shouldering through the crowd they pushed to the front and stared in horror at the captives.

"Those are the ones we shot in that meadow," Teisha said, sounding as stunned as Jordan felt. How could they be alive? I mean... you know."

"I know, but I don't know," Jordan said. "That one I shot in the head. Belle got the other in the mouth. I can see hers missing the brain but not mine." She pointed to the taller Phageian whose back was turned to the hunters. Almost as if it heard her, it turned to stare at Jordan and

Teisha. White eyes opened wider and it suddenly collapsed on the ground. The other turned, looked down, then at Jordan and collapsed next to the first.

"What the hell?" Teisha exclaimed. "They've learned to play possum."

"At least it makes it easier to do it right this time." Jordan raised her rifle and took aim, only to have a hand grab her arm and push it down.

"No... kill," Derek said.

"We have to," Jordan replied. "They'll infect everyone."

"No... kill," he repeated. "No... infect."

"Listen Derek, I don't think you understand how dangerous —"

Turning his back on Jordan, Derek signaled to six villagers and then pointed to Jordan and Teisha. Obviously he was directing them to escort the hunters away.

"You... go."

The hunters had no choice but to leave. A dozen others picked the Phageian up and carried them up the path leading to the butchery.

"You don't think they're going to cook them?" Marco asked.

Jordan shivered at the thought.

"God I hope not! I'm certainly not going to help them cut them up. Let's get back to the hut. There's nothing else we can do right now. Tomorrow we'll try to figure this out."

CHAPTER 15

THREE HOURS BEFORE sunrise, Jordan eased quietly out of the hut. The others were sleeping soundly, exhausted from the previous day's work and events. Once outside she pulled on her boots and positioned the quiver strap over her shoulder. With no villagers in sight, she slipped away into the darkness.

"You weren't thinking of checking things out without me," Teisha whispered from behind, causing Jordan to jump.

"Damn it, Teisha, scare me the next time," she grumbled. "You were supposed to be asleep."

"I never sleep that soundly. Besides, I knew you would try this. Shall we go?"

Following the path toward the butchery Jordan went off trail when they were a few hundred yards away. She wasn't going to chance crossing into the open not knowing if there was anyone stationed to guard the meat or facility.

"The trail is on the other side," she whispered. "We'll circle and pick it back up on the other side."

Teisha nodded.

A half-hour later they picked up the trail again. After following it for more than an hour Jordan began to wonder if she had picked the wrong path. They hadn't come across anything out of the ordinary. Sunrise was only an hour or so away.

"I'm sure this is the one they went up with the meat," she said, motioning for Teisha to take a break. "Surely they can't carry those baskets much farther. There was a good amount of meat in them. We'll go another ten or fifteen minutes and call —"

"ARRRGGHHH!" a voice screamed from the darkness, making Teisha and Jordan jump.

"What was that?" Teisha whispered.

"I don't know. Come on. It came from that direction."

More screams followed, although that word wasn't the best description. They sounded more inhuman, sending chills down the two hunters' backs. Teisha and Jordan crept silently up a small ridge and then dropped to their bellies. Crawling, they inched their way to a ridge. Through the shadowy light of early sunrise they spotted at least a dozen cages. Several villages were tending to the occupants.

"Those are holding pens," Teisha said. "For confining animals."

"Those aren't animals," Jordan said. "At least not what we call animals. They're Phageian."

"Why would they lock Phageian up? They should be destroyed."

"I don't know. I suppose we could ask."

"Yeah right, we just walk on in and ask the first person we meet, 'What's up?'" Teisha said, sarcastically.

"Any better idea?"

"Not really."

"So far they haven't shown any inclination for violence, even with those things. I honestly don't think it's a part of their nature. Come on. Now's as good a time as ever. Keep your bow ready, just in case." Jordan pushed some brush aside and headed toward the pens. "Hello!" she called out. Instantly the villagers stopped what they were doing to face the two hunters. They began rocking sideways, shifting from one foot to the other. "Nervous bunch, aren't they?"

"Yeah. Funny we make them nervous but Phageian don't." Teisha shook her head. "Strange world."

* * *

Jordan counted seven confined Phageian. The cages were evenly spaced, about ten feet apart. When they neared the pens the two recent captives stopped eating. Their whitish, bug-eyed expression suggested fear. Suddenly, as if on cue, they collapsed again, followed by the others.

"I'd like to know what that's about," Teisha murmured. "Damn things are worse than possums."

"They're definitely different from any in our area. They're not aggressive and seem afraid."

"But not of the villagers. If I didn't know better I'd say they're only terrified of us."

"Wouldn't you be, too?" Jordan asked. "We shot them."

"Exactly, which means they can think. How's that possible?"

"I don't know. Maybe whatever causes Phageians is changing. Maybe they have better immune systems."

"Well, the last thing we need are smart ones. Uh oh." Teisha nodded toward three villagers moving in their direction. Zee was in the lead.

"What... want?" Zee asked, stopping a few feet away.

"Hi, Zee. Ummm..." Jordan was somewhat at a loss for words. She didn't want Zee to suspect they were spying on everyone. "We were... hunting and... heard noises. We thought it might be more Phageian and decided to check it out."

Zee cocked her head slightly to the right. Jordan blushed. It was impossible to read her expression but the hunter felt like a child caught in a lie.

"Der... rick... say... you... eat... meat. You... want... meat?"

"No... I mean yes, but we weren't looking to kill anything. Just wanted to see what was wandering around." *That sounds so lame,* Jordan thought.

"That's the best you can do?" Teisha whispered.

"Yes," Jordan said. "Feel free to jump in anytime."

"No, no. You're the boss."

The woman's eyes moved from Jordan to Teisha and then back to Jordan.

"Meat... bad. No... eat... meat," she finally said. Then she motioned for Teisha and Jordan to follow her. Walking to the first cage on the right, she pointed to the Phageian lying motionless. A chunk of raw meat lay on the ground. He was the one she had shot in the meadow.

"He... eat... meat. Meat... bad. He... bad." Walking to the next cage, she repeated the same words. The third cage was different. The meat was partially cooked, although the middle looked raw. "He... eat... meat. Meat... bad."

"Okay," Jordan agreed, not knowing exactly what she was agreeing to. "Eating raw meat is bad and partially cooked is bad."

Zee nodded and moved on to the next. Inside was a Phageian child, probably in her early teens when she had been turned. At some point she had moved to the far side of the cage unnoticed. Although she was still lying down, her arm was wrapped protectively around a bowl. Jordan saw small chunks of cooked meat and plants.

"She's eating a stew," Teisha exclaimed, unable to contain her surprise.

"Meat... bad. Plant... good. She... better. Bad... not... bad. Soon... eat plant. No meat."

They're weaning them off meat, Jordan thought. *Like babies off milk.* The last three confirmed it. Two female

Phageian were huddled in corners, more interested in their food than the hunters. The last had risen to his feet and stood motionless by the barred door rocking backing and forth. His arms hung limply at his sides. His unreadable blue-white eyes roamed around the compound as if searching for something.

"What happens to him?" Jordan asked.

Motioning to the two men standing slightly behind her, Zee stepped aside, pulling Jordan and Teisha with her. One villager opened the door. The other reached in and took the Phageian's arm, escorting him from the cage. The Phageian walked obediently out and was led toward the path leading to the village.

"He... us."

"You're taking him to the village?"

"He... us."

"Oh, you mean, he's one of your people. You isolated him here, like a quarantine. Did he get bitten by one of them?" Jordan asked, pointing at the other Phageian.

"No... bit. Not... quar... tine. Not... us. Now... us."

"I think she's telling you this guy wasn't a villager," Teisha said. "But now he's going to be. You know what that means?"

"I know what it sounds like, but I don't believe it. He was probably just sick and they thought he was infected. Phageian don't eat anything but human flesh... and certainly not plants."

"A week ago, no one could have convinced me Phageian were afraid of humans, but we know those two are. We believed they only eat humans. That's animal meat in those cages and those three are definitely eating plants. This entire village is weird, but things are beginning to make some sense."

"Yeah. We need to get back to the others. Warn them," Jordan said.

"Warn them?"

"That these people are infected. Eating plants may be controlling whatever caused the disease, but they aren't cured."

"Okay, but they clearly aren't dangerous. They've had plenty of opportunity to attack us if they wanted. I'd even say they go out of their way to avoid touching us, so why the warning?"

Why indeed, Jordan thought.

"Wrong word, but the team needs to know."

"Carlos is going to love this. He's been bitching about this place from day one."

"Yeah." Jordan turned to Zee. "Listen, Zee we're sorry we intruded here. We're going to head back to the village now. Maybe help your people with some of the chores."

"Jor... dan, Ti... sha... no... hunt?" Zee asked. "Jor... dan... warn... team." Zee walked away, leaving two stunned hunters behind.

"Well that was embarrassing enough," Jordan said, aware her face had turned bright red.

Teisha laughed so hard her stomach began to hurt.

"You deserved that!"

Giving her friend a withering look, Jordan stomped off muttering to herself.

* * *

Carlos took the news like the asshole he could be.

"I knew there was something wrong here!" he yelled, glaring at Marco and Thomas. "We're living amongst a bunch of Phageian freaks. Hell, you're even treating them like family, helping with the chores. What next? You going to fuck a couple?"

Before anyone could stop him, Marco slugged Carlos, knocking him on his butt. Reaching down, he yanked him to his feet and hit him again.

"Stop it!" Jordan yelled, jumping between the two men. Teisha and Thomas each grabbed a hunter, trying to yank them apart. "Marco, turn him loose."

Shoving Carlos away, the hunter stormed away.

"Asshole!" Carlos said, swiping his bloody lip with the back of his hand.

"Shut up!" Jordan said. "You deserved that. If we didn't have to head out in a couple of days, I'd let him beat the crap out of you. I'd even help."

"What are we going to do now?" Thomas asked.

"Nothing except be a little more cautious around them. They may not know they're infected. In a few days Carlos will be well enough to travel."

"I can travel now if it means leaving this place," Carlos said.

"We keep to the plan and the routine and you stay off that foot as much as possible. If you do something stupid, it will only delay us more. The rest of you continue helping with the chores. I'm going for a walk. I need to think."

"What about Belle?" Teisha asked.

"I'll talk to her when I get back."

CHAPTER 16

PULLING THE CURTAIN aside, Jordan stepped into the dimly lit room. Two villagers sat on each side of the entrance. Neither glanced at the hunter. Their gazes were fixed on the still figure lying on her side with her back to the door.

"Belle?" Jordan called out keeping her voice low. The girl didn't move. Walking over to her, Jordan touched her shoulder lightly. "Are you awake? We have to talk. We'll be leaving here soon. Hey!" Turning Belle over, she gasped and jumped backward. Unblinking blue-white eyes shifted slowly in her direction. *Shit! What the hell's happening to you? Stupid question.* There was no doubt what was happening to Belle. For the first time in years, Jordan felt completely at a loss. She ran from the hut into the light, unsure what to do. *Breathe,* she thought, trying to control the rising panic. *Breathe!*

* * *

Teisha leaned on her hoe. Sweat ran down her forehead and into her eyes, making them burn. Gardening was hard work, she thought, and definitely not a job she ever wanted to do after she left this place.

I can't believe these people are Phageian. There has to be another explanation. Unfortunately, there wasn't... at least nothing that made sense. *If it walks like a duck, and talks like a duck...* The problem was the villagers didn't walk or talk like the normal Phageian. Definitely not talk. Shaking her head she straightened, arched her aching back and glanced toward Belle's hut. Jordan was standing outside bent over, her hands on her thighs. Teisha frowned. Something was wrong. Dropping the hoe, she checked to see if anyone else had seen Jordan's distress. The villagers were focused on their chores. Marco and Thomas were nowhere in sight.

"Are you okay?" Teisha asked, striding purposefully toward her friend.

"It's Belle," Jordan said, taking a deep breath. "She's turning."

"Turning? Turning what?" When Jordan didn't answer, Teisha ripped open the curtain and rushed inside. Dropping to her knees, she leaned over Belle. Jordan joined her.

"How can she be infected?" Teisha demanded angrily. "Unless they did something to her."

"Why would they do that to her and not us?"

"I don't know. Maybe because she's a child. There aren't that many children in this village... or haven't you noticed?"

"Of course I noticed, but when have we ever seen very many children among Phageian? They either don't survive the infection or the attacks."

"Well, they were quick to separate her from us when we arrived. Why just her?" Teisha asked, dropping back onto her butt. She draped her arms over her knees and stared at Belle.

"I assumed it was because she was wounded."

"Carlos was injured. They didn't take him away."

"Carlos had a sprained ankle. Belle was bitten by a cat and was bleeding. You know puncture wounds get infected easily."

"So the water they put her hand in must have been contaminated."

"I don't think so. They used the same water on your cut... and I nicked my finger when I was cutting meat. They brought me water to wash up with. It was warm but not hot enough to kill bacteria. We'd be infected if it was the water."

"We're adults. Belle's young. We have stronger immune systems."

Jordan shook her head.

"I don't think that's it. All of us have been exposed to more than enough water to contaminate us and we've eaten the same food. We're missing something... something that happened..."

"The cats," Teisha interrupted. "That's the only thing that's different. She was bitten by that damn cat."

"Cat bites can be bad, but..."

"Think about it, Jordan. The villagers don't like cats. What if cats also transmit the disease and these people know it?"

"Why aren't Derek and Zee afraid of them? None of this makes sense." Frustrated, Jordan motioned for Teisha to follow her. "Let's get something to eat and..."

Teisha gave Jordan an expectant look.

"And?"

"We'll have to move up our time schedule. We'll move out tomorrow. Don't say anything to the others yet."

"They're probably not around anyway, except for Carlos... and I'll be damned if I want to listen to his mouth right now," Teisha said.

Leaving, neither hunter noticed the two other villagers enter the hut behind them.

* * *

When Jordan returned, she saw Belle sitting up. It took a few moments before she realized the girl's hands were tied behind her back.

"Is that necessary?" she asked the two villagers sitting by the entrance, already knowing the answer. "Stupid question," Jordan muttered. Belle could no longer be trusted to control the urges that would eventually control her cravings.

"Belle!" Jordan shook her shoulder. "Can you hear me? It's Jordan. Do you know who I am?"

Belle looked at the face inches away from her.

"Jor... die?"

"Yes, it's Jordie. I need you to concentrate on what I'm saying. Can you do that?"

"Jor... die, I... feel..."

Jordan waited for Belle to finish the sentence but realized she couldn't find the word she needed.

"I know. Do you know what's happening to you?"

"I..." Belle's eyes seemed to search Jordan's face for an answer. She looked at one of the villagers standing by the entrance. "Like... them?"

"I don't know. Maybe."

"Not... like... them." Belle shook her head. "I... I want... to go... home."

Stooping, Jordan cautiously reached out to touch Belle's cheek.

"I'm sorry. We can't chance you infecting anyone."

"Not... die... here. Die... home."

"Even if we could take you, there isn't enough time now, sweetie," Jordan said, tenderly. When a tear trickled from Belle's right eye, Jordan couldn't hold back her own.

"Jor... die?"

"What?" she replied softly.

"I... hunter... yes?"

"Yes."

"Hunter... oath. You... promise. Hunter... infect. Hunter... die."

"Hunter oath, Belle," Jordan whispered, her voice choking.

"To... morrow."

"Tomorrow." Reluctantly Jordan agreed to the unspoken request.

"Jor... die?"

"Yes?"

"Not... sad. I... hunter. Hunter... death. Member... me."

"Always. Do you want me to stay here with you?" Belle's head dipped once. "Belle? I'd like to ask you something. Can you give me an honest answer?"

"I... try."

"If I hold you for awhile, could you tell me if the craving begins?"

Belle looked down for several seconds, seeming to consider the question. When she raised her eyes, they were almost completely white now. Slowly she moved her head from side to side.

"No."

Taking a deep breath, Jordan rose to her feet and walked behind Belle. Kneeling, she reached under the hunter's arms and wrapped her own around the slender waist.

"Then I'll figure it out on my own," she said, leaning her chin on Belle's head. They stayed in that position for several hours.

CHAPTER 17

THE HUNTERS HUDDLED around one of the many fires the villagers kept burning during the night. Deep in thought they said nothing, each trying to resolve what needed to be done with their own consciences. Seeing how quickly Belle's condition was deteriorating, Jordan had instructed Teisha to tell the others while she stayed in the hut.

"Squatting here and saying nothing isn't going to resolve this," Thomas said, finally breaking the silence. "We know what needs to be done."

"And what's that?" Marco asked. "We're talking about Belle, not one of those **things** these people have in their pens."

"We can't take her with us. She's already turning. That means she's infected. Hell, all of us could be now. No one knows for sure all the ways this stuff spreads."

"We know it has to be through a bite or open wound. Has she bitten any of you?" Carlos piped in.

"No."

"No."

All the replies were the same.

"Scratched you?"

The answers were still no.

"Then if we are it's because of something else. Since no one seems to be showing any symptoms I'd guess we're okay," Carlos said. "Our only concern right now is what to do about Belle."

Marco cursed under his breath.

"I don't like where this is going. Don't expect me to shoot her," he said. "I'll go along with whatever else you decide." Standing, he disappeared into the hut.

"This is ridiculous," Thomas grumbled. "If any of us had been bitten on this trip none of us would hesitate to kill the person... before he or she turned."

"And I wouldn't hesitate on the trip back," Carlos added.

"I would hope not! What about you?" Thomas said, turning to Teisha. "You've been awfully quiet. I say we do what has to be done. Every one of us would want that if it were us. It's a mercy killing."

"Belle's a child," Teisha said quietly.

"There are no hunter children, remember? The day she left Destiny she became a woman. A hunter like us," Marco said.

"It's not that easy and you know it. None of us knew what we were getting into when we first chose this trade. It was going to be a great adventure, fighting the bad guys, feeding the people. What child doesn't worship a hunter? Belle's no different. Turning thirteen didn't make her magically an adult. Neither did we when we gave her weapons and knowledge."

"Jordan should be part of this discussion," Carlos said. "It's not our decision to make. When is she —"

"I'm here," Jordan said, stepping out of the hut and passing the two villagers guarding the entrance. "And for once you and I agree on something, Carlos. When she joined us she accepted the responsibilities and the consequences." Jordan took a moment to make eye contact with each hunter. "The only reason we're having this discussion is because it's Belle, right?" Reluctantly, everyone nodded. "Then we do what we have to do... and we do what Belle wants us to do. Tomorrow we're leaving.

Once we're away from here..." Jordan's voice cracked from the overwhelming emotions she was feeling.

"You can't even say it!" Teisha said, angrily. "Don't we have any say in this?"

"This isn't a democracy. Belle wants to die like a hunter. She's asked that we honor the oath."

"Great! A child making an adult decision." Teisha tossed the stick she had been holding into the fire and stood. "And whether you all want to admit it, she is just a child. Still, if that's what she wants, that's what she'll get, but I don't have to like it."

"No, you don't," Jordan said. "Neither do I." Turning, she walked back into the hut where Belle was being kept. Her hand rested on the hilt of her sheathed knife. The others looked at each other, hopelessness and helplessness in their eyes.

CHAPTER 18

SUNRISE WAS STILL HOURS away when the hunters stirred and began preparing for their journey home. Although they hadn't found a new area for their people, there were several possibilities. The abundant wildlife provided enough food to sustain them for several years if they used their resources wisely.

"How do we handle Belle?" Teisha asked, once everyone was ready to leave. "You know we can't turn our back on her."

"I know. Tie her hands in front and attach two leads to them. I'll take one, you take the other. We should be able to control her movements if we keep her between us," Jordan said.

"For a while, if she cooperates. What if she doesn't? We're traveling in daylight. If she becomes unmanageable, it could attract other Phageian. What then?"

"We deal with it like we've dealt with everything else."

"Jordan..." Teisha rested her hand on her friend's shoulder. "No one here is questioning your decision. If that was one of us in there, we'd be grateful you cared so much and had the strength to keep a promise... but we still have to plan this out. Not just for our sake, but for Belle's. If we die before we kill her, she'll bear the brunt of our failure until someone else destroys her. No one will honor her like we will."

"I know. I'm grateful to all of you." Jordan looked into each hunter's eyes, her own glistening with unshed tears.

"Once we're a few hours out..." She couldn't finish, nor did she have to. Everyone nodded. "Teisha, you, Thomas and Marco get her ready. Be careful. She's been calm so far but the rage can come at any moment. I need to tell Derek and Zee we're leaving."

"I'd say they already know," Marco said, pointing at the crowd moving toward them. As usual, Derek and Zee were surrounded by cats. The large yellow-and-white one was trotting slightly in front, its tail held high.

"Wait here," Jordan told the hunters. She had only known the leaders for a few days, but in that short time she had learned to recognize subtle differences in their expressions and body language. Today they walked with a purposefulness she had never seen before. "Good morning, Zee, Derek," she said cautiously.

"Jor... dan leave?" Derek asked, looking beyond her at the others.

"Yes, our six days are up. We need to get home before the cold sets in."

"Cold. No... cold," he said pointing at himself.

Jordan's lips curled up at the corners.

"We're not so lucky. It can kill us."

"Not... good. Take... food," Derek said, motioning to two villagers who were carrying several small bundles.

"Thank you... for everything. I hope we can repay your kindness one day."

"One... day... today," Zee said, surprising Jordan. The hunter was never sure what the woman's role was in the village. She appeared and disappeared like an apparition, rarely speaking and never staying long in any spot.

"You... go. Child... stay."

There was no doubt Zee was referring to Belle.

"We can't leave her here," Jordan replied. "She's infected."

"Child... stay," Zee insisted.

Jordan shook her head.

"No, she has to come with us. All of us..." Jordan swung her arm around to indicate her team. "We made promises to each other. If anyone became infected we'd destroy them before they became Phageian. Belle's infected. We owe her that."

"You... owe... not... important. Belle... stay. We... care... for... child."

"No!" Carlos exclaimed, coming up to stand next to Jordan. The other hunters followed. They had been quietly listening to the exchange. "We're not leaving her here with you. I'd rather see her dead first."

"Child... dead... already," Zee said, her blue-white eyes never leaving Jordan's face. "You... destroy... dead. We... save... dead."

"We've seen what you —"

"Carlos! Shut up! We're not breaking our word to Belle," Jordan said, noticing the villagers were beginning to rock back and forth, a clear sign of agitation. "Zee, I saw what you did with those two Phageian. It was amazing, even honorable. This village, your people give us hope for the future, but you aren't where any of us would want to be. I can't imagine not feeling anything. I don't know if you remember what love is but it's not something I would give up even if it meant surviving the plague." *I wish I knew what you're thinking,* Jordan thought, searching Zee's face for some indication the woman understood. She saw nothing.

"Child... stay. Jor... dan come. Walk. Talk," Zee said, leaving no room for debate as she strode away.

"How much longer are we going to put up with this?" Carlos asked. "We should just get Belle and leave. It's not like they're that much of a threat." When Derek turned emotionless eyes to stare at Carlos, the hunter dropped his gaze. "I didn't mean that how it sounded," he mumbled.

259

"Carlos... angry," was all Derek said.

Jordan followed Zee. They disappeared into her hut.

CHAPTER 19

"JOR... DAN..." ZEE POINTED at a wooden crate in the corner. "Sit." She moved to a small chest next to it. Raising the lid, she removed a package wrapped in a rough woven cloth and handed it to the hunter. When Jordan unwrapped the object, she found a blue notebook and an old, cracked leather journal inside. Opening the notebook, Jordan could barely make out the faded words, Chronicles of a Property Manager.

"I don't understand," Jordan said, glancing up.

"No... portant... now," Zee replied. Taking it back, she pointed to the journal. "Portant."

The faded label was dated almost three decades before. On the first page was the name Zoie Morales, Chief Security Officer, Pharmaceutical Horizons. "Read," Zee ordered.

"Zee, we have to leave soon," Jordan said. "I don't have time for this."

"Stay... read," Zee insisted.

Realizing she wasn't getting anywhere, Jordan relented.

"Okay. I have to tell the others. Can I take this with me?"

Nodding her head once, Zee clasped Jordan's hands and folded the journal shut.

"Read... good... understand. Child... stay."

"We'll see. Thank you."

261

* * *

By the time Jordan returned to her team the sun was up. Many of the villagers had returned to their normal chores. The hunters were gathered in a circle in front of Belle's hut. Two villagers continued to guard the entrance.

"What's up?" Teisha asked, spotting Jordan before the others.

"I don't know. Zee gave me this to read."

"We don't have time for this shit," Carlos said. "The morning's half —"

"I doubt if we'll be able to leave unless I do what she wants."

"This doesn't make any sense. What's so important about that?"

"I don't know. Maybe nothing, "Jordan replied, "but I won't know until I read it. You guys might as well go help the villagers with their chores. Teisha, you stay with Belle for now. The rest of you set up a schedule to relieve Teisha in two hours. No one is to go near her, though."

"What a fuck —"

"Damn it, Carlos, can't you just do something without complaining? A few more hours off your ankle will do you good."

* * *

Jordan walked to a fallen log on the edge of the forest and slid to the ground, using it as a back rest. She didn't want to be disturbed. Opening the journal, she turned to the second page. It was obvious the entry was a continuation of another journal.

9-23-12 Professor Franklin Langley arrived today. He appears to be everything I heard about him. What a misogynistic ass! I don't think he finds women very useful. Still, if we can figure out what happened to J and T, I'll put up with his arrogance. The professor has indicated the cause of their illness is probably a bacteria infected by a virus (note to ask Victor again for the scientific name). Second theory — rabies. Will talk to locals to see if J or T was bitten by anything. Personal files show no record of complaints.

09-24-12 Spent the day looking for possible rabies sources or anything in J or T's personal effects that might help us discover the cause of their sickness. Found nothing. Langley spent most of the day spying on bugs and giving orders to the locals and employees. I'll try to contact dad tomorrow to get this jerk recalled. What a waste of time and money.

09-26-12 Nothing new to report. I spent most of the day trying to avoid Langley. Victor wasn't so lucky. Dad asked me to put up with the asshole a few more days.

09-27-11 Langley was to leave tomorrow but heard about some butterflies John was interested in. Bug people! They're all crazy. He says he wants to check them out so he'll be extending his stay another day. Nothing to report from locals or employees about J and T. No one else has come up with their symptoms. I received a message from the main compound that their behavior hasn't changed since they were transported there almost three weeks ago.

09-28-12 Langley returned with two jars of butterflies, raving about a new species. The man is nuts. Poor butterflies. They're better off dead. I'd like to figure out a way to release them but then he'd probably want to stay another day to catch some more. Sacrificing a few butterflies to get rid of Langley is worth the loss.

09-29-12 Langley and Victor left today. Good riddance to Langley. Camp has settled back down to normal routines. The Company is sending a new shift to replace the old. They should arrive tomorrow with my replacement. Dad has ordered me back home to resolve some security issues. I'll leave on Thursday. Can't wait to get out of this place. I feel like partying.

Jordan yawned. There were numerous gaps between dates.

10-5-12 Victor phoned to say J and T were dead. Professor Langley has returned to the States with samples of J's brains. Victor refused to tell me how the men died. Remembering a comment Langley made about putting them out of their misery, I think he may have convinced Victor to do something terrible. I intend to follow this up once I'm back home.

10-10-12 Dad called. Langley has J and T's symptoms. He attacked several people after being admitted to the hospital. The doctors said he passed out in his home the day he returned. He's in isolation.

10-23-12 Dad called. Langley escaped isolation yesterday. No one's found him yet. Horizons is sending out security teams to track him down. This could be a liability issue if anyone discovers he was working for us prior to getting sick.

10-30-12 Several people reported with symptoms similar to J and T. Scientists believe a bacteria may be causing the disease. They're calling it Phageian's Disease. I remember Professor Langley using a similar word. So far antibiotics and antiviruses have been unsuccessful in treating the infected. Maybe Langley was right. Maybe it's not just a bacteria or virus. Maybe it's that bacteriophage thing.

12-12-12 Haven't had time to write. News agencies reporting worldwide epidemic. People being advised not to panic. Yeah right!!!!!! Dad has ordered extra security for all our facilities. People are starting to panic.

The next entry was over a year later.

03-5-13 Found this journal today. Epidemic is pandemic. Millions dead. Scientists still haven't found the cause. People are terrified. At this rate, humans will be extinct in less than three years.

01-6-14 Tomorrow we're heading north. There are rumors of safe cities with walls and militia. Everyone we know is either dead or Phageian. God willing, we'll find some place safe. I know it's foolish to continue this journal but it provides me some relief and hope. If humanity survives, there will be a record of who caused this nightmare and what happened to Derek and me. Thankfully he was able to make it out of the Los Angeles compound before the rioters broke in.

Jordan wasn't aware of Teisha's arrival until her shadow blocked the sunlight.

"Find anything?" she asked.

"I'm not sure how important it is now but this explains how the infection might have spread. Unfortunately, the journal picks up in the middle of something so it isn't clear where it came from. Look here." Jordan pointed to Derek's name and then flipped to the first page. "Zoie Morales. Zoie is Zee. She and Derek go back a long ways."

"You think they were lovers?" Teisha asked.

"Maybe. It doesn't say, at least so far, but there was something between them a long time ago and I think it's still there. They run this place as a team."

"So I noticed. Do you mind if I read over your shoulder?"

Patting the ground next to her, Jordan shifted slightly to angle the journal in Teisha's direction as she plopped down next to her. Giving Teisha a quick outline of what she had read, she flipped back to where she had stopped reading.

I don't know the date, not that it's important anymore. Derek and I were attacked this morning while filling our canteens at the river. Three children caught us by surprise. At first we thought they were frightened. Maybe they were. We both got bit. I wonder, do Phageian fear? I don't know but these kids are afraid. They're huddled near the cave entrance we're camping in. I think they know we're infected now. They show no aggressive interest in us now.

Today We're heading out tomorrow. Going to follow the river upstream, north. We've decided to take the children with us. What else can we do? We can't go to any city now. The people will destroy all of us. Maybe we'll find a place we can build a home, safe from humans and Phageian until we find out what's going to happen to us.

Came across an abandoned asylum by a town yesterday but decided to avoid it. Several Phageian were wandering around. They probably wouldn't attack us but we can't take the chance, even if we are infected. We'll keep moving upstream. Derek denies feeling any different but his eyes are already turning white. The way he looks at me I suspect mine are too. I feel, I don't know how to describe it... just different... like I'm losing myself. I look at him and the kids and feel almost nothing or... I'm scared. They did this to me. Those kids I mean, but Derek should have seen

266

them. I know it's not his fault. I should have seen them too. I keep telling myself that I won't lose my humanity. I won't... not feel.

Derek talkt about kiling the childrn today. Was it yesterday we saw twon. Killing us to. I wont. I cant. Thots jumbled. It woud steel the last of our humnity. Somthings wrong with my thots. I wont kill the chidlren. I l kill Drek first.

3daze. maybe far enuf from tht place. What place. Far enuf. We found r hom.

Zoie's entries grew more scribbled and sometimes unintelligible. There were moments, however, when her thoughts were coherent even if her writing was awkward. The final entries gave Jordan a clearer picture of Zee and Derek's determination to survive and their struggle to keep their humanity.

Day agian Feel strang. Derek say too. Chilrn ok. Hungree. Cant thnk of nythg bt hman meet. Derk,me, no. chldern no mmet. Forc childrn us eat plnts. Fwnd clr clr space. Bldt home.

cravnins gonne chldrn derk me good plnts good

2 arrved. No intrsted in us tryng fede plnts

Cats cats. Cats not like chldrn cats bte chldrn. Derk me cats like yllow white cat lead

Tird cnt think well Mabe last tyme rite hom mnay biggr. Mor come. We grw foof. we serviv. 1 day at tme.

"Wow!" Teisha said. "That explains a lot but leaves a lot of questions unanswered. I can't believe that eating plants kept them from completely turning. And what's with the cat? It can't be the same one that bit Belle."

Jordan shook her head.

"Not unless it's a Phageian cat, and that's a scary thought. Cats can live a long time but she's probably a descendent. Derek and Zee have survived a lot. They

267

created this village without needing walls. We still hide behind ours."

"Yeah. But how? Have they really found a cure? Or is it some genetic resilience to the disease? For sure they figured something out that science couldn't."

"Like you said, more questions than answers. At least it gives us hope," Jordan said.

"So where does this leave us and Belle?" Teisha asked.

"I don't know." Jordan closed the journal and rose to her feet. "Have everyone meet me at the hut. I need to talk with Zee."

* * *

Jordan found Derek and Zee near the garden watching several workers dig up the soil. Before reading the journal she really hadn't thought of the two as anything but the leaders of the village. Now she looked at them with a new respect. They had made a home for themselves and their people. And there was a subtle intimacy she hadn't picked up on before.

"Zee, Derek, can I talk to you?" she asked. Emotionless eyes turned to stare at her. Jordan handed Zee the journal. "This is about you two... and this," she said, gesturing around the village. Neither acknowledged her observation. Jordan sighed. "I don't know how you accomplished all of this but you've done an amazing job of building this place and you've made us feel welcome." *In your own strange way,* Jordan thought. "You've also given us hope that there might be a cure for people."

"Jor... dan friend," Derek said. "Jor... dan stay. Co... pan... en stay."

"We can't. Our own people need us, now more than ever."

"You... go. Child... stay," Zee said.

268

"I... I need to talk to the others. We made her a promise. And to each other. Just as you two did to each other and the children when you first came here. Ours was that if any of us became infected we'd kill the person before they turned Phageian. You understand what that means."

"Kill... Der... ek. Kill... me." Zee put her hand on her chest.

"Of course not. You really aren't Phageian." Swiping her hand through her hair, Jordan looked back toward the hunters standing by Belle's hut. "Well, you are but you aren't. Listen, I can't make this decision by myself. I'll talk to the others, but it's up to each of them to decide."

"Jor... dan." Zee reached out to touch Jordan's arm, surprising her. "Child... stay. Child... family... here. Not... yours... now."

Without thinking Jordan, patted the hand gently. The skin was cool and pale.

"I'll see what I can do."

* * *

The hunters were talking amongst themselves, their voices low.

"Have you explained everything to them?"

"Yeah. It's all very interesting but what's that got to do with us or Belle?" Carlos demanded.

"They want her to stay here... be one of them," Jordan said.

"Over my dead body!"

"Carlos, you're such an ass!" Thomas growled. "Let Jordan talk."

"Look, I don't know what's right or wrong, but no one can deny this is the safest place we've ever been. Belle would fit in and be safe here."

269

"So you're saying we should leave her with these... these things," Carlos said. "No matter how well they get along or how many vegetables they eat, they're Phageian."

"And no matter how good a hunter you are, you're an idiot," Teisha said. "Belle is more like them than us. These people get along together better than we do."

"Because they have no feelings... no souls."

"Since when did you become the expert on souls? Belle has a second chance at life."

"Fuck you, Teisha. This isn't life. It's some... some crazy weird parody. I'd rather see her dead than living as one of those emotionless **things**."

"Look who's talking," Teisha replied. "You've been on her case since we first started out. I'm not surprised you're so anxious to kill —"

"You bitch!" Carlos lunged at Teisha but was grabbed by Marco and Thomas.

"Let him go. I'll carve his —"

"Stop it!" Jordan yelled, fed up with the continual bickering. "Carlos, you're quick to point out that these people don't have feelings. Well, if you're an example of what feelings are about, they're a hell of a lot better off than us. Why are you so anxious to kill Belle? Because she isn't who you want her to be?"

"We took an oath," Carlos mumbled.

"Yes, and it was based on what we knew about Phageian then. Things have changed. We know there are some who are different. I don't know if they have feelings like us but I can't help but believe they must on some level. Why else would they want to keep us from taking her? They know what we're planning. They don't talk much but they aren't stupid." Jordan turned to the others. "I know I normally make the decisions but this is different. We took an oath. Each of you has to decide for yourself what is more important, your oath or Belle's future."

"It doesn't seem like much of a difference, Jordan," Thomas said. "Either way she's dead to us."

"To us, yes... but dead, no. These villagers, they have lives. Maybe not what we'd want but at least they don't live in fear every day. They are more of a family than we are."

"That's true. What the hell! I already said I wasn't going to be the one to kill her."

"Marco?"

"I'm with Thomas."

"I'd like to come back one day to see her, even if she's just a gardener. I don't think she really had it in her to be a hunter," Teisha said.

Jordan turned to Carlos.

"It's up to you."

"I gave my word as a hunter. I'll keep my word as a hunter."

Pulling her knife from her sheath, Jordan flipped it around and held it hilt first to Carlos.

"Then do it now," she said. "No one will stop you and no one will think less of you if this is truly about your oath."

Carlos looked at the knife and then at each of his comrades. Finally he looked at Zee and Derek. Neither gave any indication they would interfere with his decision.

"I have my own knife." Spinning, he stormed off, ignoring the villagers guarding the entrance where Belle was held. Minutes later he emerged, glared at the group and disappeared into their hut. The others followed without saying anything. True to Jordan's word, each had made a choice. Each would have to live with it no matter how painful it was.

CHAPTER 20

SAYING GOODBYE WAS harder than Jordan had ever imagined, even though she was anxious to get home. Derek was waiting outside their hut, which was unusual. Jordan estimated it was still a couple of hours before sunrise. Normally the villagers didn't stir that early.

"Food," Derek said, holding out several bundles. "No... meat."

Jordan smiled.

"That's okay. I think I'll stay away from that for a while. Thank you, Derek. Where's Zee? I'd like to say goodbye."

"No... see... Zee. Zee... there." He pointed to the path that led to the butchery and the pens.

"Oh." Jordan wasn't sure what to say, feeling disappointed. "Well, would you tell her I said thanks?" Derek stared at her, his blue-white eyes giving no clue to what he was thinking. "Goodbye," Jordan said, turning to her team. "Let's go."

"Wait, Jor...dan. Zee... give... this." Derek handed Jordan a small bundle wrapped in worn brown hide, probably deerskin. "Zee say take."

Jordan recognized the object as one of the books Zee had hidden away in her chest.

"I can't take this. It belonged to her family."

"This... Zee... family. That... no...more," Derek explained. "Take... yours. Go."

Knowing it was useless to argue, Jordan took the bundle and tucked it in her small pack. "Okay, but I'm bringing it back later, after I've finished reading it." Derek nodded and then left to join the small group of villagers standing a few yards away.

The hunters walked to the edge of the clearing before stopping to look back at what they were leaving behind.

"Do you think we'll ever come back here?" Teisha asked. "I'll be glad to get home but I'm going to miss these people. Why, I haven't a clue."

"Me too!" Marco admitted.

Jordan nodded as she watched Derek shuffle toward other villagers who were gathering for the ritual morning meeting. She had seen them do that seven times and still didn't understand what was happening. Words were rarely spoken but everyone understood what needed to be done, even the newest member. He had been assigned to tilling the gardens.

"I'll be back," she said. "There's a lot we can learn from them."

"Not me!" Carlos headed into the woods. He clearly wanted all of this behind him.

"Do you think he'll ever get over his decision?" Teisha asked.

"One day," Jordan said. "We all eventually learn to live with ourselves. Come on! The journal hinted about a town lying three or four days from here. Maybe closer, depending on how fast they were moving. We know it's not the way we came. They followed the river upstream so we'll follow it downstream. If it's like she described, it could be just what we're looking for."

Following Carlos, the hunters disappeared into the woods, their thoughts already on what lay ahead of them. Jordan thought of an old phrase her mom had said to her as a child... something about 'miles to go before they sleep...' only for her it was miles to go before she was back in the arms of Felicia. Jordan had decided that once their people were resettled in a new place, if they found one, she was cutting back on her hunting trips. Gardening didn't seem like that bad a trade at her age.

EPILOGUE

"Are you really going to give up hunting?" Felicia asked, handing Jordan a steaming bowl of vegetable stew. The hunter had returned home the night before, too tired to do anything but fall asleep once she had washed up. The next morning she gave Felicia a quick rundown of their expedition before reporting to Eli. Hearing of her return, he called for an emergency meeting of the Council.

The food situation was reaching a crisis stage. People were starting to panic, some threatening to seize the remaining supplies by force. It didn't help that two teams were unsuccessful in their search for a new home and the other was still missing. After Jordan made her report, the villagers were more optimistic. Fear and desperation turned to hope. Anger was replaced by optimism. By the end of the meeting, everyone was feeling good.

"Probably," Jordan said, savoring her first warm meal in several days. "After we're settled in our new home. Thank god Zee kept that journal. It provided the clues we needed to find that place."

"I never thought I'd look forward to living in a sanatorium," Felicia said. "Although it somehow seems fitting. It's a crazy world out there. How long do you think it'll take to move everyone?"

"Five or six weeks. Maybe less. My team will split up. They'll lead small groups consisting of different tradesmen. Once the other hunters know the way, things will move quickly. Eli and the Council will organize the people and do the assignments."

"It's going to take several days for the first group to get ready," Felicia said.

"I know. Teisha's agreed to head out in three days with a work crew. They'll secure and clean the place up. By the time —"

"What do you mean by **clean**?"

"It was a secured facility, Felicia. Some of the patients were never released. There're probably thirty or more skeletons in some of those cells. "

"That's awful! Who would leave people like that?"

"Desperation makes us do terrible things. If the facility and town were overrun..." Jordan shrugged. "I'd rather die of thirst than get torn up by a horde of Phageian. Anyway, we'll never know. What's important is that the basement is loaded with pallets of canned and dry goods, enough food to feed us for a year, maybe longer. There's also a warehouse nearby, filled with boxes. We didn't have time to check it out." Jordan yawned.

"You ready for bed?" Felicia asked.

Jordan shook her head. Her eyes wandered to the notebook lying on the table. Picking it up, she opened it slowly, not wanting to damage any of the old, yellowed pages.

"Something troubling you?" Felicia scooted her chair closer and leaned her head on lover's shoulder.

"Not really. I was just thinking about Zee and Derek. It's hard to believe our people share a common past with a small village of Phageian. I hope everyone remembers that once we're re-established."

"We'll be there to remind them," Felicia said. "Are you still thinking about what happened to Belle? Any regrets?"

"I'll always have regrets, but I know she's in a better place."

"That doesn't make it any easier. I miss her."

"Me too." Jordan's voice choked from the unshed tears. She had tried unsuccessfully to put Belle out of her mind. Her priority was the living, not the dead.

"Do you think you'll ever go back to that village?"

"One day. After things settle down. Besides, I promised I'd return this to Zee. I don't think she intended that I keep it forever."

"I wonder why she gave you the chronicles instead of that journal you told me about."

"I don't know. Maybe it's her way of saying I'd be welcomed back. She's a hard one to figure out. You know, I managed to read this on our trek home. It... I don't know, it made me think about you, and us." Jordan turned a few more pages before stopping to pull out an old, yellowed envelope. Opening it carefully, she pulled out a letter and unfolded it. "This in particular." She began reading aloud.

I feel like an old woman unable to do the things I once dreamt about, and yet I am so young, so filled with dreams. You sit there in your favorite chair, only a few feet away, pretending nothing is wrong, and I pretend with you. All I had to do was reach out and tell you how I felt and you would have understood. Sadly, life has a way of making the foolish wise when it is too late, and the wise, shy. That is now me. I loved you before we ever met. We were words in a chatroom. And yet, somehow we connected. We gambled on instincts, on luck and on our personal faith in ourselves that the world was there to be explored and conquered. Well, conquer it we did and we've paid a price. I am losing my memory and you are losing me, at least a part of me. I love you, Suze. I love you with all my heart. There are years that separate us but there will never be distances between us. We are blessed with our memories, and when mine fade, when I become too forgetful and no longer seem to know you, believe in me. If I never again say the words "I love you!" never doubt that I do and always will.

Felicia frowned.

"I don't get the connection. Whoever these people are, they are nothing like us."

Jordan set the notebook on the table and wrapped her arms around Felicia, pulling her close.

"They're everything like us. I don't mean literally but what a love they must have had. We have that. I love you, Fels," she said, her voice husky with emotion. "This made me realize how much I've taken your love for granted."

For several moments the two women sat silently, each lost in her own thoughts. Finally, Felicia pushed slightly away from Jordan.

"I think we both have... And on that note, you need to get some rest. Tomorrow's going to be a busy day," Felicia said.

"Good idea."

"Jordie? When you return the book, would you take me along?"

Jordan pulled Felicia to her feet and nudged her toward the bed.

"Sure. I think you'd like Zee. You two have a lot in common."

"How's that?"

"Well, for one thing, she's a gard'ner." Jordan ducked when Felicia threw a pillow at her.

"Ha! Very funny! But you're right. I was actually thinking more about Belle, though. Even if she doesn't remember me, I'd like to see her again."

"She'll remember you, Fel. She'll remember you."

A Time

for Change

THE HOWLING IN THE distance seemed to be getting closer. Shawna pushed the curtain aside to stare at the distant mountaintop. Spring had arrived early but the snow-covered peaks still glistened as the early afternoon rays darted between the swift-moving clouds.

"They're more animated than normal. I hope it doesn't have anything to do with Phageian," Shawna said, letting the curtains slip from her fingers. She turned to look at the woman lying on the small cot a few feet away. "Is there anything I can do to help you?" The gold-flecked eyes were filled with so much pain Shawna could barely contain her unshed tears.

"No, it's manageable at the moment, and I wouldn't worry about Phageian. Even wolves don't mess with those things. The pack would be long gone by now."

"That's good to know. How about some cool water or a little soup? I'm making a nice brothy stew."

"Not right now. Maybe later."

Shawna sighed. What good was she if she couldn't help her best friend? As a Healer, she had the ability to ease pain; cure it if necessary. Perhaps that was the problem. **Necessary** was often subjective and even her gift had its limitations, especially if the patient was uncooperative. Sometimes her friend Roxxie could be so frustrating. Shawna wished one of her Sisters was around to advise her, but she hadn't seen a Singer in years. Perhaps she was the last of her kind. The thought was frightening.

"Are you all right?" Roxxie asked.

"I was just thinking."

"About the Sisterhood?"

Shawna made a wry face.

"You're always so perceptive. I'll bet some people find that annoying."

"No one's complained yet, and I wouldn't worry about your Sisters. They can take care of themselves."

"I know," Shawna said.

But even they can't cure Phageian or themselves if they become infected.

The Sisterhood of Singers was a small group of women gifted with the unique ability to cure illnesses and diseases with song. Their mission was to move humanity toward enlightenment by helping individuals who could most impact its future. Often this meant saving the worst of the worst. Governed by a series of Laws, the Sisters understood that progress occasionally came at a terrible price. The **Law of Balance** declared 'To move forward, one must step backward.' In simpler terms, evil and good were of equal importance; neither could exist without the other. The most horrible atrocity brought about changes for the better; at least that was what they thought until the Phageian pandemic outbreak. Nothing good had come from that! Even the Singers' skills were useless against the dead.

"Why do you continue to put yourself at risk?" Shawna asked, deciding to change the subject. "Take a break for a while."

"I could no more do that than you, Shawny. I am who I am. Besides, my risks are no greater than yours," Roxxie replied.

Shawna's brows furrowed slightly then cleared.

"Of course they are! You don't have to suffer like this. I can at least stop the pain. Why do you have to be so stubborn?"

"Stopping the pain won't cure the illness. I know you want to help but it will only delay the inevitable. The sooner this is over with, the better. Besides, the pain is tolerable, and I'm not jeopardizing your health under any circumstances."

"Healing is exhausting, not life threatening," Shawna said.

"Any time a Healer deals with the human condition, it can be life-threatening. More so now than ever before, considering this epidemic," her friend replied quietly and then flinched slightly before continuing. "These are extremely dangerous times. With the world in chaos, people are desperate to discover a cure or vaccine against Phageianism. If anyone found out about you, you'd become a lab rat, locked in some dark basement. You know what happened to Mira? She..." Roxxie didn't finish the thought, shaking her head slightly.

"What?" Nicole, Shawna's partner, had been sitting quietly off to the side listening to the two women. The Healer simply waved her lover's question off nonchalantly. "Who is Mira?" Nicole asked.

"That was a long time ago," Shawna said. "And had nothing to do with Phageian. Roxxie likes to be a bit overly dramatic sometimes."

Roxxie gave Shawna a knowing glance, even managing a small smirk. "Overly dramatic? Please, you know better. You Healers think you can save the world, and maybe you will eventually. You just can't save everyone, including yourselves. If any of you are captured, all in the Order are threatened."

"Well, I won't be forced to help anyone. Neither will my Sisters."

Brown eyes speckled with gold turned to look at the woman quietly sitting in a chair several feet away. Nicole had been mostly listening to the conversation between

283

Roxxie and Shawna. Normally reserved, she now stared intently at Shawna, her eyes never wavering from her lover's face. She clearly wanted to ask a question but for whatever reason decided not to. Roxxie kept her own pain-filled gaze on Nicole while she continued to direct her conversation at the Healer.

"Anyone can be forced to do something they don't want. It only takes the right persuasion. Would you refuse to do something if Nicole's life depended on your choice?"

Shawna turned to meet Nicole's questioning look. Nothing in the eyes gave away what her partner was thinking or feeling.

"I... I'm not sure. I hope I'd be strong enough to do what is right, even if meant her death." Again looking at Nicole, she saw the slight nod of approval.

"I would expect nothing less," Nicole murmured softly.

"I hope for your sakes it never comes to that," Roxxie said quietly and then groaned, clenching her hands into tight balls, battling another spasm of pain. "I'm sorry but I need to rest for a while. Perhaps we can talk again in a little while. It's a good way to distract me from my... discomfort."

"Of course!" Shawna exclaimed. "I'm so sorry. I've been negligent in my duties. Sleep," she whispered, gently stroking her friend's thick salt-and-pepper-colored hair.

* * *

"I wish there was more we could do for her," Shawna said, motioning for Nicole to follow her out of the bedroom and into the kitchen.

"Even Healers have their limitations. Roxxie doesn't want your help. In fact she seems especially concerned about you for some reason. Does she know something I don't?

Picking up a ladle, the Healer dipped it into the boiling pot of soup and pulled out a sample to taste.

"Hmmm. Needs a little more salt."

"Shawna?"

"Roxxie knows a lot of things about me you don't. We all have previous lives, things we don't like to talk or think about. Besides, this isn't about me or our pasts. This is about her. She needs help. I could relieve her pain."

"She's refused it. All we can do is give her our support, even if it's just our company. I'm surprised she was able to find you considering how isolated we are and the condition she's in."

"Roxxie's strong-willed and determined, not to mention she has great instincts. She's always been able to find me, even in the remotest of places. And it makes sense for her to come to me when she's in pain. I'm a Healer."

"Yes, a Healer who isn't allowed to heal. That makes no sense."

"Oh. Well..." Shawna busied herself stirring the soup. "She's too independent."

"That makes even less sense. Roxxie's an intelligent woman. She came to you for a reason. Logic says it should be because of your gift."

"You know, Nicole, not all things can be explained by logic. We're close. We've known each other forever."

"Forever? Even you aren't **that** old," Nicole said, chuckling. Healers were known for longevity, often living two or three hundred years.

"Old enough."

"Maybe I should buy you a wheelchair... Okay, okay," Nicole said, holding up her hand to ward off a mock blow. "Just kidding! Where did you two first meet?"

"Well, believe it or not, in the woods while I was on a camping trip. I had just finished a difficult **calling** and decided to take a much-needed break. The mountains seemed a great place to replenish my energy. I've always loved communing with nature. You want something to drink?" Shawna asked, walking over to the icebox.

"Berryjuice."

"Here," Shawna said, tossing her a small, corked bottle. "That should hold you for a while."

"You were saying?" Nicole asked, taking a sip.

"I was saying," Shawna continued, "I went camping. On the third evening I heard a rustling in the underbrush. At first I thought it was a bear or something."

"You weren't worried about Phageian?"

"No. I didn't know they existed until I met Roxxie. The epidemic was in its early stages. Anyway, it wasn't an animal, not that I was worried. Healers and animals have always had an affinity. We believe they sense our aversion to killing."

"But not to eating meat," Nicole teased.

"Of course we eat meat. Most Singers lean toward vegetarianism, but there's nothing like a good steak. Now, do you mind if I finish my story?"

"Sorry."

Shawna sighed and shook her head.

"No you're not. As I was saying, instead of a wild animal it was Roxxie, surrounded by hundreds of butterflies. It was like a vision from a fairytale. Needless to say, I was stunned. More so when she greeted me by name."

"I can imagine. Did she say how she knew you? And why the butterflies?"

Shawna laughed.

"The butterflies? She said she came across them in a meadow earlier in the day. They left as soon as they saw me. It actually hurt my feelings. I love animals and they usually like me. She said she had heard rumors about a single woman wandering through the woods and decided to check it out. That's when I found out about the epidemic."

"I'll bet she thought you were nuts."

"Naïve is more like it. When she realized I hadn't heard of Phageian she offered to keep me company. How could I refuse? She was gorgeous. Still is."

"Hey," Nicole objected. "I'm supposed to be your girlfriend."

"Well, you weren't around then," Shawna teased.

"Unfortunately not. Did she know you belonged to the Sisterhood?"

"I don't know and I didn't ask. Bringing it up would probably have aroused her curiosity."

"Makes sense, although I'm surprised you didn't try to find something out."

"I'm quite good at self-control, thank you. Besides, we had more important things to talk about. I wanted to know about the Phageian problem. Roxxie brought me up to speed on what was happening. We, well we sort of bonded. I liked her a lot." Shawna grinned broadly.

"Uh huh! How much is a lot?" Nicole asked between gulps of juice.

"Fifteen days and nights a lot. She knew the forests," Shawna hesitated, trying to think of a comparison, "like you knew electronics and all that techy stuff. Roxxie took me places you wouldn't believe; undiscovered caves, hidden waterfalls, ancient trees over two-thousand years old. And she took me back to that meadow with the butterflies. There must have been millions of them flying around. It was like staring at an enormous kaleidoscope. A person could lose themselves in its beauty if they watched them long enough. Then there were the other animals and plants. They weren't afraid of us. Some even allowed me to touch them."

"Animals or plants?"

"Animals, silly. Not that any plants objected." The corner of Nicole' mouth twitched. "It was a magical experience that I'll never forget. Those days with Roxxie were some of the happiest of my life. I'd like to go back there one day... if I knew the way."

"Roxxie can't tell you?"

"I asked her once, a few years later. She said she didn't remember so I dropped it."

Nicole cocked her head sideways giving Shawna a speculative look.

"So why did you break up?"

"Our destinies. I had my **callings**. She had hers."

"But she isn't a Healer. Why would she have **callings**?"

"Roxxie's a healer in her own way —"

A pain-filled moan interrupted Shawna. She and Nicole dashed back into the bedroom.

* * *

"What is it, Roxxie? Sweetie? What can we do to help?"

"Get me a different body," Roxxie replied and then grimaced.

Wolves howled mournfully, momentarily distracting the Healer.

"Don't they ever take a break?" Shawna muttered.

Roxxie gave her friend a curious look.

"You've always said they have the most beautiful voices in the world."

"They do. I'm just being foolish."

The pain-filled eyes cleared momentarily.

"Stop worrying about me, Shawny. You know this won't last much longer."

"I know, but I hate seeing you hurt like this. And telling me it won't last very long isn't very comforting. Suffering like this isn't necessary."

"It is." Roxxie groaned. "And who are you to talk? How many times have you felt such pain?"

"It's not the same," Shawna objected. "We don't feel the pain of our patients. At least not in the real sense. I sing them back to health. My song travels deep into their core to rebuild damaged cells. That's all."

"That's not all and you know it. You draw small amounts of energy from everything around you when you can, but what if there's no one?"

"We can use our own reserves if we have to. Safely, of course."

"Right! Safely. That's the key word, isn't it?" Shawna glanced uncomfortably at Nicole. There were several occasions when the Healer had returned home so exhausted she could barely walk. "I thought so," Roxxie added, nodding her head knowingly.

"That's different!" Shawna objected.

"How?" Nicole cut in. "You never said —"

"You've always known my missions could be dangerous," Shawna interrupted. "If people knew —"

"I'm not talking about those hunting you and you know it. Could you die if you used too much of your reserves?"

Shawna took a deep breath and sighed.

"It's... possible."

"Possible? And you've never mentioned this before?" Nicole glared angrily at Shawna.

"I've never really thought about it. Besides, it wouldn't make any difference. I'm not going to stop what I'm doing because of some faulty mechanism —?"

"Mechanism? You're not a machine!"

"No, she's not, but she is a Healer," Roxxie cut in. "Not even she can change that. Now, I hate having you wait on me but —"

"Oh my god!" Shawna exclaimed, seeing the pained expression of her friend. "Some caregiver I am! I'll be right back."

Dashing out of the room, Shawna headed for the kitchen.

"You really care for her, don't you?" Nicole asked.

"More than life itself!" Roxxie pressed her right palm against her chest. "Pain sucks," she murmured. "It shows, doesn't it? My caring."

"Blatantly."

Roxxie blushed.

"We sort of have a history."

"Sort of? Shawna told me you were lovers a long time ago."

"She said that?"

"In so many words, yes. She said your different destinies are what ended the relationship. Knowing her as I do, she'd never have let you go if she loved you that much. I suspect you're a lot like her that way."

"Perhaps," Roxxie said. "We were definitely in love, but too altruistic. Our missions were more important. We didn't have the courage to try for both."

Nicole looked at the open doorway and then back at Roxxie.

"Or were just too young to figure it out."

The gold-flecked brown eyes widened in surprise.

"You're very perceptive."

"Knowing Shawna, that's a no-brainer. She doesn't give up on anything."

"That's her." Roxxie seemed to hesitate for a moment, and then motioned for Nicole to sit. "Have you ever heard the word Quasiera?"

Surprisingly, Nicole nodded.

"A long time ago. My mother was a librarian for over forty years. She loved sifting through old books researching ancient mythologies and cultures. It was her passion. Whenever she discovered something especially interesting she'd get all excited. That was one legend she seemed particularly fascinated with. Mostly there were vague hints of an ancient race that was exterminated several thousand years ago. No one's ever found any evidence of their existence, though."

"They existed," Roxxie said. "And still do. The few that survived the last massacres disappeared deep into the most ancient forests. Even then they were hunted down. Fortunately, most weren't found."

"Who massacred them?"

"You believe me?" Roxxie asked, her voice filled with both wonder and pain. "It's not often I find someone so easily accepting."

"I suspect it's not often you tell this story. There's no reason not to believe you."

"People killed them. They thought the Quasiera were demons or servants of evil. Humans thoughtlessly destroyed almost an entire race without compunction and then excused their behavior as necessary, rather than admit to their mistakes."

"And what was it about the Quasiera that terrified the people so much that they wanted to annihilate this race? Your race, I'm assuming?"

"Ignorance. Fear. All the things that make them afraid of the dark," Roxxie replied, showing no surprise at Nicole's conclusion. Before she could continue, Shawna entered the bedroom carrying a tray with a bowl of soup and a glass of water.

"Here you go," she said, putting it on the table next to Roxxie. "Are you able to sit up?"

"I'll manage." With Nicole's help, Roxxie shifted into a more comfortable position for drinking the soup. "Smells good," Roxxie said. "What's in it?"

"Nothing magical. Chicken, carrots, tubers, onions, wild garlic and a few herbs that should help the pain subside a little. It won't poison you," Shawna teased.

"You'd have to hunt far and wide for something that could actually do that." A knowing glance passed between the Healer and her friend.

"So," Shawna said, "did I miss anything important? Some deep, dark secret?" She glanced inquiringly from Roxxie to Nicole.

"Nothing you don't already know," Roxxie replied, taking a sip of soup. Rather than use the spoon, she picked the bowl up and drank from its edge. "Wow! This is delicious. You're cooking's improved over the years."

"I've always been a good cook," Shawna responded indignantly.

"My point exactly. Good, not great." Setting the bowl back on the tray, Roxxie lifted the glass and drained it of water. "I was telling Nicole about the Quasiera."

"That old story?" The Healer shook her head. "I'm surprised Nicole hasn't fallen asleep by now," she jested. When Roxxie shook her own head in mock disgust, Shawna leaned over and planted another kiss on her friend's cheek. "You know I'm joking. It's such a sad story. I cry whenever I think about it. I'll go get you a refill." Picking up the glass, she rushed from the room. Nicole wasn't able to hide her surprise at her lover's sudden exit.

"She wasn't kidding about crying," Roxxie said. "Shall I continue?"

"If you want. I know you're still in a lot of pain. It might be better if you rested again. We can continue this later."

"Later will be too late. This disease is progressing faster than I thought. In a few hours I'll be gone. It's best you hear everything now. Yes, I am Quasiera, one of the last of my race. There's only a few hundred living in North America. I've heard that scattered groups exist in the remote jungles of South America and some mountains in Eastern Europe. I hope the rumors are true. If not, my species will be extinct by the end of this century. Even we can't live forever."

"Nothing ever does," Nicole said.

Roxxie nodded. "That we know of. As I was saying, I am Quasiera. It means, well, literally, 'One who touches the suffering,' or at least that's about as close an interpretation as anyone can come up with in human language."

"Meaning you're like Shawna, a Healer?"

"Not even close. We can't heal anything. Nor do we want to. There's too great a price to pay. Healers, especially Singers like Shawny, can be drawn into such dark places in the mind. Some never find their way out. They remain as lost as their patient. Another Healer might be able to lead them back to the light, if they're lucky. No, Quasiera never intrude into the minds of others, even if we could."

Nicole shook her head.

"I don't understand."

"We like to think of ourselves as teachers. Perhaps **guides** is a better word."

"Guides to where?"

"Not to where, but to how," Roxxie said. "We offer people who are suffering from extreme physical pain better ways to cope. They learn they have choices, hope for those strong enough to believe in themselves, and acceptance for the ones too tired to fight any longer."

"Humans are capable of that already. Why would they need Quasiera?"

"Why do you need Shawna? You're a capable, self-sufficient woman. Why did you partner with her? **Need** can't always be explained. It doesn't have to be logical. It can even be debatable, but it can't ever be ignored. In a way, Healers and Quasiera have a similar mission: Helping the living. We both feel their suffering and try to help. The difference is Healers cure, we can't. But we do feel their pain. It becomes our pain. Their illness becomes our illness."

"Figuratively," Nicole said, nodding her understanding.

"No. Literally," Roxxie replied.

"I still don't understand."

Roxxie sighed and picked up the bowl of soup to take a few more sips. Whatever Shawna had put into the warm broth soothed her insides, easing the pain in her chest. Taking a deep hesitant breath, she tested her body, relishing the momentary relief.

"Shawny makes a hell of a brew," she said. "She should patent this stuff. It'd go a long way to ease people's suffering."

"Healers have no interest in financial gains. They hoard their secrets just so pharmaceuticals don't try to profit from them. That's another trait you have in common with Healers. You dole out tidbits of information, but never quite disclose everything. It's annoying when Shawna does that."

Roxxie cocked her head, giving Nicole a curious look.

"You aren't very patient, are you?"

"I have my moments. Is this some sort of test? If so, I don't like games."

"It's not a test Nicole. Why would I do that? It's simply the way I explain things. If I'm frustrating you we can stop. Our story, my story, must be explained in a certain way to be fully understood."

"Sorry. Please go on. I'm listening."

"Thank you." Roxxie closed her eyes momentarily. "Where was I? Oh yes, what do we do? Our bodies can emulate certain characteristics of things around us. It's an adaptation that makes humans more comfortable. Basically, the longer I'm around you the more I become like you." Roxxie shifted in the bed, clenching her jaw to keep from groaning. "Could you ask Shawna to come in here?"

Nicole frowned. "Do you need more herbs? I can..." Roxxie closed her eyes and shook her head. "Shawna," Nicole called out. "Can you come in here?"

Seconds later, Shawna entered, drying her hands with a towel. "What?"

"Roxxie wants you."

"Really?" The Healer gave Roxxie a peculiar look. "What? I'm not giving away my soup secrets if that's what you want," she teased, trying not to appear too worried. "Have you changed your mind about me helping you?"

"No," Roxxie said quietly and then doubled over as an excruciating spasm ripped across her insides. Her breathing became more labored as the pressure on her chest increased. "I... I need to lie back down a bit."

When Shawna reached forward to touch her forehead, Roxxie jerked away. "No, you can't do that. This isn't your pain to bear."

"But I can ease it." Shawna's eyes watered with unshed tears. "Even a little would help."

"The pain's passing. I'm fine. Actually, I just wanted to tell you the soup is helping and hoped I could get another bowl while I finish telling Nicole my story." When Shawna hesitated, Roxxie touched her hand lightly, barely making contact with the skin. "Shawny, I'm fine. Really!" The Healer sighed and left. "I worry about her. She cares too much sometimes," Roxxie told Nicole.

"I know, but that's who she is."

Roxxie nodded and then motioned back toward the chair.

"Sit. There isn't much more to tell you. As I said, I don't have a lot of time left. Where was I?" Roxxie closed her eyes, clearly gathering her thoughts. "Ah yes. Our traits. As I was saying, Quasiera can take on certain traits of who or what's around them. We normally try not to. It plays havoc with our minds and bodies. Sometimes though, it's necessary. Especially with the sick. It's imperative we understand what they feel."

Nicole's eyes widened the moment she realized what Roxxie meant.

"You're not just talking about traits, are you? Your body develops the same diseases."

Roxxie nodded.

"And suffer the same symptoms. How else can we truly know what they are experiencing? It's the only way to guide them through their journey. Hopefully help them grow stronger, and if not, at least be with them until they reach their final destination."

"Do you only choose terminally ill people?"

"Not at all. We don't know where each journey ends. My last contact is doing quite nicely. It was tough on her, though. She still has a long battle ahead, but she's a fighter. Oh, and Quasiera don't just help humans. All living things concern us. Plants are a bit awkward, but even they need assistance now and then."

"How can you help a plant? Your biological make-up shouldn't be compatible with them."

"That's actually an erroneous assumption. The fact that we are able to replicate within ourselves something that is inside another entity... well, that seems inconceivable. Yet we do. Who or what that entity is becomes insignificant, don't you think?"

Nicole sat quietly for a few moments considering the question.

"I guess it makes sense in a crazy sort of way. What happens to Quasiera after their journey ends? You're still in a lot of pain so you obviously can't return to your old self and start over."

"What makes you think that?" Roxxie asked.

"You'd have done it already. Suffering serves no purpose. If your last contact has moved on and is getting better, why aren't you?"

"Things are never simple. Obviously if she died, I'd be dead. Some I've helped have died."

"So what prevented you from dying then?"

Roxxie shrugged.

"Resilience. Luck. Who knows? Sometimes we run out of both!"

"Is that what's happening now?"

"I don't know. We never know our fate any more than those we help." Roxxie hesitated for a moment. "That's why I need to ask a favor of you."

"What?"

"Leave me alone for a while. Don't let Shawny back in here for two hours. When you do, if you can't awaken me, take my body into the woods and lay it by the stream. It's imperative I be naked. No clothes, nothing human or manmade must touch me. Shawna will want to. She'll be upset but under no circumstances must she be allowed near me once I'm placed on the earth. Any contact would kill her. Besides, there's nothing she could do to help me. Promise me!"

"I can do that. Then what?"

"Nothing. If Quasiera are near, they'll find me and take me home."

"And if they aren't?"

"In the end, it won't matter."

Roxxie closed her eyes.

Standing, Nicole walked to the door and then turned back to look at Roxxie. The woman was lying on her side with her eyes closed. They didn't need to be open for Nicole to see the pain Roxxie was in. The face said it all. Nicole hoped she would be able to sleep.

* * *

Shawna looked at the clock nervously.

"It's two hours."

Nicole motioned for Shawna to lead the way and followed her back into the bedroom. Roxxie appeared to be sleeping. When the Healer rushed over to her friend to check for a pulse, she found none.

"No!" she whispered. "No. Please, Roxxie, wake up! Don't do this to me!"

Nicole walked over and gently nudged Shawna to the side. She rechecked Roxxie's vitals and found nothing.

"I think she knew this would happen. She asked me to do her a favor before I left. She wanted us to take her body into the woods by the stream."

"Why?" the Healer asked, her voice choked with emotion.

"I don't know." Leaning down, Nicole picked Roxxie up, shifting her weight so she could cradle her in her arms. Roxxie was a slender woman, probably not weighing even a hundred pounds.

"Let me..." Shawna said.

"That's okay. She's not very heavy. Grab that flashlight. We may need it later."

Silently, Shawna followed Nicole into the forest. Roxxie's body was lowered onto a bed of leaves beneath an old oak tree. The sounds of animals and the bubbling stream filled the early night air. Nicole backed away, pulling Shawna with her.

"I have to tell her goodbye," Shawna said. Tears streamed down her cheeks.

"Say it from here. She said we were not to touch her."

"But —"

"No buts, Shawna." Nicole wrapped her arms around her lover and held her close. "It was her last request. We'll wait here for a while to see what happens. If Quasiera are near, they'll come for her."

"And if they don't, what then?"

"Then we leave her."

"I'm not going to do that! This isn't how it's supposed to happen."

"I know," Nicole replied softly. "I know."

An hour passed without either speaking. A small orange butterfly flitted from the dark forest, its wings flapping furiously. Passing over the still form lying on the ground, it hovered for a few moments and then flew back in the direction it had come from. Minutes later, another butterfly arrived, repeating the first one's behavior. Seconds later, it was joined by a large, white butterfly. Suddenly the air was alive with thousands of orange and black fluttering wings.

"Those are the same ones we saw in the valley," Shawna whispered, not wanting to draw attention to the two of them. "They have to be."

"Normally, I'd say it wasn't possible, but Roxxie wasn't normal," Nicole said. Both women jumped when a long, mournful cry broke the still night, followed by several more. Nicole and Shawna looked nervously around the clearing, searching for signs of the wolves.

"They sound close." Nicole drew Shawna firmly against her.

A low groan startled them.

Spinning, they looked toward Roxxie's still form. The white butterfly had settled on Roxxie's cheek. After taking a few steps, it rose into the air and soared away. Within seconds, all of the butterflies disappeared back into the forest.

Distracted, neither Shawna nor Nicole noticed the body had shifted. Now on its side, curled into a fetal position, it twitched and jerked several times, then again lay still. Another groan, barely noticeable, caught the women's attention.

Roxxie's arms and legs stiffened. Thighs trembled and began thickening while the calves shrank disproportionately. The hands and feet transformed into round padded paws with sharp, pointed nails. Her jaw and nose became an elongated muzzle with long canine teeth protruding between closed lips. Salt-and-pepper-colored hair sprang up from the skin, eventually covering Roxxie's entire body with a lush, thick coat of fur. From the base of her backbone, a long hairy tail emerged. The transformation took only minutes. When it was over, the sleek, lean form of a wolf lay where once there had been a woman.

Breaking free of Nicole's embrace, Shawna ran to Roxxie and wrapped her arms around the animal's neck.

"Don't!" Nicole called out, her reactions too slow to stop the Healer.

"You scared me to death," Shawna cried out, ignoring Nicole's warning. "The last time wasn't like this."

"Transformations are never the same," Roxxie growled, nuzzling Shawna's neck with her nose. "This one was worse than normal, but I'm fine now."

"Thank goodness," the Healer said, turning back to Nicole. "She's beautiful, isn't she!"

Nicole glanced at Shawna and then back at Roxxie. She had heard of shapeshifters, but never believed in their existence.

"You've seen her do this before?"

Shawna nodded.

"Once. It wasn't this bad. I thought you were dead," the Healer said, turning back to Roxxie.

"That is always a possibility, Shawny. I'm sorry I worried you so much." Roxxie licked Shawna's cheek.

"I don't understand," Nicole said.

"It's the only way Roxxie can recover from an illness."

"Quasiera don't suffer from human diseases," Roxxie explained. "We're immune to them and most other illnesses. To feel and understand another species, we must become that species. The down side is that we are very vulnerable to their afflictions. This is our purpose! Why we exist! We help when we can, those we can. After each journey we return to our natural state. Our bodies reject the disease. We are whole again, if all goes well. Of course, it doesn't happen overnight and is quite exhausting. I must return to my pack to complete the recovery."

Nicole remembered that Roxxie had mentioned her pack once before. Strangely, she hadn't thought much about the use of the word.

"How long do you have to stay a wolf this time?" Shawna asked.

"At least a year."

"A year? That's such a long time."

"We've been apart longer. Besides, in Healer or Quasiera time, it's the blink of an eye," Roxxie teased.

"Maybe, but in my time, it's too long. I'll miss you." Shawna hugged Roxxie again, kissing her forehead. "I love you so much, Roxxie. Maybe you won't have another case between now and then."

"For you, this once, I'll ask the alpha Mother for a special favor," Roxxie promised, her bright eyes gleaming with humor. "Take care of Shawny, Nicole," the wolf growled. "Or I'll have to show you what pain really is."

"I don't need threats to make me protect Shawna," Nicole said.

The wolf moved around the Healer and stood directly in front of Nicole.

"Quasiera never threaten." The hard glint of her eyes reinforced her words but quickly softened. "Take care of yourself, too. You're the only one who can really protect her from Phageian, and herself." Walking toward a group of the trees, she stopped at the edge of the darkness.

"Roxxie," Nicole called out. "Can I ask you something before you leave?"

"Of course."

"Just before you... morphed into a wolf, thousands of butterflies showed up. Did that have anything to do with your transformation?"

"Butterflies?"

"Yes, orange and black, except for a large white one. It landed on your cheek."

Roxxie raised her nose and sniffed at the air.

"Ah, that one! We've crossed paths a few times. She's my lucky charm. If she's hanging around here, you'll be safe. Where The White Mother flies, there are no Phageian. I must leave now. Stay safe."

Loping away, Roxxie disappeared into the darkness. Several wolf howls greeted her.

"Sounds like she's going to have company on her way home," Nicole said. "Let's go home. You've been keeping a lot of secrets from me. I want to know what else you've been hiding."

Shawna nodded. Turning into her lover's arms, she smiled.

Be safe, Roxxie! Shawna thought.

Always, my friend. Always!

About the Author

FRAN HECKROTTE lives in the sunny South with her husband, Howard, her dogs, Sophie and Skipper, and numerous other critters. Her life experiences include living in Alaska for almost three years, gold-panning, bull riding, scuba diving, flying, training gaited horses and more. After spending five years in law enforcement, she switched to construction and eventually opened her own property management company, Orphan Homes Property Management, LLC. She has replaced her motorcycle with snow skis and a warm beach. Her favorite city is Montreal. Hobbies are too numerous to mention but she loves to interact with her readers. Email address: novel_ideas_publishing@hotmail.com.

About the Editor

ALEXA HOFFMAN-I currently live in New Mexico with my partner and our two cats, enjoying 80-degree days in March, green chile on everything and hot-air balloons in the early morning throughout the year. My life is about to change, though. We're moving to Manhattan to be closer to both of our families and for her to attend grad school. The difference in locations will be like night and day — no more warm winters and open spaces!

It's not my first time living on the East Coast; I studied English and biochemistry in college in Pennsylvania, graduating in 2002. Since then, I've worked as a newspaper reporter and editor and now I'm a manager in a company that focuses on content marketing, social media and PR. In my spare time, I edit for authors and publishing companies and do marketing/PR for another company — good thing I enjoy challenges! I write when I get the urge, but a hectic lifestyle (and sometimes writer's block) curtails that quite a bit.

My partner and I love to travel, especially outside of the U.S. I rock climb as much as possible — indoors, for now. Hiking, running and other outdoor activities keep me sane. Reading, doing crossword puzzles, watching movies and exploring the world around me fill in the sparse moments in-between everything else.

If you have any questions or are looking for a copyeditor, feel free to contact me at auth2b@gmail.com. If you just want insight into my weird mind, follow me on twitter (@auth2b).

About the Cover Artist

PATTY G HENDERSON is an author, publisher and artist and all-around bohemian at heart. An independent author, she launched her own publishing imprint, Blanca Rosa Publishing. She writes Gothic Historical Romances and has published three so far, THE SECRET OF LIGHTHOUSE POINTE, CASTLE OF DARK SHADOWS and PASSION FOR VENGEANCE. She has also penned four Brenda Strange Supernatural Mysteries, THE BURNING OF HER SIN, TANGLED AND DARK, THE MISSING PAGE and XIMORA. Comfortable wearing several creative hats, Patty is an accomplished artist as well as author. She's done popular book cover artwork for many mainstream mystery and horror authors and lesbian authors via her graphic arts business, Boulevard Photografica. In addition to a nearly complete immersion in indie writing and publishing, Patty is a Star Trek geek, attending Star Trek conventions and costuming from the show. She is active in animal charities and has devoted two anthologies where profits have all gone to several animal charities. Patty can be reached via her author web site: http://www.pattyghenderson.com or check out her graphics and book cover professional web site: www.boulevardphotografica.yolasite.com

**Thank You for Purchasing and Reading
Odyssey of the Butterfly**

Novel Ideas Publishing, LLC

http://www.novelideaspublishing.net

www.ingramcontent.com/pod-product-compliance
Lightning Source LLC
Chambersburg PA
CBHW071247170626

46809CB00001B/113